About the Author

Paula Guildea lives in County Dublin, Ireland. she teaches Esol and creative writing, and spends time with family. Paula has a BA Degree in English literature, a Higher Diploma in further education and a MA in creative writing.

Want

Paula Guildea

Want

Vanguard Press

VANGUARD PAPERBACK

© Copyright 2024
Paula Guildea

The right of **Paula Guildea** to be identified as author of
this work has been asserted by her in accordance with the
Copyright, Designs and Patents Act 1988.

A CIP catalogue record for this title is
available from the British Library.

ISBN 978-1-83794-173-5

This is a work of fiction. Names, characters, businesses, places, events and
incidents are either the product of the author's imagination or used in a
fictitious manner. Any resemblance to actual persons, living or dead, or actual
events is purely coincidental.

Vanguard Press is an imprint of
Pegasus Elliot Mackenzie Publishers Ltd.
www.pegasuspublishers.com

First Published in 2024

Vanguard Press
Sheraton House Castle Park
Cambridge England

Printed & Bound in Great Britain

I would like to dedicate the book to my children, Cassie, Madison (Hooley), Tristan and Rían.

I would like to acknowledge the English department at Maynooth University. In particular the MA creative writing course, and the lecturers, Belinda McKeon and Oona Frawley, whose creative input was invaluable to me.

Prologue

Some words follow people around, not like a label, but still plastered to the skin...

Chapter One

It wasn't as if honey, or something sweeter, was there to attract the insect. A light prickly tarsus climbed in and through the leather strap of Darcy's sandal. A summer foot on display, unprotected, but for the straps. She had poured sugar into a cup, stirred diligently and sipped three dainty mouthfuls of creamy, warm cappuccino. Now, she wanted to swat the tiny pest before it made a home under the sole of her bare foot.

Totting over newly painted pink nail polish, the insect paused, as if deciding, where next. Darcy patted her foot. Opposite her, Mina was launching into her lecture, there was no avoiding it, insect or not.

Mina chatted and Darcy drifted intermittently, in and out of tail-ended syllables. Failing to decipher the missing pieces, while replacing missed words from Mina's facial expression and animated hand gestures instead. Mina spoke with passion about idealism on the anchor cast of hope, or something to that effect, philosophizing in her usual manner. Darcy nodded, yes, in agreement and hoped Mina did not notice her half-hearted attempt at faking concern.

Mina's shoelace was open. It lay a limp snake on the path, getting squashed by Doc Martens and Nikes. The half-emptied sugar wrapper blew off the table onto the ground below, as grains of sugar sprinkled the road like salt on chips. Darcy wanted to catch the wrapper but it moved faster than her reaction, even on a mild day like today.

At last, the insect disembarked.

Darcy tuned in.

'It seems a lot to ask, y'know,' Mina said, touching the corner of her mouth as though crumbs remained. 'She's basically giving you an ultimatum because her mother's a head doctor. It's textbook, y'know the type, always analysing. Ugh. Sounds to me as if she's just mimicking mama's words. Anyway, haven't we covered this before, this same topic?'

Mina sagged, half-hunched, then grimaced peculiarly. 'Come to think of it, the whole thing is a weird love triangle, you'll have people talking.'

Darcy smiled across the table at her best friend, silently agreeing with her words of wisdom.

'You can't win,' Mina asserted, 'I'd leave things the way they are for now. The break will do you good, you and Jessica. You know that yourself.'

'But I don't want a break,' Darcy sighed, 'I don't want another break, and that's the problem. Our last split, you remember that, well, that should've been our last. We've been in a prolonged break-up ever since. I'm not stupid, I know it's the typical heart-over-head scenario. It's bloody draining. I'm drained.'

Her tongue traced the inside of her cheek, where torn tissue, from chewing the night before, caused mild discomfort. The movement triggered an awareness of sorts, a question even, that wasn't there before, but, as was often the case, Darcy chose to ignore.

For now, the delicate skin held on to the pain, and Darcy worked, as Darcy often did, at pretending it wasn't there.

'I really don't know what to do, and I've to work in an hour. I don't know which is worse, being bored at work, or having too much time to think. Why do I get myself so wound up?'

Mina's eyes narrowed, and her shoulders lifted, as if questioning Darcy's predicament.

'Maybe, she's not the one, and it's that simple, only your incessant need to choose a woman who possesses certain traits tends to have disastrous results. Your idea of perfection, or should I say, the perfect woman, is unrealistic, which just adds to the strain that already exists.

'And I'm not being flippant, can you just take what I'm saying on board.'

'Pass me your phone a minute,' Darcy urged.

'What, why?'

'Just gimme it, I need to check something, I'm not asking to keep it, just for a sec.'

Darcy wanted to check an Instagram profile but was in constant fear of touching her own screen

15

accidentally while scrolling.

'No, I will not be party to such nonsense, finish your coffee and get to work. My God, Darcy, she slept with a guy, with a man you know, a boy-man. If that isn't reason enough for moving on, then I don't know what is… you were exclusive, right?'

'I guess. I mean, who knows?'

'Ugh, stop being so desperate, next you'll say she had your permission.'

As Mina regarded her censoriously, Darcy picked up her bag and searched for a vape.

'You're gay, you're not bisexual and you've told me that you want the same in your partner, that's why this is so gross.'

'I was hardly that adamant, was I?' Darcy frowned, 'Sounds a bit controlling, to be honest. Maybe that was the problem. Maybe I was the problem.'

'Oh, so now it's because you set boundaries within your relationship that's the issue, right? Can you actually hear yourself, you sound like a beta male.'

'That's harsh and uncalled for.'

'Are you no longer a top either?'

Flinching, Darcy prepared to retort but, instead, played along with Mina's game.

'Oh, that's a low blow, a low blow.'

Darcy endearingly smirked at Mina's indefensible query; there was nothing else she could do.

From their perch off Fitzwilliam Street, Dublin's layered tapestry was offered in an endless parade of people and their uniqueness. It was a space where fashion's rhythm played off-key and funky style appeared from behind the line of every brick wall. Bright colours adorned brighter personalities. People who were proponents of a reoccurring fashion cycle, displaying chic to the delight of some onlookers, and dismay to others who were less adventurous.

Windows above the seated girls opened, and quiet conversations floated overhead, swirling like steam from beneath an open grate of a chef's heaving kitchen.

Darcy began to play with a loose fake pearl on her arm. It had been a gift from a lover. She twisted the bead between thumb and index finger, loosely, in the hope of calmness. This evoked a memory of her as a child holding her grandmother's rosary beads and its similar feeling. Her grandmother, whom she now lived with since the death of her parents five years ago.

In the distance, church bells rang, leaving Darcy with an uncanny sensation. She was struck with the image of parishioners blessing themselves, in the height of prayer and supplication. Sometimes, Darcy, hearing the familiar religious chime, equated anything related to God, as something to push aside, bury, or avoid. Family customs, especially to do with religion, had fallen apart, the way old wood deteriorates and crumbles when restoration is no longer available, or indeed required.

Letting go of the bead, Darcy moved her cup so that it did not align with its circled coffee stain on the table, and repositioned it half-circle instead.

Her mind pondered, even in company, how life can be crap most of the time, and how an aimless path had somehow materialised as her choice to follow!

Her eyes darted from place to place as she fought hard to concentrate, not only on Mina's words, but the dilemma of moving through her own mounting confusion, thoughts she felt unable to share, even to Mina, who had been such a good friend since starting college.

Darcy sipped. 'I just think you're being too judgemental; we didn't carve out rules in stone, conformity sucks. Once you see how society manipulates every decision, you can't unsee it, it messes with your thought process,' she sighed, 'And, not only that, missy, I want to live my life, and the repercussions of *my* life, without negative comments from my trusted circle of friends.'

'Oh, dear Lord, I give up. It's so much more than that and you know it.' Mina said.

'Is it though?' Darcy attempted a sardonic smile. 'Sometimes a relationship is worth a little mishap, a mistake here and there, have you ever thought that I'm no angel?'

'Absolutely, more than once, but, my dear Darcy,' Mina shrugged in jest, 'I can only go by what you've told me.'

'Yes, I know. I dug my own grave by repeating that I'm a gold star, a fact I'm proud of and expect my lovers to treat with respect. I know what I've always said.'

'And now you've changed. Really, how does that even work, and how am I supposed to comply with changes that my brain does not compute?'

'Not changed, I know who I am but things have happened recently, that's all, things I want to keep to myself. Things separate from Jess, is that all right?'

Mina looked away as if distracted, inhaled deeply, then re-engaged. 'You need to put yourself out there more.'

Darcy felt as though she was losing Mina's interest. 'Ah, yes, that old chestnut. Life isn't all daffodils and sexual gratification, Mina. Not all of us have it worked out.'

'Why the dig?' Mina pumped.

'I'm not digging, Mina.'

Mina carped lightly, 'You should be in a different mind space, being so pent up is ridiculous. I mean, we're almost at the finish line, college is ending, just one semester left. Four years of lectures and tutorials, it's a time to celebrate. You shouldn't be so ratty.'

She released a layer of her hair and then reclipped loose strands back into place.

'By now, there should be some semblance of the future we've worked towards; it should be all coming together, the pay-off. Remember our passions, goals?' She smiled. 'Our limitations. That stupid first year's fading list of accomplishments that we haven't ticked off yet.'

Darcy sniffled, suddenly chilly.

'I never had a list, that was you. You and Kate and the others. Have I not said in the past, lists corrode inspiration, they stifle creativity; obviously, I was talking to the wall.'

'You may not be digging but, whatever it is, and to be honest I get it's something, talking about it might actually help. Blaming others is a tad immature, even for you Darcy. Maybe self-reflect a tiny bit, that's what you'd say to me, you know you would.'

'I wish it was that easy, I wish… well, I wish a lot of things and I don't believe over-thinking this one will cut it. Anyway I'm boring myself, I'm hurting my own head.'

Darcy thought about it and understood that each complication in her life had merged into one gargantuan mess. Her flawed judgement of character towered over other ramblings in her mind, but each self-inflicted complication had its own calling bell, ready to summon at will. She could not tell Mina about each of the separate issues so, instead, she lived with one unified lie. Did that make her a pathological liar? she wondered. Does a pathological liar know they're one or do they even convince themselves with their own lies? Darcy had only tried to stay protected because her sanity was at stake. It had been that way from early on. And it wasn't as if Mina had all of the background knowledge; Mina was privy to what Darcy chose to share, and not the hidden secrets. Was that such a bad thing, she thought, was she harming anyone? Her life mechanically moved forward without having her pause to enquire about said deceit, or the consequence attached to that deceit but, within that movement, it was never her intention to cause hurt, pain or confusion.

Lies helped Darcy to save face. Her lies were hers alone to protect, because, in doing so, she protected the hurt too, the main feature of her story.

That way she survived.

The last thing she needed, she mused, was to reflect on the whys of her decisions.

Mina stood.

'I'll see you later at Dom's and, please, leave this stranger at home,' Mina circled her hand in front of Darcy's body.

'I prefer my confident Darcy, bring her, okay? Old Darcy wouldn't take the shit this new you seems to revel in, it's beyond mind-boggling.'

Darcy inhaled and watched her righteous friend meld into the souls of moving shadows, as some ambled along the crowded pathway, others rushed. She thought about the pathways that were a part of the city's beloved landscape that would soon change because of corporate greed. Dublin's historical nooks and crannies, replaced with hotel developments and heartless lobbies. Gentrification sought to improve by burying Irish culture without a gravestone. A revival without a wise soul, in a soulless void of cemented vulgarity, or so she'd read recently in a popular magazine. That's progress for you.

Of course, Mina was right.

Darcy had become… utterly confusing. How's that for self-reflection?

'Can I get the bill?' The waiter affirmed with a nod.

Behind his head, hanging baskets dangled; they contained dead flowers. How odd, Darcy thought, it's summer and everything should be in bloom but these baskets have been neglected, left to dry up and choke from thirst. It doesn't seem fair.

When the waiter returned, he handed Darcy the bill.

'Can I ask why you've let the flowers die,' she shrugged, 'Maybe not you personally but someone here, the owner?'

The waiter turned, 'Oh, I think they're last years; they haven't been replaced yet. Someone comes in, a florist from across the street, as far as I know.'

'Flowers with life make a difference, I think, don't you? I mean it's just a suggestion. I didn't know it until now, but looking at those limp petals has made me sad.'

'Oh, okay, word, I guess.'

The waiter forced a grin and took the money Darcy left behind; he watched her as she walked into a lane between two streets, then, without being obvious, sniffed around the vacant table for pot or similar substances.

While chirping birds wheeled the dull sky scanning for discarded morsels, Darcy took out her own mobile phone. Chewing on the side of her thumbnail, she began to scroll the empty vessel of perfectly orchestrated lifestyles containing smiling faces and picturesque locations.

Jessica's Instagram page was an act of aesthetic hypnotism, beguiling and magical, giving surface-level pleasure to her sixteen thousand followers.

22

Jessica was past tense.

The first raindrop fell and gently caught hold of Darcy's cheek; she raised her head in surprise.

Darcy decided to go to the library quickly before work. A poetry book she'd been patiently waiting on was now patiently waiting on her. Its pages sat on a shelf labelled, "On Order".

The label was aubergine and white, a strange thing to remember but Darcy had taken note, for no other reason than mindless observation. As the light raindrops continued to fall, Darcy left thoughts of Mina and Jessica behind but, of course, without them to distract her, Darcy was taken back to earlier that day when she had wiped up tea stains from spillage caused by her grandmother's shaky hand, as she wobbled back upstairs to the comfort of her bedroom. Each tiled step contained a blot or two of browned water. She had stopped wiping a minute while listening to her grandmother's words as they descended from her bedroom, *You're a topper, Darcy, you're a topper, good girl, I'd be lost without you.* Darcy had sponged each stain wondering how fast her grandmother's dementia would progress.

Darcy did not tell her inner circle about her living arrangements, indeed, Darcy kept a lot about herself, to herself.

A phone ring chimed; she recognised the number.

'Hello… Oh really… no, I don't mind at all… no, seriously, I can change shifts, it's no bother.'

The rain's darkened mood fizzled because the impromptu shift change from work somehow neutralised mother nature's tears as Darcy entered the library with a spring in her step and no work ties to bind her. Now she had more time to get ready for the planned night ahead. Maybe she would try out that new make-up she bought online the week previous, because of a popular influencer, and paint on a smile for everyone; it might just stop them asking too many questions, she thought.

Chapter Two

Dom's place was kicking; not frenetic but certain rooms contained overzealous party-goers and recreational uppers, suggesting all needs would be catered to. Darcy stood on her tippy toes to search for her tribe, eventually finding the back of Mina's head, by a floral hairpin and fading red highlights.

'Hey.' A tap on the shoulder.

Darcy turned and faced Cruz, a Spanish Erasmus student (who extended his stay for reasons only known to him and one professor) with curly brown hair and a giveaway complexion of caramel hue, tantamount to three weeks on holiday for Darcy's chalky skin tones.

'You made it.'

'h-huh.'

Cruz's lips parted in an attempt to utter something as Darcy heard her name vibrate across the room.

'My God, how can my ears hurt when the place is teeming with people's voices?' Darcy said, while adding, 'I'm ready to leave, my bad.'

'Stay a while, you'll get used to it,' Cruz assured her, It's worse in the next room.'

Mina appeared, arms outstretched, almost squealing Darcy's name.

'Yeahhh, I didn't know you'd arrived! I thought you weren't coming, did you get a drink yet?'

'Well, everyone knows I'm here now, Mina.'

'Oh, stop bitching, I'm just excited you're here… and guess who else is?' She winked.

'Why are you winking? Stop being so childish. If Jess is here, just say it and cut out the drunken gibberish.'

'I'm so locked. I'm ready to do things I'll regret in the morning.'

'Hi, Mina,' Cruz interjected, all but forgotten.

'Oh, hi, I almost didn't see you there.' The dig did not go unnoticed. He shuffled his feet, awkwardly.

'Can I get you guys a drink?'

'Can you get me a coke, cheers?' Darcy needed her wits about her.

'A coke,' Mina scolded, 'You better have vodka in your bag to add to that, I ain't dancing on the table alone tonight, sista.' Mina danced a half-arsed move while making silly hand movements to a beat she alone could hear. Drunk on freedom and on her lack of things to worry about.

'I think you've drank enough vodka for the two of us, where's Kate?'

'Don't you mean Jess-i-caaa?' The last syllable of the name was dragged out for emphasis.

'No, I don't mean Jess-i-caaa,' Darcy answered verbatim, avoiding the urge to glance around the room.

'Well, she's looking for you, she's been asking about you. In all fairness, I was going to warn her to leave you

26

alone but I thought better of it, I mean, we're almost grown-ups,' Mina teased, Almost ready for the big bad world.'

'Almost,' Darcy shrugged. 'Listen, I'm not staying long, I... 'Cruz returned, can of coke in hand.

The music from one room swallowed the wave of another. Converse runners pranced on sticky parquet flooring, attached to souls that have not experienced grief or pain, or real hardship. Baggy boyfriend jeans, short shorts, dungarees, sunglasses and printed t-shirts rested on sweating bodies, swaying to the rhythm. The make-shift dancefloor, which was the living room, held an array of potential in its brimming enclosure, and all with not a money worry between them. Well-born, upper class, the world was theirs for the taking. With daddy's help. Or maybe that was just how Darcy saw them; who knew of their real experiences, maybe they hid behind a mask just like her. She made a promise to herself to be more mindful and less judgemental, she made a promise to try at least.

Lately, no matter where Darcy went, she thought about her grandmother, either her grandmother's condition or her grandmother being left alone. Worry, now felt like a constant companion.

On her way to the bathroom, she checked her watch.

It was okay to leave her grandmother Pat alone for a while, but not for long.

Jessica opened the bathroom door from the inside, just as Darcy reached out for the handle. They stood facing each other, a moment of unsteadiness, of cautious negotiation between ego and apathetic façade. Who would speak first, who would put their pride to one side and be respectful in the face of the past and its seedy disappointments? Remembering Mina's lecture on how people viewed her private relationships, Darcy suddenly felt naked, as if the leading lady in a show she had not been cast in; a contract she had not signed.

She knew it wasn't so, but thought voices lowered around the corridor.

'How've you been?'

Icebroken.

'I've been better, and you?'

'Same… listen, I wanted to-

'Wait' Darcy murmured, 'Not here, it's far too loud and crazy.'

Jessica nodded.

'Can we meet up then, it's not like I haven't tried calling you?'

Darcy found Jessica alluring, which had its drawbacks. Jessica with her blond pigtails, cheek dimples, and high cheekbones. Facial structure that defied how bones were meant to be. No one questioned Jessica's beauty, her physical appearance was obvious, but there was also a mystique she showed few in intimate settings.

Jessica had 'it', whatever 'it' was. She looked at Darcy and Darcy felt dizzy.

Don't do it, Darcy thought, don't get sucked in. But, of course, all Jessica had to do was lean against the architrave, blink and, as if by sheer telepathy, will the world to stop turning and it would comply.

But nothing was willed, it seemed, so nothing turned.

Who should or would confess, because confession was the theme, even if the theme had not been announced?

Darcy found herself thinking of a sign she'd seen on a recent trip to the West of Ireland. High on an electrical pole, Jesus' bloody face mid-crucifixion, ravaged by non-believers, non-Jesuits and thorn pricks. REPENT spelt out in white beneath his face, his mouth aghast in bafflement.

Darcy, in a church, her confessional box would suffocate her. A priest on high, administering his own rendition of the sacred word. *To whom atones will walk among us once again for they are welcome back into the flock.* Why did everything always sway back to forgiveness?

Suddenly burdened, Darcy felt split in two, not having split personalities, just split in two, like the orange her mother halved and put in her patterned lunch box every second day for school.

'Darcy, are you listening to me?'

'I'm sorry, Jess, it's the music, it's too deafening, and I need to use the loo, do you mind?'

'Can we talk?'

'Maybe, it's a lovely thought but… call me and we can arrange something?'

'Why not now? Let's get out of here.'

'I can't, I need to get home.'

Darcy turned to leave, but her thoughts stayed with Jessica tethered to memories of their past encounters. The lovemaking, the talks till midnight, the sharing, the passion, the way they followed one another around like a welcomed shadow, a layer of the other they unashamedly sought out for comfort. And, of course, there were the lies.

Lingering, as if glue, pulled away but not released. She turned but Jessica was gone.

Returning to the hub of the party, Darcy was dismayed to see Jay, his armed draped around some guy from their English class, dancing stupidly as if the past few weeks didn't matter. Jay, the guy to blame for everything. The guy caught with Jessica. Jay, who had copied Darcy's assignments, not word-for-word but, still, on more than one occasion. Jay, who Darcy liked but wanted to slap, had the temerity to rise above his indiscretions with an innate aloofness of casual disregard now stood central in the crowd, sipping on a can of cooled Peroni.

Yes, Jay, Jay was the guy who had slept with Jessica and so much more.

Darcy brushed past him on her way to the front door. 'Hey,' he said casually, 'Are you leaving already?'

'There's nothing to stay for. Especially now, and I meant to tell you something before,' Darcy fought to keep it hidden but her face twitched and her eyes squinted towards him in an attempt to make him smaller. She despised how his primitive power to control overwhelmed her, and the fact he had no idea of this, made things worse.

'You've impeccable taste, it's something we seem to have in common.'

Jay shrugged. 'Don't be mad, Darcy, we're young,

youth is the time for mistakes and indulgence, you know that yourself.' He winked. Darcy hated how indifferent he was, how smug.

One night a couple of months previously, he'd winked in another way. Darcy swigged on water and swallowed down the memory, not prepared for the emotions it evoked. Tender, on a basic level but also immensely annoying. She found it so hard to explain.

'There you are.' Mina sounded frustrated, 'I've been looking everywhere.' She eyed Jay with a dissatisfied frown, after all, he was a man.

'Won't you re-join us in the living room?'

Darcy shook her head.

'No, I'm going to head back to Rita's.'

A lie.

'I promised I'd help with a piece she's working on.'

More lies.

'Eww,' Mina objected, 'Rather you than me. Okay, well, I'll see you tomorrow. I don't think you're in the mood for partying anyway, so I'm not going to try and change your mind.'

'I just need to get my shit together, and I will.'

Another lie.

*

Walking back to her grandmother's house, Darcy wondered if she was anything more than an experimental plaything in Jessica's journey of self-discovery. It seemed Jessica was looking for herself and Darcy had to go along for the ride. Was that it? Darcy wondered. Was Jessica trying out everything until she'd tried it all, type of thing. Was her goal to explore each mind until an explosive epiphany illuminated 'the one' in her perpetual search for love, lust and confusion? Jessica had suggested once that everyone should draw their fingertips along different skin tones until their hand rested with ease on clustered freckles that caused a stir; be daring, be flamboyant, she'd say, be curious, don't simply, settle. At the time, Darcy thought, it had resonated as something poetic but now she wanted to add her own interpretation, which was, be an asshole to everyone until some eejit succumbs to your manipulation, without realising their mistake. Lie, lie until you realise you've dug a hole so deep, that the lights went out and dignity along with it. Not intentionally, not at all, but as if no other choice was an option. Not as romantic as Jessica's words but definitely more realistic.

Footsteps behind her, one after another, made Darcy turn. Jay, grinning, picked up speed until he was by her side asking for a light.

'I don't have a light… why are you following me?'

'I'm not following you. Moody, I live this way too.'

'You do not, you live nowhere near here, Jay.' Being outside, away from the music and the other people, sedated Darcy's previous anger towards him.

'The night wasn't what you expected?' he asked.

'Why do you say that?' Darcy felt more in control without everybody's eyes watching her every move. And, just like before, when it was just the two of them, playful in his company.

'You left,' Jay remarked, 'It's a dead giveaway.'

'Maybe I have to be somewhere, besides, it's none of your business.'

Jay chuckled. 'You can hardly still be angry with me, with Jessica?'

'Is that a rhetorical question or do you want me to answer it?'

Darcy stopped walking and turned to face Jay, head-on. 'You've no idea about people's feelings, do you?'

'That's not true, I seem to recall partaking in certain feelings that brought you joy, if I'm not mistaken.'

'I'm not having this conversation. And nothing is on repeat. I've had a taster and I'm not going back for more. You're wasting your time. We're friends, and I'm not talking about the ones with benefits.'

'Maybe you should tell your girlfriend that.'

'Jay, this is not a three-way. You're a using shit and you know it; you toy with everyone.'

'I toy with everyone, that's rich. You're the one pretending Jessica is the one to blame for doing the dirty on you; you're making her feel worthless when you did exactly the same and, on top of that…'

Darcy felt discovered, transparent, as though the game was up and perhaps the walls could fall, at last.

'Stop, just stop… '

'You need to talk to her, Darcy, you need to tell her the truth… you should to be honest with yourself too.'

Why was Jay being the voice of reason? His words were not pioneering, they did not contain new revelations in the science behind convoluted relationships and why they span in a repetitive motion without end.

'You're right, Jay, I do need to talk to her, but not to you, okay, so, please, crawl back under your rock and leave me alone. I don't need reminding of the part I played, especially from you.'

'That's mean; you're being a dick, but fine.' Jay held up his arms and then turned to leave.

He paused and raised an eyebrow. 'Just don't leave it too long, Jessica and Mina looked cosy on the sofa as I was leaving, too cosy for comfort, if ye get me.'

Chapter Three

After a restless night and texts back and forth, Darcy and Jessica had agreed to meet.

The waitress brought the coffee and asked if there was anything else.

What there was, Darcy thought, was an open universe within an insular world, consisting of two inhabitants, at a table, ready for battle, and ready to fight! But other than that, everything seemed cool!—

'I know it's over, and I'm actually okay with it now, but I need to know one thing; why the lies?'

Which ones precisely? Darcy thought.

'Who have you been talking to?'

'Oh, right,' Jessica rolled her eyes. 'Whose version of events, you mean?'

'If you like.'

'Jay, if you must know.'

'Ah, Jay, the bearer of truth. I should've known.'

'It should have been you who told me about you and him, Darcy. The irony is laughable.'

'This isn't just about him… ' Darcy shifted in her seat. 'What did he tell you?'

'Everything you haven't and thanks for that.'

'It wasn't that simple. I-'

'Don't. I don't care that you slept with him, it's that you gave me shit because I did.'

'I didn't sleep with him, we… played around, is all.'

'Oh, Jesus, as if that matters,' Jessica smirked.

'Of course, it matters, you screwed him! It's totally different.'

'No, you know what's different, saying you'll be faithful to someone and then reneging on that promise.'

'I never promised. I never *said* the words; you interpreted, you assumed. You set those standards, not me, insinuating exclusivity without mouthing the actual words, without hearing them from me.' Darcy looked down. 'That's just perception on your part, a perceived idea.'

'I know what it means, Darcy.'

'So, when I said I didn't believe in the concept of monogamy, what was your perception then?' Darcy's eyes widened.

'And my response, can you even remember what I said?'

'Yes, I remember.'

Darcy found herself thinking about the time she had painted her grandmother's garden fence; the chipped wooden slants that needed to be replaced rather than refurbished were barely nailed on. She remembered painting with light strokes but the paintbrush moved too fast to stop a bug from being caught between the soggy bristles and smudged. That was how Darcy felt, detached and unable to reform. The right words trapped in a prison cell without a key. And that bothered her because Jessica was waiting for answers she could not provide.

'You said,' Darcy revisited, 'That we were joined spiritually, like soul-sisters, sharing pleasure whenever we felt like it, without labels or expectations. Living better than our best lives.'

'And I said that that was a stronger bond than commitment and its unrealistic constraints, or something close to that.'

'Something close to that,' Darcy agreed.

'I thought I knew you better, God knows you've spoken about morals, your personal crusade at trying to fix what's broken. I've watched society dictate and you oppose it. So, morally, I expected more from you. Not from me, I'm not saying that. But, I was naive.'

Darcy felt a familiarity with Jessica because, in her company, they discovered how similar their values were.

She chose a tribe to do just that but, after a while, found she didn't really belong there. She pretended to fit in. Good grades, was sociable, and was accepted by her peers but only because she lied about her socioeconomic situation, her location and living arrangements. She fit in because she created a persona that emulated the final piece of a jigsaw puzzle, ensconced to fit into a world of like-minded people. A puzzle made up of unrealistic pieces, that if truly observed would show discord. And yet, a union of sorts, a compatible group of misfits, that thrived off one another's core beliefs and idealisms.

Sharing pains but burying the real hurt, and for the most part, that was the rub.

Darcy was an adult orphan but no one knew, because the child inside her had not mourned the loss of her parents or the gaping void their departure left behind.

Killed. Taken too soon.

And Darcy never got to say goodbye, her familiar landscape irrevocably changed, altered to include aloneness. But, not in the ordinary sense, in a rippling effect that eased intermittently, but never ceased.

'Everything comes down to happiness, Darcy, and, if I don't make you happy then just be honest about it.'

'I never said that, I just went with the flow of things, just like you did. At the time, it didn't feel like a big deal. To be honest, I still think Jay is unimportant, in the bigger scheme of things, he's inconsequential.'

'And so are we, it seems.' Jessica let her head drop.

'I don't know what to say. I thought I wanted this but maybe I'm not ready and I think that's okay. I'm trying to figure it all out.'

'Well, thanks for letting *me* know.'

'I'm sorry, Jessica, I've been living with deceit, or confusion, I'm not even sure what to label it. Em, I've been a mess and it has nothing to do with us, with you. I've been quite lost. You helped but, now, well, I guess I've been parasitic and it's shameful. I need to take a look at my morals. And I have to prioritise my mental health, Darcy sighed, 'This is a little wired.'

A silence rested.

'Wow,' Darcy lowered her head. 'I can't believe I just said that, but there you go.'

'Can I help you?' Jessica interjected.

'No, but thank you. This, whatever it is, I need to do on my own.'

*

Darcy ran tap water from the kitchen faucet until it cooled. She filled a glass to the top, sipped a little, and then replaced it on the draining board. The day had promise, it always had until hazy flashbacks occurred or an insignificant moment became reclaimed by regret.

'Gran, do you need anything else, while I'm free, I might put a wash on?'

'What, love? Oh, wait, Darcy, yes, I'm coming,' Pat called from the landing, 'I need cigarettes, love, can you get me some?'

'Gran, you don't smoke, you haven't in years.'

'I most definitely do, sure I was smoking with Carmel next door by the wall yesterday, just pick me up twenty, here… there's a tenner.'

A tenner, Darcy thought, you won't get far on that, it's not the eighties.

In the absence of patience, Darcy added, 'Gran, you really don't smoke anymore.'

'Well, I want to,' Pat added abruptly.

39

The conversation was over, the debatable part anyway. Darcy would accommodate her grandmother's wishes, this once. She smoked an odd blunt every now and then herself but the taste of nicotine made her throat gag—the high not enough to overshadow the stale aftertaste.

Darcy knew her grandmother had begun smoking again, not because of a past addiction but a much more recent encounter with a neighbour, at their dividing wall, and with his medicinal dope. *Give us a drag of that,* and another and another, until Pat craved the nicotine inside the spliff and bought twenty to smoke behind her garden shed out the back. Straight plumes of smoke momentarily merged with the air but not before Darcy caught sight of its hazy heavenward evaporation.

Now, Pat demanded a pack, for a tenner no less. Darcy assented to her grandmother's demand and did what she was told, half dismayed and half in acquiescing begrudgery. Darcy let herself have few pleasures yet never understood why or cared to examine the reason behind that fact, or why she was now thinking about it instead of the things at hand. Then, bemused, she examined why Pat would want to smoke again. Surely there was no pleasure in the cigarette stink, she thought further, wafting up the stairs and down the hall, impregnating the wallpaper that already held decades of musky, dusty, stagnant odours, not paying rent, but there for eternity. Darcy was, once again, reminded that she missed her home, her parents and their non-smoking, "clean cotton" Yankee candle-smelling rooms. Of course, Pat wasn't thinking clearly, or pragmatically, or about wafts, smells or even lung damage! Pat's world was getting smaller day by day, so Darcy tried compassion, even if that meant putting her own discomfort aside.

Darcy, like most students, held a boring summer job. Actually, Darcy worked most weekends during winter too. In a chocolate shop, a posh one, whose customers never ceased to amaze her. Their superior attitudes and entitled placement within life's stratification tier system, a free pass, to ignorance. Except for one or two, who replaced class distinction with seasonal weather chats or, on a rare occasion, economics. Darcy impatiently rushed them along either way. She thought about her ideal customer and realised it was a given to complain about the people walking in and out of the shop door.

She had her regulars though and they were characters for sure. Entertainers without a stage. Darcy packed chocolates individually, requested by a customer with red gloss lipstick.

'Can you be particularly generous with the women-y chocolates please dear, and a pink ribbon, as it's for a girl?'

Darcy tried to hide her thoughts on the discriminatory request, behind a fake smile and rehearsed nod. She, herself always disliked the colour pink. She remembered questioning why she was supposed to like it, as a child. The assigned gender colour preference as opposed to liking, in her case, navy blue or dark green.

The banality of the rote working routine ever criticised because of its lack of satisfaction or meaning, but nonetheless, repeated each working day. Darcy moved from left to right, picking up smooth and heart-shaped textures and then handed over the box of carefully ribboned goodies. The lady grinned tightly, exposing thin-lined red gloss on her teeth. The breeze swirled from the open door and lifted the lady's receipt behind her, the printed paper overlooked by lady red lips, or disregarded without a thought. Darcy walked out front to bin it, then wiped the cover of her phone with the clean edge of her apron. A couple walked in then, laughing and genuinely happy. They looked totally loved up and Darcy felt a pang of jealously because of their closeness. Holding her pain as if a pause button pressed, she walked back behind the counter to box sweets, while feeling boxed in.

Chapter Four

It had been a week since the party and the disastrous coffee date with Jessica when she messaged asking to meet up again, as friends this time, she'd said. Darcy was apprehensive but agreed. In truth, Darcy missed something about Jessica, something intangible, which made it hard to pinpoint. The week apart, feeling regretful may have contributed to her confusion. Maybe it was the sex, nothing too mysterious about that, but, no, there was definitely something else.

Now, in work while she waited for closing, she wondered if her clothes smelled of smoke as she sniffed her blouse, pulling back her head slightly, just in case. Jo Malone's Lime, Basil and Mandarin filled her nostrils, the lotion rubbed on in copious amounts after this morning's shower.

Just in case.

Sweet, woody, pleasant smells were better than no smells at all, or so her mother used to say. Her mother, her guiding light and inspiration, ash-boned who now smelled of nothingness. Sprinkled, instead, over moving leaves and landing where soil opened up and digested, not only her remains but her beauty too.

The front door opened a little, held agape by a regular and her frowned expression.

'Do you have the salted caramel with a dust of cocoa in yet, the rather big ones? I called yesterday.'

'No, I'm sorry, Mrs Wilson, there's a delivery on Friday, do you remember I told you that when you enquired? Come back then, I'll put some aside.'

'Oh, right, I see, so you don't have them in, no, you're absolutely sure?' The disappointing look insinuated incompetence, another insult Darcy cast aside. If there was one thing Darcy knew for certain, challenging ignorance was pointless because it had a comeback only the ignorant could understand.

'Like I just said, Friday. Come back then.'

Mrs Wilson grumbled something; her words got lost in the vacuum of the closing door.

Some customers were blatantly rude, some, but Mrs Wilson always carried with her a canvas bag with her pet dog's face embroidered centrally, in bright colours of rusty, burnt orange and cornered with flecks of off-white grey. Darcy had once owned a dog with similar features. The poor thing had to be put down. Spaces, Darcy thought, even concrete walls that most people are used to, hold memories that other people ignite, trigger, alight, memories that they are totally unaware they've aroused.

In truth, Darcy was looking forward to seeing Jessica again, as if the short time apart had somehow erased the bad aftertaste left by their last meeting and replaced it with an excitement taken from their earlier romance. Those first days when anything was possible. Except, this time, they were meeting at a protest for women's rights. Not walking laughingly around the Ticknock fairy castle loop, melting ice cream running down their arms as their tongues raced to catch the mini smarties and chocolate flakes, cascading in its creamy streams before the coated sweets reached the sleeve of their jumpers. While reminiscing, Darcy could now easily conclude that Jessica had been an unwitting rite of passage to early adulthood in Darcy's life.

During the honeymoon period, Darcy had sometimes watched Jessica walk ahead, observing the way her hand lifted to replace the dangling ear pod, fallen from the left lobe and resting close to her breast, hence igniting Aqualung's melancholy number, "Remember Us", featuring Sara Bareilles's spectacularly haunting vocal tones. Jessica would turn and smile while pressing in the vibrating music to deafen all else. Jessica also read prose from books she thought Darcy ought to know. Repeating certain sentences that sang off the pages and heightened the mood, in a way mere conversation never could. Maybe it was Jessica's orating, her perfect enunciation, tone and facial movements, that made the hairs on Darcy's arms tingle when she read.

But that was then. When the magic moments held the good times.

Darcy wondered if Jay had ever been treated to a recital of Yeats or Dickenson, or other classical literary pieces she revered. Remembering as a child how her mother would encourage she learn. She wondered what

45

both Jessica and Jay saw in her. She struggled to identify her charming qualities, to understand if some expansion of herself was visible to others but sat on her blindside, perched, holding all the cards, dictating one reveal after another, just so.

Jay had since gotten in touch. Just late night stupid Jay texts. Funny, dull at times, witty but entertaining all the same and with no real harm. Darcy, while lying in bed, watched a tiny spider weave a thin web along her bedroom ceiling, and told herself texting Jay was harmless fun, that she was single after all. She could do as she pleased.

One minute, Darcy had been busy with her own thoughts of isolation and the amusing reasons why, and the next, her phone lit up, as if time was running out. All in the same week. Why could one dirt-bird not exist without the other? And, why, after many debates between the sub-conscious mind and the cognitive—let's manage our day-to-day life—part of her head, did Darcy still have no idea what she was doing?

As Darcy closed up shop for the day, she decided to walk home instead of catching the bus. As she got closer to the row of houses on her street, Darcy watched her grandmother's neighbour, Maryann, come out her front door just as a supermarket van drove close to the curb and halted outside Maryann's gate.

Within earshot the conversation between Maryann and the driver of the van travelled allowing Darcy to hear the exchange as she neared.

'Ye can't keep taking the shopping trollies, Maryann Gibson.'

'But I need that one, eh, that's mine. I always use it!'

The driver's assistant and temporary trolly relocator pushed *Maryann's* trolly into the back of the van. Attaching it to other shopping trollies found abandoned around the estate and surrounding areas.

'Maryann, it's not yours, for feck sake, there's hardly any left in the shop because you locals keep presuming ownership.'

'You locals, the cheek of ye, sure you're a local yourself, if your da saw you now he'd be ashamed for ye.'

'Can you not just get the delivery man to deliver your messages like everyone else... save me the hassle of having to drive the van around like an eejit, playing spot the trolly.'

'And what about me frozen peas, sure, by the time they'd get delivered they'd be soft and mashed.'

'Would ye stop it, not at all, there's special bags for that.'

'Well,' Maryann insisted pointedly, 'Now that you've taken me trolly, you may give me a lift to the shop, ye hardly expect me to walk when you've transport, me poor ankles.'

The driver rolled his eyes up to heaven but did not deny Maryann access to the trolly kidnapping van. Darcy smiled to herself at Maryann's cunning comeback, knowing full well another shopping trolly would take pride of place in Maryann's garden half an hour later. There was something charming about living in an old, mature estate; everyone looked out for their neighbour and oldness was incomparable, so competition was obsolete. No one gave a damn what the Joneses did, said, wore or owned. They looked out for each other. One person brought in the bins after the work men lined them along the path, and another kind neighbour mowed the lawns, hedging the verges so they were uniformed and level, tidied and neat. Sometimes he would tip his straw hat to Darcy in the morning, or give a wave in passing while walking in the evening with his wife; and their fluffy white dog. People shared history and Darcy really liked that.

Darcy nodded as Maryann drove by, then exhaled the day, dragging from the now, half-empty, raspberry-flavoured vape, before opening the front gate.

As soon as Darcy walked inside the house, she thought something was off. Putting the pack of twenty cigarettes on the hall table, she caught a faint smell of burning or previously burnt toast.

'Gran, are you in?'

Darcy walked into the kitchen and was met with black-stained kitchen cabinets, a dark grey ceiling above the oven and a frying pan with loose charcoal sausages, burnt to a crisp.

Pat appeared, looking disorientated.

'I forgot to turn the frying pan down, Darcy, I went upstairs and I must have fallen asleep, I'm not sure but, well... '

'It's okay, Gran, we can fix this, it's grand, a bit of fairy and hot water will do the trick.'

'The bloody fire alarm went off, sure that would wake the dead and I ran and almost fell but I managed to turn it off, an' all. I opened the windas wide and that helped, but you probably need to spray that lavender stuff you like, that choky stuff. Oh, I'm sorry, Darcy, am I losing it, am I?'

'Not at all, Gran. Don't be worrying, come here.'

Darcy pulled her grandmother close and scanned the area. A death-trap waiting to happen, if not by the blackened hot plates then by the cigarettes on the table.

'I think we need to make an appointment to see Doc O' Reilly, get some advice, eh.'

Pat nodded. 'I think that's best.'

'Have you eaten?' Darcy smiled, 'Cos those sausages don't look very appetising, do they? Let me make you a sandwich.'

*

The day of the protest march arrived.

We're meeting at Parnell Street, if you're still interested, not just a text but a phone call. Darcy, split in two, but not by split personalities, replied, *sure, I'll be there, what time?*

She sat staring into space with her phone resting in her hand. The weight of her life, her real life pushing her body, bones and all, into the cemented concrete floor, under the coarse carpet of her grandmother's living room floor. She would soon be a post-graduate student. One semester left to finish; the black mortarboard hats would fly high into the sky. A ceremony to celebrate a student's accomplishments and completion. Where family could gather and be proud. A time of happiness. Only Darcy had no parents and a grandmother hardly able to remember her own name, who would soon forget stolen beach days, or rolling down the hill of a Martello tower, or a first kiss or last handshake, or of having had a baby girl, or burying a husband, or of dancing while others danced too. Soon, Pat would have a blank canvas, with no colours or brush to paint with, or content to paint about.

Life was changing and the only thing Darcy could control was a decision to rekindle a friendship with a past lover, who changed like the weather, unapologetically.

Two-thirty, that's perfect. See you then.

'Of course, I'll keep an eye on her. Pat is in good hands,' Maryann assured Darcy as she ran for the bus. 'You have my mobile number anyway, so just call.'

Sitting on the bus that smelled nasty, Darcy scratched her knee even though it wasn't itchy and associated the imagined itch with apprehension. That, layered with feeling like a fool, caused a steady show of no confidence. Darcy sought to build a protective wall around her emotions but ended up with a fence that would collapse if gently leaned on.

What am I doing? she thought, retracing old steps expecting to find unspoiled ground, who does that?

Half the population, apparently.

At each bus stop heading into town, crowds of women, transwomen, non-binary, girls and supportive men hopped on. The bus doors closed them in like sardines, flanked by other sardines in a moving tin. Darcy already knew why Jessica chose a neutral playing field to bounce blame back and forth. Only Darcy didn't really feel like having that type of conversation. She only hoped Jessica was ready to move forward, without the obligatory chat-fest and tired explanations. That old ground doesn't need rehashing, she thought.

The sound of people's voices buzzed in Darcy's ear. She looked out the window at passing shops, passed by people on a bus ready to stand up for women's rights in America. As her gaze shifted and re-entered the upstairs bus deck where she sat, Darcy noticed an unopened tampon on the floor between a transgender woman and a flamboyant female. Their feet circled it in a protective hug. Darcy felt awkward and refrained from drawing their attention downwards. She didn't want to offend anyone by just assuming and the bus was full of well-intended, judgemental individuals who would collectively cancel anyone's ass vocalising opinions that didn't match their own, inadvertently or not! So, she tried to shift her perspective by clearing her mind.

It may have been the setting, the impending protest or Darcy's lame attempt to avoid thinking about Jessica, but she found herself reading the other passengers on the bus. What were their political views? Did some of their opinions replicate her own? Maybe some but not all. She didn't follow the crowd on every occasion, which was something that upset people, namely her peers, more than once. She wondered if believing in free speech was now offensive and if it was still okay for people to be whatever or whoever they wanted. Maybe *cancel culture* needed cancelling, she thought, at least until another, more fitting and inclusive fad became popularised. The irony, Darcy thought, a culture that claims to exemplify inclusion but sometimes, most times, excludes popular opinion and rational thinking, like one shoe fits all. Before a minute, Darcy found herself debating an inner voice as if that part of her mind was a separate entity, concluding with the statement: Okay listen, if society stays keeled off balance, then it, by nature, reproduces inequality allowing cultural insensitivities to germinate, manifest and evolve! In essence, just staying the same, with the same issues, just named differently, unresolved.

Damn, Darcy thought, and they call this generation, she observed her fellow travellers, the aware ones.

The bus's movement catered to her musing, swaying her gently, as she replayed thoughts she'd often questioned.

What's so wrong with wanting to live in a world where acceptance is not just a word thrown around in conversation, or a YouTube upload, but an action with cause and effect? Not just an ideology from a textbook, worn out from turning pages and fading print, but a script played out in real life. Not just a discussion that, once it ends, is neatly put away and kept on a shelf until next time, but a lived experience by a movement intelligent enough to see it through. *Is it not the same for everyone here,* she thought.

Is peace not what we all want? To normalise love between consenting adults, that ultimately advocates positivity. Darcy's inner voice warned her against the tone of the conversation, citing, even if her life had a propensity toward darkness at the present moment, darkness was not resident in a permanent parking space. And the population of the world would grow, expand and experiment with or without her lame opinion on how it should evolve. As the bus slowed, it jarred Darcy into the present moment.

When the bus stopped, everyone moved as if a herd of stampeding baby elephants parading towards one meeting point. The unused tampon flattened underfoot.

Darcy joined the queue and thought she spotted Mina up the road, she tried moving her head to get a better look but the crowd swallowed the sea of faces and the moving steps pushed her forward but in a slower flow. Painted logo banners held up blocked her view anyway, so she stayed on the path towards Parnell Steet and her initial proposed destination.

And then, of course, the rain joined in, but only trickles, staying for the chorus and not the whole song.

'Darcy, Darc, over here.' Hands waved, painted nails, a bright green sheen as if beaconed light, guiding sailors home, through a heaving rain storm. Darcy followed the familiarity of the voice and, before long, was face to face with Jessica. Her ex.

'Come on, it's bloody packed down here, keep moving, a bit up there to the left.' Darcy followed Jessica's navigation through the masses and wondered if she would navigate the conversation with such grace, later on. If things remained platonic, then the need for digging deep and pulling apart (again) may be unnecessary.

The protestors, with synchronised assertiveness, shouted anthems of support against (male-dominated) government decisions on women's bodies and their reproductive organs.

American politics was always up for debate, especially the country's choice of president. Darcy watched a YouTube clip recently where the latest commander-in-chief almost fell asleep while speaking to crowds from a wooden podium. Mispronouncing words and including words from the auto-cue, like, *repeat line*. A man, once respected in his homeland had now become a laughing stock.

Give me Michael D. any day, Darcy thought. A poet and an endearing character, not afraid to speak up about Ireland's ongoing housing crisis. Not that much would come of it, because talk is cheap. And if there's one thing a politician is good at it's cheap talk, she thought. Between homelessness and the cost of living in Ireland, the Emerald Isle needed redirection, and an interjection of common sense—give Mary Lou a shot. That, or give the reigning politicians a right kick up the arse.

As always when it came to supporting controversial issues, Irish people came out in their droves, ever the supporters of the underdog, they marched, hoping to change the world but having no real control over the outcome.

Darcy wasn't particularly political, or at least she hadn't intended to be but in her opinion women always had to explain or defend or push for, or give up something for, therefore always having to oppose in some regard.

Who would have thought, that *anyone* had the right to decide what should happen in someone else's functioning, able-bodied body? Darcy wanted to make a stand for women. Not unborn women or unborn men, just women. Who really were the backbone of society. Some would say she was a TERF, which, of course, was ridiculous as her darling Kate, one of her best friends, was a transgender woman, assigned male at birth but now fitting into her life with acceptance. Kate became who she was meant to be and being around her had given Darcy a different type of insight. Especially on how one person can be alienated for their choices, skin colour and gender, all at the same time. Darcy had watched Kate transition and stood by her side when she needed a friend.

Darcy's decision to proudly support women was not derived from a matriarchal standpoint either. It wasn't about a power trip. Remembering the late Maggie Thatcher, a powerful female who had an iron temperament. Darcy thought about the iron lady's reputation, and her public disconnect from the coal miners, whose lives she destroyed. Lest we forget her lobbying for a known criminal, a man whose abhorrent crimes were pompously discovered. Learned in history class during a political economics debate on notorious leaders, without the pervy affiliation, obviously.

So, no, Darcy's main objective was not to put women on a pedestal.

Darcy simply wanted equality.

It was their turn, *the turn of women*. The turn of the woman.

Women were, most definitely coming into their own.

But Darcy was still aware of how opinions differ.

The funny thing about honest opinion, she thought, is as soon as you give it, you're attacked as if your words burn. Like Dante's inferno on an extra hot afternoon. More often than not, opinions stay in a person's mind space, a safer arena than partying in the outside world and facing attack. Darcy had held her tongue, had become smaller to allow louder voices. Even now, as she walked, her deliberate silence spoke volumes.

Afterwards, as the marchers dispersed into smaller clusters, Jessica asked Darcy if she would like to grab something to eat. Town was packed so they decided on a prepacked sandwich deal and a walk up to St Stephen's Green. The early evening was pleasant enough and the open space wouldn't feel claustrophobic.

Just in case.

They sat on an empty bench, its paint mostly chipped. Better not to speak first, Darcy thought, especially because she didn't want to direct the conversation into depths neither could swim up from. Jessica seemed open though, jovial even, or maybe that was just wishful thinking. You could never tell just by looking at someone, maybe the eyes would sometimes give something away but, not today, definitely not today.

After all, in her own words, Jessica had told Darcy, *you hurt me.*

So, Darcy ate her egg and onion quietly, in anticipation, while observing Jessica's two different coloured Converse—unpaired, quirky, but not Jessica's idea, stolen from a new slick magazine most likely. Jessica was a non-conformist fashion icon in the making, compared to her own plain attire. Faded navy shorts and a white tee with Metallica printed across the front, an anti-fashion statement piece not worn for anything but convenience, and not a subtle shout-out to any current movement, shoe Doc's and spotted pop-socks, which were an afterthought and certainly didn't match; hardly mattering but part of her null meanderings.

After eight minutes.

'So, what have you been up to, how's work?' The pigtails moved and the dimples followed.

The work question, the most pedestrian question to ever grace a mouthpiece, along with the weather question, or summary, or statement. The safest way to begin in any language. Darcy was compelled to answer with something just as dull.

'Oh, it's grand, you know same ole, same ole.'

'Any mad stories about funny customers, I miss that.'
Jessica grinned.

And there it was, an opening to the past, an introduction within the first paragraph as if an "inciting incident" in a gripping narrative. The reader, wholly engaged, even before the sub-plot has picked up momentum.

'Yes,' Darcy chuckled, 'There's been plenty of them… and, you, how have you been?'

'I've been over-thinking, arranging circumstances to fit with falsehoods that keeps me sane, the usual. I tend to lean into the obscure. That hasn't changed.'

Darcy let the silence sit a moment, then said. 'Sylvia Plath once said, "If I didn't think, I'd be much happier", so you're in good company.'

'Ah, who doesn't love a bit of Sylvia but you know that didn't end well.'

Jessica scrunched up her face, then said,

'Listen, I know this is out of the blue but my brother is having a ridiculous engagement party at our house, out the back garden actually and I'd love it if you would come.'

'Me!' said with a surprising pitch, on purpose. Darcy was genuinely shocked.

'The emphasis is a bit dramatic, but, yes, you, Darcy.'

'Sorry, I didn't mean to sound dismissive. I'm taken aback, especially after our last meeting, I was cruel. Not intentionally but I was hurtful all the same. I'm a fuck-up.'

'Oh, we all are,' Jessica shrugged, 'Just look around, we're all trying to build a place of respect, better than the last generation, but-'

'That endeavour comes with its own set of problems, right?' Darcy put her sandwich wrapper to the side.

'My sentiment exactly.'

Mina appeared then across the green with a couple of other people, her head bobbling between the thorned rose bushes earthed together in a raised flowerbed. Mina, who always, mostly, sometimes, made Darcy feel good. Who, since meeting on the third day of the first week of college, had helped Darcy fit in. She walked in her usual way of *I love life and life loves me* attitude. Even back then, in the old days, when Darcy felt at a distance in the middle of passing conversation and interrupted sentences, Mina lifted whatever situation needed that extra umph.

Jessica bent forward to wipe something stained off her shoe. 'You don't have to decide now, it's not until next weekend anyway.'

Mina was getting close.

'I've never met your family though, why now, I mean, I'm not trying to diss the invitation but we never did the family meeting thing.'

Closer.

'That wasn't me, you said you weren't into the whole meeting parents, I just went along with it to keep you happy.'

Darcy could not, as yet, manage to say the words, *my parents are dead. They were killed* together in a freak accident. So, she said instead, *Getting to know a partner and being committed to them before committing to their family is important to me.*

'I'm not saying I want to meet your family, I'm suggesting you come with me to a family gathering, it's no big deal, just say if you don't want to.' Jessica propounded.

'I never said that, Jesus, Jess. It's confusing, this, whatever it is. I will go, I want to, it just takes me a minute, that's all.'

'Cos you've things going on, I get it.'

'Are you being facetious, seriously?'

'Stop being so easily triggered, God, we're like an old married couple.'

'Oh, my God, you two are so cute,' Mina said as she reached the bench. 'Is the romance back on?'

'You sound like my Auntie May, give over.'

'You're not going to believe what happened, Rita, you know Rita right, she got hit by a flying bottle, while marching, a glass bottle. She needs stitches, some dickhead on the side path.'

'My God, that's awful, but it doesn't surprise me, I did see a few people getting rowdy. It's very rare these things are completely peaceful, even though most people try to be respectful.' Mina said.

'It's always the way; a few ruin things for the greater good. Rome wasn't built in a day and all that, some people have no vision. No purpose.' Darcy added.

'Yeah, it's bloody awful.'

Darcy stood.

'Guys, I'm sorry but I have to go. I need to get home.'

'I thought we'd grab a cocktail at The Lucky Duck, I've missed watching you puke martini expresso, after two or three?'

'Ha-ha,' Darcy calmly retorted, 'Not today, I can't. I've been gone long enough as it is, I just gotta go.'

'Have you a hidden real life robot doll you need to feed data to, naked and needing to be plugged in?' Mina laughed loudly at her own childish joke. 'You're giving serious enigmatic vibes.' She added, 'It's a little freaky.'

'And you're a little tasteless.' Darcy smiled smugly.

'You love tasteless and you know it.'

'Maybe, but I still have to go, catch you guys later.'

Chapter Five

Opening Pat's bedroom door slightly, Darcy relaxed once she saw the outlined figure of her grandmother's resting frame. Closing the door, while attempting to ease the creak caused by a loose nail she intended to mend, she went back downstairs to think. The air of the city centre still on her skin, she sought refuge from the bed cover brought down from her bedroom, a creased quilt that separated her calves as they rested on the sofa.

Jay texted as if they were a couple; Darcy texted back as if she was the man in the relationship. Absent, with cursory answers few and far between.

Come over to my place and watch a movie, he'd ask.

Two hours later.

I can't, Darcy answered. Unsure why she was even entertaining him and his ego for that matter. Darcy, in the midst of thinking, wondered if both Jess and Jay had become detraction mechanisms to conserve her world of insularity. Positioned to stop her from thinking about the real issues needing her intelligence and care.

Adjusting her ear-pods, Darcy lay back on her bed and thought about attraction. The meaning of the word. The limitation it created if used in the wrong context. Exactly who did Darcy find more attractive, boys or girls?

Neither?

Now, that was a sobering thought, but it was also fabricated. People intrigued her, regardless of their gender.

Imagine being labelled greedy over confused, Darcy mused, bewildered.

She felt inadequate as a partner because, since the death of her parents, there were pieces of her own *being* missing. She knew she could just about manage to function but, beyond that, every complication that stood in her doorway, she ignored, dismissed or pretended wasn't there. She had become complex in a simple world, having lead a simple life intentionally. Maybe you need to talk to someone, she thought, maybe you need help. Maybe play that song you like or look up distraction on that app you have, just do that.

So, she thought again about attraction and what it meant.

Raising on her elbow, she checked the dictionary app on her phone, keying in *attract…* while the autocue filled in the rest.

Attraction: the action or power of evoking interest in or liking for someone or something.

There was something that Jay did she found attractive. The way he worked his environment, his personal space, as if shared with an afterglow or something just as hypnotic. But she was attracted to Jessica in an utterly different way. Essentially, she was attracted to both of them though, but what did that mean? She had sex with lots of women, sex was fun but she had never experienced sexual penetration with a boy. Right then she asked herself if that was an option, a desire, but she couldn't answer, she didn't know. And that was the problem, in a world of black and white, you were supposed to know, you were directed by political correctness and ideology to know. You made up your mind and then you weren't allowed to change it, or even consider changing it. Which was quite amazing, in the pondering sense of the word. Darcy assumed she had made up her mind about a lot of things, how naive to have felt so right and been so wrong.

She lay back and rested her eyes, hoping her overactive mind would join in in her assumption about rest.

A knock, no, a tap on the front door woke Darcy up. The room was quiet but for the light tapping. The sun had lowered, casting a shadowy hint of dusky coral through the drapes. Darcy, suddenly anxious, made her way towards the rapping sound.

A neighbour from across the street was holding Pat's arm gently, a fretful look on her face. Darcy's grandmother appeared shaken and thrown, her skin a lighter tone than usual. Her nightdress hung loose under a house coat that was buttoned incorrectly, causing it to look slanted.

'Heya, Darcy, I found your gran up the road, she was wandering, looking to find Mrs Costello around the back. I tried to explain that Mrs Costello is long gone but, well, she was insistent and got a little agitated, she-'

'Thank you, Mora, I fell asleep for a minute; I didn't hear her go out.'

'Oh, not at all, I understand, a young girl like you left to mind...'

'Come on, Gran, let's get you inside and make you a cuppa.'

Darcy thought she might die from embarrassment, from her own carelessness and the fact her grandmother was knicker-less walking around the estate looking for dead people to have a catch-up. And, of all the people to find her walking aimlessly, Mora Byrne, the biggest gossip in the town.

Darcy led her grandmother through to the kitchen and then dialled the emergency doc.

Despondency loomed, long after the doctor left the house. The tablets Pat had been previously prescribed doubled in size and requirement. The doctor had also suggested a proper thorough examination of Pat's declining faculties, where, after cognitive specialists gave their opinions, a subsequent brain scan, an MRI, would take place. Darcy looked on as her grandmother, sitting out the back, lit another cigarette while one sat in the ashtray, half-smoked.

*

Meeting at the grounds of Trinity College to visit its old library and see the Book Of Kells had to be the most fashionably unfashionable thing to do, for a date that wasn't a date. But Darcy needed the safety net of the public and their bouncing bodies, with stacks of books, to act as dividers from her life, and the facing of it, and the not facing of it.

Kate was coming too; Kate who had warm brown skin that Darcy envied, and was almost six feet tall, walked with the grace of a queen, queer as anything and colourfully outrageous. Kate, although flamboyant, dressed conservatively for the occasion, walked through the archway entrance and raced towards Darcy, a big grin on her face.

'I'm thrilled, delighted, I've never been, have you, and it's on my bucket list, as mundane as that sounds. Do you have the tickets?'

'Jay is coming too.'

Kate looked idly around, bemused.

'Not Jay, *Jay*?'

Darcy had skipped warning Kate about Jay beforehand because Kate would have declined the invitation. Kate's circle were open-minded, forward-thinking creatives. But a man deemed manipulative might not be in favour. And Jay was, well, Jay was Jay.

'So, you got me here under false pretences?'

'No, no, I have the tickets, just three and not two. Please don't be mad.'

Darcy faked innocence by becoming wide-eyed and doe-y; pouting her lower lip.

Kate put her head back in horror but when it returned she giggled. 'Oh, feck it, let's go in and explore things less antiquated than Jay's thoughts on morality, but you owe me one, Darcy, you really do.'

Jay was a respectable ten minutes late. His curls danced all over his head as he casually entered the hallway of the Berkeley Library.

He nodded towards them, with the hint of a smile. Which was so him.

'Kate, hi, what a surprise.' He mused.

Kate barely nodded.

He turned to Darcy, 'I didn't realise this was a mini reunion of people who dislike me, yay,' he smirked but not in a nasty way.

Kate retorted while blinking her false eye lashes. 'Jesus, we're not even inside and you've made this about you, how nuanced.'

'Children,' Darcy injected, then trumped, 'Remember, we're final year students. We hold ourselves to a certain high standard, don't let the side down.'

'Oh, shut up, Darcy.'

Kate and Jay let out a casual chuckle.

After queueing and viewing the famous book, Jay walked over to another library in the college, so Darcy followed him. It was a place where the literature section housed classics from all documented periods, ages and talents. By then, Kate had given some excuse or another about having to leave. Darcy eventually found Jay, by some shelved leather-bound books pretending to be well-read and distinguished. Holding a book, half parted on either side.

He recited as she walked towards him.

A perpetual lust anchors my will,
I lay, I sleep,
I am part of you still.
In the swell I drown, unless
Unless, unless you stand
And tend our ground.

'Are we alone?'

'No, Jay, the library has readers, book returners and staff at every turn. We are not alone.'

'I meant Kate-free.'

'I know what you meant, I was teasing.'

'And flirtatious.'

'No, wrong again, I'm being nothing other than cynical ole me.'

'And that's your problem, Darcy, identity, or lack of, you haven't a bloody idea how cool you are, how open-minded, how attractive, how...'

'Do you like poetry? Or was that reading before a ruse of sorts?'

Jay laughed, a genuine chortle, 'I'm not that clever.'

'Shouldn't you be standing at the sociology section studying Durkheim for your finals?' Darcy ribbed.

'Oh, Jesus, no. Plenty of time for that in late September. Let's grab a beer, or at least a latte, this place is outrageously pretentious.' Winking that wink.

'Why should I go anywhere with you? I still haven't forgiven you for telling Jessica our secret. I should kick you in the shins but you're not worth the pain.'

'That's old news. Come on, one beer.'

In her mind, Darcy protested against the idea. Chewing the inside of her mouth gently, as her thumb pressed in the skin, she contemplated her reasons for meeting Jay in the first place. Might as well get hanged for a sheep, as a lamb, and all that, she thought, an idiom that transgressed Darcy's usually problematic inner discourse. Also in that two-way, one-person conversation was the glaring and obvious truth that Darcy proposed a challenge for Jay. She knew that, she wasn't stupid. He wanted to bed her and his ego informed him, probably on the daily, that if he persisted, he just might. She argued this point within her head, with herself and, as she turned to leave, was still unsure which side came off best.

Following Jay out, he held the door open for her like a perfect gentleman.

*

Waiting for the bus home had its advantages. Darcy could curse to herself without having to explain to anyone the reasons why. She seemed to be going through a rebellious episode. There was something about being in Jay's company, something stupid, as if her own story was in him, trying to write its way out. On some strange level, they shared challenges but they were tacit, hovering in the ether somewhere unprovoked, they remained unspoken. Which was so silly and unsubstantiated. It was a dubious form of justification, she had told herself at the time, for sitting across from him as he checked his phone.

While sipping coffee, he had tried to grab her hand, and not in an affectionate way, not in any type of ownership way either but as if wanting to connect, physically connect in a way that would make a slight difference. She had pulled away, not wanting touch but wanting something that remained a mystery, even to her. There had been one or two subtle incidences of inappropriateness, a delicate gaze, the passing of a tattered beermat, dampened from its coarse environment, accompanied by a purposeful touch.

But nothing striking or remarkable.

Jay made Darcy look as though the game being played was already won. He was blissfully unaware of the choke hold, around her neck, secured there with her own bare hands.

Darcy continued to let her mind wander, she examined her challenges while asking what they were exactly, or could they even be labelled?

Was she capable of affirming true feelings? Could she keep denying reality? Did it not feel better to say she was right about nothing being right, or fixed, or fixed in, or having preference. Like a building but not the scaffolding.

Wouldn't that need less explanation?

And yet, there she was, letting him smile at her, as his curls moved and rested on one side of his face, having her resist the urge to replicate Barbra Streisand in *The Way We Were*, a movie she'd watched a few nights before, when

Barbra gently placed Robert Redford's character Hubbell's hair to one side. *Your girl is lovely, Hubbell*, words to confirm the end of what could have been, but never would.

An ending with no doubt but full of doubtful wonder. Unlike her ending which still had motion, and moved with tireless ambiguity.

Darcy, instead of touching Jay, thought about the repercussions that would follow such an intimate thing. And then she focused on the touching and the not touching which was what really mattered, and underneath that, the question of the touch.

Did she want to be touched by *his* touch? And, of how, not too long ago, she had promised herself no, never again, because she fancied women. And that was that. But now, he was in her thoughts, the thoughts that linger, not thoughts that you'll never forget, just the flimsy ones that rest awhile then blow away.

They say youth's foundations are laid in the present, in the present reality, in the now, where everything is felt in the rawness of the moment. But Darcy craved escapism, to a reality that was not the realness of her life. That made her think about revaluating the choices she had made in recent days. But thinking of it made her wobble on her feet, and in doing that, her feet wobbled.

A man walked by and made the most disgusting sound that Darcy had ever heard. It woke Darcy from her analytical daydream. She asked herself why men had to inhale phlegm as if it was an escaping convict getting sucked back into prison, then spit it out, and ruin all that was nice about the world.

Darcy hated men, sometimes all men but not old men who smelled good. She liked old men who smelled good, the smell, not the man, like his presentation, the way he presented himself to the world, his sliver beard groomed and slick. Not like some men who were desperate to be forgotten, stuffy, stained and musty, their smell associated with cobwebs in a cellar that has not been dusted in centuries. From smells, Darcy's thoughts changed to things around her likes and dislikes. Like, when people laughed without reason; a useless laugh. This irritated her more than it should but she was powerless to change it. She liked reading a book in a park with no noise, as well as bus rides in silence, a blissful rarity, an anomaly of sorts in today's fast paced society. She liked riding passenger in the car her mum used to drive, as people she let pass, waved to thank her. But she hated the noise of a bouncing football, whose bouncer was a happy teenager with a group of his angsty friends. She hated too, the noise of her granddad's T.V. when she visited as a child and, because he was half deaf, had to sit through an episode of Game Of Thrones with her hands over her ears for the duration. But she loved walking bare foot along the edge of the ocean on a winter's day, or a summer one too. On occasion finding whole sea shells to put in a glass jar on her grandmother's conservatory windowsill. She enjoyed watching a toddler laugh, a hearty laugh at a parent doing something comical. Watching these clips on a screen by scrolling through her phone at night, having spent an inordinate amount of time online, when she should be trying to sleep. And she loved the orange Mickey Mouse t-shirt Jessica had given her for their six-month anniversary, and she seemed keen, and even liked, spending time with men who confused her, and that she hated, apparently.

Years later, her mother would say, hardly anyone waves thanks when you let them pass anymore.

As the bus pulled up along the side, Darcy realised she had been thinking utter rubbish for the last half hour to avoid what really needed her attention, she mused happily on how wonderful the mind was for such a thing.

Chapter Six

Pat was sitting in her usual spot by the back window in the kitchen when Darcy got in.

'Did I ever tell you about the time I used to sell strawberries from a Silver Cross pram, now, you know what type a Silver Cross is, don't ye; the big wheels, three of us kids would fit in it at once. Little legs dangling over the side of it?'

'Yes, Gran.' Darcy pressed down the button on the kettle.

'Anyway, my da had glasshouses out the back and.'

Darcy had heard this story umpteen times already but she was learning patience and how to be patient.

She made coffee because she had begun to hate tea, tea stains, tea bags, tea bags left in the sink, tea stained rings left after the many half-filled tea cups were left on any space available, cold, and still containing a tea bag. The cup of used tea bags that filled a big mug, covered in old tea seeping from the used tea bags piled on top of one another, all because her grandmother had stopped realising how unhygienic it was. Darcy felt queasy every time she saw the mound and steered away from the countertop harbouring the towered brownish pile, wanting to complain, to scream, in fact, but reminding herself she was only a guest. A permanent guest in an old dwelling space, but a guest all the same.

'Well, I never complained,' Pat continued, 'I sat there on the side of the road until every strawberry pundit was sold, no matter what the weather. It could be lashing out of the heavens and me and the sisters couldn't leave until all the punits were sold.'

'You have mentioned it once or twice, Gran, how are you feeling today, here, take your tablets.'

'More tablets, are you sure?'

'Yes, Gran, every day, it has to be done, to make you better.'

Of course, that was a lie. Pat would only get worse, not any better.

'I was just here thinking about that time I sold strawberries for my da, have I ever told you about the time I was almost stoned by passing children from a nearby estate, bitches they were?'

Darcy sat down and smiled at her grandmother, as the light of the drawing evening caught her grey, fading complexion.

Life was so fickle, so circling and fast. Beginning with innocence and the inability to judge, or fail. The middle part happens and then, the beginning comes again with the brain's regression, as if a baby once more. Learning to walk with innocence and the inability to judge, or fail.

Darcy's eyes welled up with tears but her grandmother did not notice, instead, she reached for her tea-bagged tea cup and, in mid-conversation, sipped.

'Oh, I almost forgot, while I have you here. There's a senior citizens' dance coming up and I want a soft body wave in my hair. Make an appointment for me. I've already bought a ticket from Maryann, she's selling them for the bingo.'

'Is that so, Gran?'

'Ye never know, I might even pick up a man.'

'Well, I don't know about another perm, don't you remember what happened last time?'

Darcy did not what to remind her grandmother but perms and thinning hair did not mix well.

'I haven't a clue, but I think I'd be gorgeous, don't you?'

'Sure, leave it with me. Your hair might be too short but I'm sure the stylist can work her magic.'

*

The next morning Darcy wiped milk up from the counter, tiny drops she'd missed when making coffee in the small back kitchen in work.

While staring out the window, transfixed towards the sky, she let her mind travel, and it chose backward.

The story behind how she and Jessica first met, was a thought Darcy often played on repeat and as work dragged on, Darcy silently reflected on the past. From the many social clubs introduced in the first year of college, she had joined the same one as Jessica. The "human rights and wellness club". The club was in its infancy but its members, an eclectic mix of nerds and activists, shared many views on equality, equities unevenness, the effects of racism, abortion law, gender inequality, the #metoo movement, spirituality, among many more. Without giving it a name, Darcy admitted, in times of deep contemplation, she'd hooked up with a group of political leftists who loved to debate current affairs and hear their own voices. Of course, Jay and two of his friends were also members, joining out of curiosity, with the ultimate goal of getting laid.

(Which he did, eventually.)

In the weightlessness of those first days, those vapid meetings, of awkwardness and tip-toeing, the room had space for everyone. Darcy gravitated towards Jessica, and her metal blue water bottle and yellow eyeshadow. They did not speak to one another immediately but, instead, acted coyly.

Later that day, Darcy found a note in her bag and from there, Jessica's penned words opened a place for dialogue, not only about political views but of who she and Jessica were, as opinionated, feeling humans in the world.

'Sorry, but are those boxes of chocolate prepopulated?'

A customer had walked in and asked a simple question while pointing in the direction of the stacked boxes.

'Prepopulated?' Darcy asked, dumbfounded.

'You know, prepacked,' the customer confidently expressed.

How odd, Darcy thought, a term she had never heard before about a routine part of her job, robotically done without thinking.

'Oh, prepacked. Yes… yes, they are.'

'A plethora of choice, how nice, although I only really like the dark ones.'

Darcy grinned.

Jay passed by the shop window, his head glued to his phone, until he realised where he was, then he backtracked and open the shop door.

'I was just passing by.'

'No, you were not,' Darcy replied, with an air of *don't gimme that*.

The man in the shop interjected, annoyed. 'Excuse me, sales, ah, girl or em person, or whatever, but I'm in a rush.'

'Oh, sure, sorry. Which prepopulated box did you require?'

Seven minutes later and Jay was reaching over the counter to try and grab a Manon chocolate from the cooled display cabinet.

Earlier that week, during a chilled conversation, everyone agreed that the problem with living in a small city was that every academic, every creative used the same stomping ground, perused the same book stores and ate at the same trendy food halls. There was nowhere to hide. Most of her fellow students frequented the shop, so having

Jay visit was not a big deal. The fact that she was happy to see him, was a big deal.

'There's cameras, would you stop messing, you'll get me sacked.'

'You haven't replied to the camping WhatsApp group, and you've opened it, so don't use that pathetic excuse.'

There it was again, the cool, nonchalant, I worry about absolutely nothing attitude.

'Some of us have to earn a living, Jay, some of us have responsibilities.'

'Oh, God, pass me the violin, you always look so chilled Darc.' Jay bit into the smooth white casing of the silky coffee-filled sweet. 'If you're that stressed, then all the more reason for getting away. Anyway, we go every year, what's the problem? Isn't the camping trip the first place you and Jess got it on?'

Darcy gave an exaggerated sigh, she narrowed her eyes and said, 'Isn't the camping trip the first place *you* and Jess got it on?'

'Whoa, steady… you know that's not true.'

The place, the where, the why had stopped bothering Darcy.

'Come on, say you'll go, it wouldn't be the same without you, and you know you can trust me.'

Trust, what the hell did that mean? Darcy thought, as Jay walked over to the wide window, at the same time a new customer entered the shop, and as Darcy readied their order, she tried to pull apart the concept of trust, she wondered who really had the notion figured out. Certainly not some twenty-somethings, with a proclivity for making misguided judgments and mistakes. What did they understand about trust, commitment or loyalty? They could hardly trust themselves. So, how could anyone ask to be trusted, in the I-won't-do-the-dirty-and-break-your-heart type of way? Only a foolish person would believe such a stupid claim. And anyone who believes there's justification for blame while a person does something they don't truly comprehend is a gobshite. Plain and simple. Darcy had been a gobshite, a right one.

The customer left, happy with their purchase.

'I'll answer the message this evening, when I get in,' Darcy said.

'Good, cause it's West Cork. Toscan du Plantier's house.'

'You're not serious, we'll never get away with that.'

'Well, it's not an official camping trip, so who'll know? It's what we do anyway, show up and see what happens.'

'I suppose; is Kate, Mina going?'

'Mina, of course, sure she's the deviant who started it all. Remember, she needed research for her forensic psychology assignment. So, she convinced everyone a trip to Naul, Co. Dublin, would get her a first, and we all fell for it, because of the introduction of Jägermeister, and a local book reading, slam poetry event. God, you forget everything, Darcy.'

'I didn't forget it, I was thinking, thinking aloud; I know full well who organised the first trip. I helped, for feck sake, but it all started by accident, really it did.'

Darcy had not seen Mina since the march, so she decided, if for no other reason than spending time with her friend, that she would go.

'Do it then, while I'm standing here, accept the invite on the WhatsApp group.'

Since first year, a group of students went camping together in camp sites across Ireland, mostly counties that had literary or music festivals on at the time. A cultural expedition that made them feel like involved, participatory students, reciting old poems by the camp-fire while dancing to old folklore tunes, played out of tune by merry hopefuls. All in the name of student life.

The theme surrounding these outings emanated by sheer accident when someone from the group (Mina) drunkenly suggested they explore an abandoned house that someone died in. Someone who was murdered in, to be precise, because it might give insight from a visceral interaction as opposed to learning from a book—and get her a first in her essay.

First-year students did a lot of reckless things, but this was fourth year, and Darcy and most of the initial group still participated in these clandestine adventures. The annual gathering was a great way to re-connect with everyone and get drunk, accidentally stumble on an old book store unobserved by prying eyes, and talk camp-side until the early hours.

Of course, Darcy's grandmother was healthy back then, falling apart at the seams from old age, but her mind was intact. Now, Darcy had to ask Philomena, Pat's new carer, if she would look after Pat for a couple of nights. Her going, really depended on the outcome of that discussion.

As Darcy closed the shop for the evening, a text came through from Mina and Kate, they were having drinks near Dawson Street and would Darcy join them. One drink wouldn't hurt and might even set her up for a good night's sleep. Darcy's grandmother was never far from her thoughts but she had already asked their caring neighbour, Maryann, to keep an eye. In all truth, Darcy searched for excuses to stay away from home lately, ashamed as she was to admit it.

In any event, she had a confession to make to her astute, opinionated and forever-giving-advice-she-did-not-want-to-hear, friends.

About Jay, about playing around with Jay, about lying to Jessica and about, no, she would stop there. The conversation would include more than enough convolutedness for one meeting. As Darcy entered the pub, she felt exceedingly nervous about Mina's reaction.

'I heard it, I mean Jesus, a man giving his opinion on transwomen's intellect, as if balls give him the… ' Mina looked up, 'Oh, hey.'

After hugs and ordered drinks, Mina resumed her debate on gender identity and how patriarchal society in general blatantly confused issues about gender, because of their bias and uninformed opinions, while neglecting to mention that an opinion does not override a feeling, a genetic calling of sorts, that no one but the person feeling the feelings within their body could comprehend. Darcy had established a long time ago that the world functioned on a spinning globe of continual trial and error. Most societies ran life trials, as each new issue appeared but only until they got bored and not because they found a solution.

Gender identity was certainly the topic on trial in almost every objective, cultural conversation dominating the moment. And of course, everyone thought they were right, and people in the opposing field, were wrong.

'To insinuate that gender identity is just a fad, a fashion accessory, it was so insulting to the trans population, alluding that intelligence is a drawback, or to suggest people should follow *his* views on what he deems normal, was sickening. I was so annoyed, I had to turn him off, what a cretin.' Mina stressed.

'What is wrong with some people.'

'Old mind-set and dated perspective, isn't it the same for every generation? The forward thinkers whose ideas get dissected, bear the brunt of the hostility, until change is woven into society and becomes the norm.'

'It still comes down to choice anyway.' Kate added.

'I agree, but choice is the catalyst for change and that's the bottom line, the fear surrounding that.'

'But fear of what, an imagined boogie man, sorry,

boogie woman?' Kate scoffed, frustration caught between the squint in her eyes.

'Fear that their archaic ideology might be threatened, that the nuclear family might be up for a redo; that scares the shit out of people. The loss of control.'

'But that ideal has been evolving for years, Mina, no one really cares about mam, dad, two kids and a dog anymore.' Darcy determined.

'My point is, these topics should have never been an issue, most things that we as women face, most of our challenges should never have been issues for men to figure out in the first place.'

'Well, no one will think for me,' Kate insisted, 'Think for me, or make choices concerning *my* body, the notion of it is insane.'

'Yes, yes,' Mina said, 'Your body, your choice, especially as a woman.'

'Yea,' Kate said, 'But I'm a transwoman, and I'd like to add that I'm very proud to be part of that particularly gorgeous and inspiring group. It makes me feel special, and my journey super interesting…'

'Yea, I get that.' Mina said, 'But you're still a woman Kate.'

'Yes, but a transwoman, don't tell me what I identify as, I know, and I love who I am! I'm a delectable delight.'

'Yea, yea, I'm just saying…' Mina huffed, with a rather rambunctious overtone.

'Give her space Mina, ' Darcy added, 'Kate has as

much right as anyone to decide what's right for her. Just be an ally, without such a strong opposing opinion.'

'I am! Of course I am. Spatial navigation is not the issue. Am I not allowed speak now!' Mina added.

Darcy shifted in her seat. She sipped her Whiskey Sour, and inhaled. 'Okay, so… ' she began but was cut off mid-sentence.

'I don't like the sound of that,' Mina intoned, 'can we not get too serious, I mean, about personal things, please, not after the day I've had.'

Darcy sat back into her pent-up tension, the words caught in her throat.

'Shut up, Mina, and let her talk,' Kate moved her open hand towards Darcy, as an invitation to speak.

'Guys, this isn't going to be pretty, I've been an idiot and you are not going to like me very much after this one.' Darcy coughed, gently.

In unison, Kate and Mina arched eyebrows.

'Are we talking murder?'

'Worse.'

'Just spit it out; I can't take suspense when it could be interesting.' Mina scoffed.

'It's about the reasons Jessica and I called it a day, actually, the human reason why. Jay, to be precise.'

'Him again. What is it this time?' Kate asked.

'I fooled around with him a bit, a while ago, I was too embarrassed to say anything and then the shit with Jessica and I just… '

'Oh, that,' Mina said, 'We already know about that, boring, next.' She drank a mouthful of beer as if uninterested, waving her hand back and forth to initiate the conversation move on.

Kate, wide-eyed, expressed dismay, but vocalised… nothing.

'Have you accepted the invite to the camping trip? I need numbers,' Mina asked.

Darcy felt flabbergasted, then deflated.

She had finally plucked up the courage to share her deception and had been shot down just as fast. The conversation continued but without Darcy's concentrated presence.

Mina had been too blasé, too direct, which could only mean she did not want to have the conversation while Kate was there, but the conversation was pending, just on hold.

Two cocktails later and Darcy sat outside the pub, checking her phone for bus times. Both Mina and Kate had left together ten minutes before and left Darcy feeling isolated from her own spirit, along with the alcohol and the spirit from the alcohol. She felt pissed and pissed off simultaneously.

Aloneness seemed to call to her, whispering promises of solitude and calmness. She was about to decline the camping invitation when a text from Mina appeared on her screen.

We need to have a chat…

Aloneness, instead of slipping away, remained, as if residue left on the sole of her shoe after standing on a chewy sweet on a scorching day. She inhaled and put her phone in her bag.

Mina the conversationalist had been her support system when the words they shared were intimate and telling. Mina was Darcy's first real friend in college, the person who brought wine and King crisps, chocolate-covered peanuts and small yellow bottles of rescue remedy.

Just in case.

Darcy had issues, deep running issues, that internalised as habits she simply ignored.

Habits that had formed inside her, formed without warning. Appearing incognito, too unidentifiable to label, like a rare gem, coved and undiscovered in a bleak cave. But just because she labelled these moments habits, in her heart Darcy knew each one was a form of depression.

A slight heavy head in the morning, a darkness, not black but grey, lingering as if a lone cloud deciding to pitch up and block the sun. She avoided naming it because to do so would give it power. But, when the grey metamorphosed from doubt, into self-doubt, as if a cunning, mercurial chess player, Darcy knew she was in trouble and that the obvious signs of mental illness had artfully curled up beside her and were now sitting safely in the pit of her stomach.

Chapter Seven

A walk in the park stress-free was something attainable for most people but, for Darcy, the imminent discussion she was about to have, weighed her down like the stones Virginia Woolf used to take her underwater. Time lapsed, then, eventually, Mina rounded the corner and joined Darcy on the bench, catching, as if planned, the minute between awkward and worried.

They were friends, they were good friends, the type to tuck, not sweep but tuck nonsense under the carpet. They'd both faced each other's misunderstandings, disagreements that bent but did not break, fraught with precious neglect but not unsurmountable; the type of problems friends wanted to fix instead of letting go. They were both dogmatic, but not towards each other. Towards each other, they had always been kind.

Until…

Darcy looked down and noticed the button on her shirt was open. Inside the fabric, a dark mark stained the inside of the material. When Darcy tried to remove the stain, the smudge caused a deeper impregnation. A light breeze and the stain but forgotten.

As Mina turned, and smiled half- heartedly.

'I'm not here to argue, I love you and I want to say that right off the bat, okay.'

'Sure.'

'It's not that you lied to me about Jay.'

'Lied, I didn't even get a chance… '

'Wait, please, I don't want to make this about him, this is about us, our friendship, who we are as people, and I need to say things to move on from it.'

'I get that, but moving on means I get a chance to explain too.'

'I just don't get how, for the last four years, you've been a lesbian, an activist, a feminist, a spokeswoman for equality, a liberal, someone who… '

'Why are we talking about someone I was four years ago, a shadow, a phantom?'

'Because you introduced yourself as the type of person I could relate to.'

'Well, four years ago I believed wholeheartedly and with passion that America could never have a worse president than Trump, but, there you go, I was wrong.'

'Who gives a shit about Trump Darcy, he's a million miles away, and will probably be voted in again anyway!' Mina preached, while sighing heavily.

Darcy held her hands out. 'What I mean is, things change, the world changes, thoughts, opinions, vibes, beliefs, knowledge, it all changes. I'm trying to grow as a person, allowing others to do the same.'

'But you've marched for lesbian rights, a staunch supporter and… '

'Can you hear yourself, Mina, do you know how ignorant you sound? Do you know you're offering your friendship with conditions? Do you understand that you're pressurising me to be something I'm not, to fit your mould?'

'My mould; it was you who stood proud in your identity, in your sureness, how can I be blamed for highlighting the fact?'

'Because, by doing so, you're contradicting everything we stand for. Freedom, and the right to be who we want to be.'

'I stand for that, it's you who doesn't, I mean, how can you be so confused about your sexual preference?'

'Who said anything about sex, or who I fancy? Did you ever think I might just enjoy Jay's company?'

'No, because Jay is an idiot.'

'You ask people to stop judging and it's all you do. I don't think you've had one proper conversation with him, Mina.'

'I don't need to; I know a narcissist when I see one, he's egotistical and vain, all the traits you said you dislike in a person.'

Darcy knew Mina had an issue with men, with all men, but she had never pushed her friend for more information as to why.

'And you think Jessica was perfect for me?

'I never once said that.'

'You know, *I would support you* no matter what was happening in your life.'

90

'I am supporting you, I'm here, aren't I? I just, I just don't want you doing anything you'll regret.'

'Like experiencing life, you mean? Or going with the flow of instinct, of desire?'

A moment that caused pause.

Across the green, a flower patch, flattened by children running over it, a desire path with no infinitive direction, the earthy soil underneath, a mattress for the multicoloured petals loosened or broken off distracted Darcy for a brief moment. The flowers disconnected from their stems and source of life, looked as though a listless rainbow, not unlike Darcy. She was brought back to a time as a child, summer evenings, running through corn fields, being chased, as laugher hummed, causing the same flatness as corn stems parted, forced to let children through, and sunbeams follow.

Darcy never wanted to do things to make other people feel bad, just herself feel better.

'You can hardly stand on a podium and scream for marginalised people now, can you?'

'I think I can because, in some ways, we're all marginalised. We're all pigeon-holed into separate groups because society dictates that, and people are afraid to break the status quo, the structure of the world they live in, in case the changes affect them in other ways. Some people, not all people.'

'Maybe I need to re-examine my values a little.'

'Maybe I need to call myself bisexual.'

'That greedy word, ugh.'

'Can we hug?'

'We can hug.'

'It's at this juncture that I should probably tell you I'm going to Jessica's house this weekend, some engagement party or something.'

'Oh, Darcy you need help, you do, and I'm here for that.'

They giggled, comfortable again.

'I'm not even sure why I said I'd go.'

'It's not too late to change your mind, it never is.'

It would probably take another conversation, one, over a bottle of wine, to really feel okay again, the okay that has innocence attached, the okay that's shiny and planted in newness from oldness, just fed with fresh air.

So, it was just as well that both women cared as much as the other about their relationship. So that both would put in the effort that was needed to, not only understand the other's opinion but respect said differences too.

*

When Darcy walked through the front door of her grandmother's house. Pat was putting milk in the fridge. By just looking at her, Darcy knew something was not quite right. Not only were Pat's clothes on backwards, but they were inside out too. The labels, as if the edge of a neck scarf around her neck, flapped about as she moved. It wasn't until Darcy was fully in the kitchen that she realised

Pat's hair was much shorter, that the perm done recently was all but cut away. Hesitant to upset Pat, Darcy chose to ignore the obvious until she figured out the means by which Pat had butchered her new hairstyle.

'Hi, Gran, how have you been today, did Philomena bring the shopping?'

'Oh, hello there, stranger, em, I think so, I just noticed there was no milk so I popped up to Supervalu there.'

The last time Darcy had been in Supervalu, one of the shop assistants, a local girl, had asked Darcy was her grandmother all right. *She seems a bit disorientated and she keeps buying bread-sticks, too many breadsticks, if ye ask me, well for one person, y'know.* When Darcy went back home that day, sure enough, one of the presses, had stacks of breadsticks, one packed on top of the other as if preparing for an apocalyptic ending or near miss, in which the mere sustenance provided by empty breadsticks would suffice.

Opening the fridge, five litres of milk, sat in the door tray shoulder to shoulder as if soldiers anticipating battle on the front line.

When Darcy was out, at work or socialising, she could not keep a watchful eye on her grandmother, the worry of it stayed with her like an insect bite causing a constant itch. Only for the fact of Philomena and Maryann's helping hands, Darcy would have to consider a different option. But that would be a last resort. Darcy had every intention of taking care of her grandmother until she could not anymore.

'Oh, do you know what I forgot, a lotto ticket, would you get me one when you're out… oh, and breadsticks, especially breadsticks, we're running short.'

Since a neighbour's recent win on the Lotto, Pat had insisted on buying a ticket every week. That was one of the things not slipping her mind, as yet. Thereafter, Darcy often wondered, *Do people who win big on the Lotto still buy a Lotto ticket?*

Pat's neighbour across the road had been part of a family syndicate that won the lotto. Winning a massive amount. Apparently, members of the family picked the same numbers for years, buying their tickets from a local country shop every Sunday. Not all members of the family participated in the draw but, when the numbers came through, the winning siblings included the absentees. Darcy thought that was a pretty amazing thing to do, so generous and inclusive. Sometimes she would stare across the road at the millionaire's house and wonder why he had not put up new blinds on his windows. His curtains hung bland, with cream lining, housing the empty windows, within draped stillness, that created a shadowed effect for the passing world to gape through. Or why chipped whitewash paint hung, attached by cobwebs, from his outside wall, crumbling at the corners, begging for attention.

He obviously did not care about blinds, he could buy a million blinds to pin to each rectangular shape seeking cover, if he wanted to. And, as for the paint job, she had seen him paint his wall annually, like everyone else on the row. He was probably too busy planning a holiday with his family, Darcy mused, and who could blame him.

Darcy sometimes thought about such mindless things, to fill an empty space in her brain.

'Hey Darcy, Darcy love, can you go to the credit union for me please?' Pat shouted from another part of the house.

'I need a letter and they said you need to pick it up for me. Something like that, I'm not quite sure.'

'Sure Gran, gimmie a sec.'

*

By the time she returned from the errant, the quietness felt heavy and the street felt empty. Darcy thought, just for a moment that she'd jumped off the bus at the wrong stop; that maybe her estate was further up. She side-stepped a pile of tipped out cigarette butts and walked over the neighbour's newly cut grass verge. The front gate was wide open and as she wiped down the hairs that stood gently but stout on her arm, Darcy noticed her Grandmother's front door was wide open too.

'Darcy, Darcy!' Maryann was behind her, frantic. 'Your gran, she's gone missing, we've all been out, the whole row has been searching. She came to me looking for you, and I asked her to wait until I grabbed my coat, then…oh, where could she be?'

Darcy's first thought was the ocean.

The flow and pull of the heaving waves, their powerful drag. The way they swallowed the water back, along with anything else caught up in the swell. She could hear the pebbles at the edge of the sea, she felt them rest and move, move and rest. She could hear the wind howl with a fierce determination, whipping hair and clothing

into a frenzied dance. She felt the salty spray from the churning waves sting her face, like the ocean itself was trying to convey its restless energy. As the gusts carried with them the scent of the sea, a pungent reminder of the untamed forces at play.

Stop! Darcy thought, Jesus, stop being so solemn. Pat hated the sand. The beach would be the last place she'd go.

'Have you searched the alleys?'

'I think Jonny and Frank have gone to look. I saw Marion heading to the shops, you know how your gran likes those ready-made dinners, I'm not fond of the mash myself but…'

'So Marion is gone to look for her too?'

'Yes.' Maryann sighed, 'Can ye think of anywhere. A place she might have mentioned Darcy?'

The graveyard, Darcy thought. Pat, over a cuppa recently had regaled Darcy with a yarn about her mam as a teenager, taking a pound shop bought Ouija board to the graveyard with a group of friends, to invite the dead back for a conversation!

Maybe, Darcy surmised, the chat had triggered something for her gran. Maybe.

'Let me just make a flash of tea,' Maryann said, 'And set that recorder thing for the news, and I'll be with you.'

'No, no,' Darcy replied, 'You've done enough, I'll head out on my own. I have an idea.'

'We might have to ring the guards soon.'

'I understand, I know.' Darcy nodded.

The iron gate had rust near the bottom, and as the gate opened with the dust that had gathered under the hinge, it made a gritty sound. The harsh noise only added to Darcy's pent-up irritation. On her tippy toes she scanned the gravestones. Not all the headstones stood erect. Time and neglect had caused some to topple. Darcy imagined those fallen stones, cracked and broken would have many stories to tell. On some, soft green moss hung like a blanket, tucking in and holding onto tales of the past.

Pat sat regally on the side of someone's grave curb, her legs folded, dragging on a fag. Her thin, lined lips, outlined, then layered with luminous pink lipstick. Rouge on both cheeks, plastered, like Aunt Sally from Worzel Gummidge. One slipper dangled, loose on her foot as it moved up and down, like the worries of the world were a world away.

Darcy stood still and watched her a moment.

Pat wore a nightdress that was practically see-through!

Her thinning, shortened hair was pushed back by a hairband; the fine texture wispy and delicate, albeit almost bald.

'Gran, what on earth are you doing here? It's getting late.' Darcy said.

97

'Oh Darcy, there you are, I knew we were meeting here. I thought I got the time wrong, but no I was right. I'm always right.'

'Maybe,' Darcy spoke, 'maybe you had a little dream, you could've dreamt that we were to meet. Whose grave is that anyway?'

'What? It's your mothers! Don't you recognise it?'

'No, Gran,' Darcy sat down and made her gran scooch-up. 'I don't think it is.' She put her arm around her gran's shoulder.

'Well, there's a lot of people I know here so what's the difference.'

A gate opened in the distance and a man walked in to the graveyard. It was the millionaire, he waved over.

'Did you say you'd let me cut your hair Darcy?'

Pat's words miffed Darcy. 'Cut it?'

Pat held up a small professional shears. 'I brought your Grandpa's scissors, he was a great barber in the Congo in the 1960's, a great solider too. The best.'

'Okay Gran, let's get you home, it's late. Let me text Maryann.'

'Why would ye text her?'

'To book her in for a trim.'

'What?' Pat looked surprised.

'Never mind, come on, let's go.'

Pat sauntered through the lined graves, reading the odd gravestone as she passed it by.

'There ye are Pat, ye had us worried for a minute.' The millionaire said, with a warm grin.

'Sure, where else would I be?' Pat answered, nonchalantly. Unaware of the havoc caused.

'Good to see you too Darcy, it's a fine evening.'

Darcy smiled, 'It is.'

'It's late now though,' Pat added, 'too late to be out. Come on Darcy, get a move on, why ye said meet here is a mystery.'

Darcy cast her eyes heavenward, endearingly and with an appreciative smile.

Chapter Eight

Jessica's parents were both psychiatrists and her brother, Tom, a radiologist. All of the -ologists and Darcy a chocolate seller. The psychiatrists were all about *naming* everything. *Be transparent*, had been their advice when Jessica had asked for it. They lived in Dun Laoghaire, in a Georgian house with an enormous back garden. As Darcy walked through a rose- flowered archway, she wondered to herself why she was here. A tightness in her throat gave way to a slight trickle, as she loosened the top button of her blouse.

Immense greenery and an array of colour offered up by the multitude of flowerbeds and perfectly planted flowers presented a picture-perfect picture. Guests gathered in small groups, engaging in small talk, to while away time before the real party began.

Darcy noticed other people her age, or lack thereof, but not anyone she would associate with. Just an odd familiar feature in the sauntering passers-by.

Who would she mingle with while Jessica busied herself being popular?

What exactly was the occasion? Oh, yes, Darcy recalled, it was Jessica's brother, Tom's engagement party. Darcy found an empty table and positioned herself to people-watch. As if the watching of people might ease the disillusionment that the people created being them, or just the pondering of it, of the people watching, for Darcy, might do the same, because her disillusionment was truly heightened.

A family gathering.

A family.

A mam, a dad, two kids and a dog. Ouch.

Suddenly, the edge of darkness swept in. Once it was only the edge then Darcy knew she could manage it. The edge was like a pointed finger, tapping her on the shoulder, an initial warning to say, *if you're not careful, a sucker-punch will be next.* Darcy knew the initial signs, the rudimentary stir. Anxiety had a way of casting a shadow. The shadow insisting it followed you around, wearing a dark coat, heavy and impenetrable, so no light seeped through, opaque and miserable.

The night previous, Darcy had curled up on her bed in a ball of anguish. The silent tears had come uninvited as if a dam wall cracked, waiting to burst. Seeing her grandmother slowly shrink had been the instigator, but what followed was every guilt-ridden incident Darcy had ever lived through. Each memory hurt. Her home hurt. Her job hurt. Her friends hurt. Her loneliness hurt. Her skin hurt. Her future hurt. Then, the self-hate, as if a volcanic eruption, its hot lava spewing insults, as if her internal dialogue was a co-host in her own destruction, her depression, part of a masterplan to make her small, where each imperative organ had agreed to play its part. The weight of her life was like a slow death. An illness that would chip away, as if a broken machine only working to keep itself entertained. Darcy knew she needed help but she had not admitted that to herself.

She could not, because life would not allow such an admission. Lying was her option.

And so it was then. More lies. Darcy reached for a glass filled with alcohol and let the liquid slowly calm her nervous system, and infiltrate her mind with deception.

'Hey,' ever so sprightly, Jessica appeared.

Like nothing ever happened, a catch-up chit-chat flowed freely, back and forth, back and forth. Like the old days without the love.

'I suppose you'll camp with Kate and Mina; that makes sense.'

'And what about you?'

'I've already agreed to stay in Dom's tent, only because he has a six-man tent and all the gear. A porta loo and all. I literally just have to show up. And the smell of his socks and feet will get zipped up when he sleeps.'

'I don't think this trip will beat last year's, do you?'

As soon as the words were out, Darcy wanted to retract them. The rumour that Jessica and Jay fooled around on that trip had reached Darcy one drunken pub-crawl. But Darcy was not trying to dig. She was in protection mode, the carer of her own heart.

'We can always make it better, we can do what we

want, except get too political, we all know what happens then.'

'I heard on the radio that the government will stop charging women for the pill, well, women of a certain age. So, I suppose that's something.'

'Oh, Darcy, ever the crusader of impervious women's causes, yay for the feminist, a little win is better than no win at all.'

'Somebody has to care, women deserve that agency, at least.' Darcy susurrated.

'Sorry?' Jessica uttered, slightly miffed. 'I care, but not when it's men making the adjustments to rules created by them in the first place. It's embarrassing.'

'I don't agree with you.' Darcy added, 'There are men out there that see with open eyes. They see women's issues as universal and not just with singular vision, they stand on the side of women. You should try it.'

'Ouch, is Darcy feeling a little argumentative, a little defensive today, too many wines?' Jessica teased blithely.

'I may have but at least I'm not acting like a pompous twat.'

Jessica giggled, unfazed by the insult.

'That's better. Being overtly cantankerous suits you more.'

'I have a sane rationale, that's all. I don't harbour unconscious bias either.'

'Prim and proper.'

'Are you going to take anything I say seriously today?'

'How can I, the world has become too serious. I'm all for women,' Jessica used air quotes to emphasis the word women, 'But I don't need to shout it from the roof-tops like Mina and the rest. And you're so broody anyway, confounding all my suspicions.'

'Mina knows what she's doing, Jess, she isn't pushing an agenda that doesn't have substance.'

'Okay, okay, I give up, whatever… ' Jessica took a huge mouthful of her drink. 'Come with me, I want to show you something.'

Jessica walked ahead as Darcy followed within an inch of her, her flowy, floral-printed skirt moving to allow movement, in between. She rounded the corner of an old out-building and the second Darcy caught up, she felt positioned and pushed up against the wall. Lips familiar but for the taste of strawberry daiquiri, searched her own. Tender but hungry. Her face cupped first and then released by one hand. The other under her shirt. A tongue, finding its way, entering a mouth, penetrating, eager and in control. Small tender kisses on the neck, wet upon the exposed part so sensitive to touch. Darcy began to ache, as her body moved submissively in whatever direction Jessica urged with sound, with approach. There was a newness to her touch, an urgency, as if something missing, had now returned. Returned to a hidden place, as the two women remained hidden. Out of sight, out of judgement and in the outsideness of it, a space to teter.

Jessica pulled away smiling, leaving a taste that Darcy licked from her own lips.

'I'm sorry, don't hate me. I had to kiss you, I've missed kissing you so much.'

How weird, Darcy thought, to kiss someone again after they've kissed someone that you kissed without their knowing, and the knowing of it, that was tied to ambivalence. A full circle of hypocrisy. But, standing face to face, not even fully understanding what just happened, Darcy realised the unpacking of the event, needed putting away for another time.

'I don't know what to say.'

'Nothing needs to be said, Darcy, stop being so sombre. Let me get you another drink. My parents should have the guitar out by now anyway. We can sing away our blues.'

Relief, that was how Darcy thought she should feel. There had been an inconspicuous desire to be kissed but relief sat with other emotions in the audience at an auditorium. In a performance called: Doubt. Maybe even in the back row of the dress circle, with a restricted view. Darcy felt a little used.

Indeed, by the time Darcy and Jessica returned, her family sat around playing musical instruments, singing happily, on this happy occasion.

A family.

A togetherness. A place Darcy now felt out of place.

Envy now sat together with relief, eating popcorn. The auditorium darkened for the show to begin.

There was a time when there had been sing-songs, family time and togetherness. Darcy was part of something just as real. A weekend-trip with her family to Donegal, Rosguill camping site. Crystal blue seas, golden sand and Irish accents, guitar playing camp-fire singalongs and roving children, feeling free and feeling freedom, in the gated community. A communal firepit where flames danced in harmony with the camping vibe. Long grass and sprays of wild flowers and freshly painted white fences. In a place beneath the vast canvas of the night sky families mixed, and then tents became homes as the rhythmic lullaby of gentle waves created an ethereal symphony that serenaded weary children to sleep.

A memory now, like all the rest.

As a dainty lady approached, Darcy side-stepped the memory, and blinked with fervour, while wiping the top of her lip, she focused intently as the woman drew near.

'Darcy, isn't it, I'm Muireann, Jessica's mum.' Her hand extended.

Ah, yes, Darcy thought, the head doctor, the adviser, the lady responsible for rearing a liberal, slightly narcissistic daughter, who hugs a lot.

'Oh, hi, yes, I'm me, pleased to meet you.'

'Jessica has told me so much about you.'

'Oh, I can imagine.'

'She speaks very highly of you actually, I'm surprised we haven't met before.'

'Me too, I guess time just slips away, I know we had planned a meeting, a few times at least, but something always came up.'

'Well, you're here now, I hope you can sing, we sing a lot here.'

'Me, oh, no, not a note.'

'Everyone has a note inside them… oh, here she comes, Jessica, Jess.'

'You have a lovely home Mrs-'

'Oh, call me Muireann, only my patients call me Mrs Galloway and, speaking of patients, if you ever need to talk Darcy, about anything, anything at all. Just pick up the phone, okay? I'll listen.'

'Why the serious faces, you two?' Jessica rosy-cheeked and flushed joined the conversation. But it was too late, Darcy had had enough.

'I have to leave, sorry to say but it's getting late and I'm opening the shop in the morning, so-'

'I'll leave you two, then… It was so nice meeting you at last, Darcy, don't be a stranger, now that you know where we are.'

'Oh, surely you don't have to leave just yet. Things are heating up; people are puking in the corner and falling into ditches and all sorts.'

'I have to get an early night.'

More lies.

Darcy felt suffocated, overwhelmed. In silent prayer that an earthquake would, shake the ground, invoke terror and send everyone scurrying for cover, and her into a deep hole.

'I will text you, we can chat that way, if you're not too plastered that is, go, go and enjoy the rest of your night with your family, enjoy it while no one is fighting or being obnoxious.'

She turned to leave, which left Jessica standing in her own confusion. And it was in confusion and the sharing of that particular emotion that Darcy understood, was the only thing that made them compatible now.

The bus was empty, the top deck with rows of empty two-seaters. Darcy had her choice of smelly seats. Feeling rather melancholy, she put her head against the window. As the bus wheels turned, so too did her mind in relation to the kiss hours before. What did it mean? Perhaps it meant nothing. What was a kiss anyway, it was hardly a meeting of minds, of morals, of future goals? It was merely another reason to over think.

That obligatory heart shape someone draws with their fingertip, after breathing on a bus window, appeared before Darcy even realised what she had done.

And the thinking of it, and the trying to not think of it, was almost too much.

The relationship between Jessica and Darcy had soured. Lust still lingered, as lust often did, but equality, balance, vulnerability, commitment, longing, and effort— they were all missing. Like opening an sealed Easter egg as a kid and the small candy-wrapped sweets weren't inside.

Looking out the window as the bus passed, Darcy watched windowed compartments of different connective interactions play out as her eyes flickered open and shut.

Teens training, holding hands in a circle as if a human daisy chain, the football net their backdrop, as the sun continued its lonely decent. People queuing outside the cinema, laughing at one another's silly jokes before deciding if, this time, they would have butter on their popcorn instead of just salt.

Dogs on leads, walking their owners, tongues hanging out, tails wagging, trying to avoid joggers, who believed they owned the path. Some, if not all, then definitely a few, thinking what a nice evening it was.

Darcy thought again about Jessica, her kiss, their coupling, but resolved to forget about the encounter. The complication attached to the kiss would not be worth the hassle. But the kiss had been lovely.

The kissing had always been quite lovely.

The bus stopped. Darcy's eye followed action from below. Yelping puppies in a basket and attached to the basket, a small sign that read *For Sale Twenty Euros Each*. In that same second Darcy wanted to run down the winding staircase of the bus and scoop each puppy into her arms, preventing their mistreatment, or neglect or every negative thought that had managed to enter her brain regarding the puppies' welfare. As if it were no one else's responsibility but hers to be their savour. Of course, the bus moved away and the side street soon became as if a hazy mirage, in the evening twilight.

Darcy searched in her bag for lavender hand cream and applied the lotion, skin on skin, hoping to induce the type of calming effect promised in an article she had read recently about natural fragrances and their benefits.

The yelping puppies, the very image of them at least replaced, albeit temporarily, by the image of Jessica and her flowy, floral print skirt.

Chapter Nine

Opening the front door, the first thing Darcy noticed was her grandmother on the floor. Two slippered feet, one resting upon the other, one slipper slightly off at the heel but unmoving. Why would her grandmother be lying on the floor, still, like a plastic mannequin waiting to be dressed for an early morning window display?

'Ahhh, ah.'

'Gran, Gran, what happened, are you hurt?'

In a moment of panic, the panic gives permission to be idiotic, it almost insists upon it, *be an* idiot, it says, a complete twat, say stupid, obviously stupid things, that state the obvious. The most common of these enquiries being the redundant question, are you okay, when someone is most unequivocally not!

'I fell, I think I fell and hurt my arm. Is your mother here, can you get her for me, please?'

At the hospital, hours later, Darcy sat bedside, sobbing quietly, ashamed that Pat now had her arm in a cast and was sedated because of the pain.

Pain, Darcy thought, her frail grandmother had been in pain, while she was out exploring her options. Sitting in the room, the clean clinical room, Darcy could still smell faint cigarette smoke from her grandmother's short hair. She was thankful the hospital bedroom smelled of cleaning products and antiseptic because, lately, living with her grandmother had been like living in an old pub bar, where the stale smell of used butts and ashtrays remained long after the establishment's patrons had left.

She was glad of the clean air, glad that Pat was in bed being watched, being minded, being not so much *a burden*. And then she pinched herself, actually dug her fingernails in for being so mean and having mean thoughts about the grandmother she'd neglected and left to fall, on the cold kitchen tiles, with her short self cropped hair, and break her arm.

Her own nails split the skin on her wrist. She raised her arm to her mouth and licked away the evidence. The metallic salty taste of blood rested on her tongue.

She thought a minute about walking outside to the car park and not looking left or right before stepping onto the road, then she thought about how strong a branch would have to be to hold her weight.

Just in case.

Darcy's phone chimed in her bag.

Hey, I just got your message, I'm gonna come over there and see you.

No, honestly no. That's not necessary, I'm okay.

I'm coming, I'll bring coffee.

Darcy had no idea, none at all, why she rang Jay of all people. Maybe it was because he would not ask too many questions. Jay was coming over, to be some form of comfort, the type with no ulterior motive. None on display anyway. He was bringing coffee so they could sip it to fill in the lull their inadequate pleasantries might not cover.

*

'I'm not trying to be nosey, really, but you never mentioned you lived with your gran before. I had no idea.'

Jay was being friendly, enquiring but not in a prying manner, not in an intrusive way. Jay did not have that in him. And Darcy knew that, that he wouldn't push, or overstep.

'It's a temporary thing. She has a carer and she left early, she text me, but I never saw the text, I was out, so our lines got crossed and now this.' Darcy shrugged before pointing to Pat's hospital bedroom. Looking for comfort but not wanting physical touch.

Hospitals had become overcrowded and because of staff shortages patients were only allowed immediate family to visit.

Jay had still come though, he had still come to listen.

'Is there anything you need?'

A new life.

'No, no, the coffee is all I need, thank you.'

'You'll still make the camping trip though, right? I mean, she's here being looked after?'

The trip had completely slipped Darcy's mind. Darcy could not decide now. She had not slept properly and felt discombobulated. I could actually get out of the trip over this, she thought, but then thought better of it.

113

'Yeah, I guess. I think they're keeping her in for a week, for observation and to carry out certain tests.'

'Well, then. I think you need it too, the trip and she'll be fine, in the best place and all that,' Jay said reassuringly.

'Yeah but what type of granddaughter would I be, popping off to a festival while she is in hospital?'

'The cool type. I don't think she will mind Darc and I'm sure there's other relatives willing to visit.'

Being sure was one thing but being right was another. In reality, there was no one else. Darcy was the only one left. The lone survivor but for an ailing grandmother hanging on by an erosive thread.

'I was gonna walk home and take a shower; I could use the company if you're free. No pressure.'

'Sure, I'm not working until this evening.' Jay smiled.

'Work, damn, just gimme a minute. I need to make a call.'

Darcy, who hardly ever called in sick to her job, was convinced to take a week's leave, they could manage and she deserved a break. Stopping to buy milk and air freshener, Darcy told Jay that the house might not have been aired out in a while and to expect a stagnant, musty smell, to which he laughed, citing his own living space in comparison, followed by the words *not to worry*. In recent weeks, Pat had taken up smoking at least thirty a day, while pottering around, closing every window that Darcy had opened earlier that day. Ash falling on the carpet as she moved from room to room.

As they walked towards the front door, Darcy, once again, thought about her motives in contacting Jay. Maybe, she surmised, that in life, people required other people, specific people for certain jobs, for certain situations, for unexpected events or for expected events when required. She was that person for other people, called especially to avoid candid conversations. And the reaching out, for the most part, was an ongoing thing, a mutual thing and each living person was participating in these exchanges on a subconscious level, never asking why but moving with intuition, trusting in its esoteric power, without question or reservation.

Darcy's rambling brain slowed as she entered the hallway.

Suddenly, she felt the heaviness of exhaustion, and could hardly stand.

She wobbled, light-headed but that intuition, so to speak, meant Jay reached her before she fell, embracing her firmly until he navigated the space and found a sofa to lay her down.

Chapter Ten

The days preceding and the day of the camping trip Darcy cancelled then reaffirmed her place on the train and the subsequent shenanigans that would bring. Eight college students on their summer break, meeting up to cause havoc, but, for Darcy, she was along for the ride to escape reality. Maybe the others were too, in their own way, harbouring secrets, keeping secret personal struggles close to their chests. Who could really lay claim to knowing someone else's meandering of the mind? Or the truths veiled beneath a haze, meant as a diversion.

The seating was detailed so as not to cause any awkwardness. A pre-booked mapping of bums on specific seats, a thought-through dynamic to avoid discomfort and awkward silences. Almost everyone in the group had messed around with one another at some stage in their years together. A fact that was intimately incestuous in an odd acceptable way that seemed to escape the scrutiny it deserved. An allyship, on a form without signatures. But a few hurt someone, and that was the jagged edge. The dense, dark perpetual cloud, even on a sunny day.

'You can drink alcohol, sure they bloody sell it on that cart thing they bring around and there's a bar at the back of the train. How can they tell if it's theirs or your own, get it down ye? Down the hatch old boy?'

Dom, ever the androcentric pussycat, the man that has to be a man, in the stereotypical sense of the word, gripped a beer can in one hand, unintentionally causing a dent. And, facing him, Jay sat, perplexed, not his usual upbeat sarcastic self. Darcy assumed he was acting reservedly to protect her feelings. As if two peas in a pod. Knowing she was an emotional wreck and hoping to show his support, tacitly.

Darcy had asked that he not wallow because she had made a promise to herself to enjoy the trip, two nights away without any loose commitments, and all that that entailed. If she could manage, could muster that, the managing of it, with some effort, then so should he. The nights before, when he had minded her and she had let him, there was no exchange of appreciation for what he had done, because the right words escaped her and she was fearful, in a weak moment, of articulating her truth. A realness, set, as if a ruby, a precious gemstone, in a velvet case, in a protected glass display box, guarded by butch men with machine guns, that she could never disclose, expose or reveal.

While she rested on the sofa, under a banket he had found and draped over her, he had busied himself opening windows all over the house, an inch on each, hoping to let in fresh air. But what escaped from outside indoors was used air, from an old estate, reproduced. An elderly couple's fire lighting, even in summer, burning banned turf and polluting toxins already swirling through the heavy evening mist. A smoky barbecue with sizzling steak and hot dogs, fried onions and burnt butties, charcoal chicken wings and firepit coals. The aromas of an active estate, where fresh air, as if encased in a dome, was non-existent. Dogs barked constantly as man's constant companion polluted the air another way.

But Jay had opened the windows as a caring gesture and Darcy, being elsewhere in her thoughts, had forgotten to thank him. She had forgotten to say, that the kind gesture stung, like a pain from a cut; as if appreciation was cause for getting stitches, or a bandage or a cast. And that the voice she used to say thank you usually came coupled with a voice that gave a reason, and that particular voice was lost, she had lost her voice. So, she looked at him instead, in hope of saying thank you with her eyes. In hope of catching his gaze before alcohol and stupidity took the place in his memory of her, a few nights back, when he had minded her and she had let him.

Now, as the passing rays of sunshine made him blink, he laughed at whatever Dom said next, a kind of false laugh, to fit in, held together with a hesitancy that only Darcy noticed. And the moment moved on, just like the train.

'Are you okay, Darcy doo?' Mina's pet name for her when she was tipsy, 'You seem distracted. It's such a pity Kate couldn't make it, isn't it. I think the new hormone she's taking isn't sitting well in her stomach?'

An approbatory nod and then Darcy said,

'I'm good, I'm just anticipating the hangover, how old am I?' Darcy put her plastic glass of wine on the table. 'Y'know Kate is most definitely naked right now and engaging in sexual pleasure, while we're stuck here, in this stuffy carriage with Dom's farts and his massive ego. The hormone tablet situation is only an excuse.'

'He is bloody gorgeous though, if I didn't love women I would definitely go there,' she whispered, as if anyone could hear her over the constant exchanges across the train tables, and a tad afraid in case someone did.

'It's okay to say he's a bit of all right, Mina, he's built like an Adonis and, in all fairness, he can hold down chat.'

'Slay, but only as long as it's about GAA or the players on the Irish Rugby team.' Mina added with an emphatic grunt, curling her nose up at the mention of sport.

'Not true, I've heard him, on more than one occasion, explicitly, no, that's the wrong word. I've heard him recite Daffodil, word for word, honestly.'

'Stop, Wordsworth?'

'Well, not the whole thing, but at least a few verses, he was very eloquent, actually.'

'I wandered lonely as a cloud, that floats on high o'er vales and hills.'

'Shush, Jesus, he'll hear you, I gave my word, I wouldn't sneer on this trip.'

Darcy laughed, 'Well, you didn't promise me and, anyway, you hate poetry, especially the romantic era. I'm surprised you even listened to poor Dom's rendition without blatantly yawning.'

119

'I yawned under my hand, he was concentrating too much to notice.'

Darcy saw above Jay's head on the train, poems adorned the walls above the luggage rack. Each train carriage framed poems or prose by revered Irish writers, to teach and enlighten the younger generation about Empire and love and unrequited love and towers, and famine and about uprising, and political opinion, and Godot and about Innisfree and Maud and making bread and freedom and of Dorian and beauty and The Dark and of Dedalus and of a beautiful isle, robbed of its wholeness by greed and the Black and Tans, buggers and all, their brutality and their disregard and their stealing of language, and the spoken Gaeilge word, native until spoiled by uncultured barbarism. And their giving of English, which was handy- while the Catholic church and its hypocritical members turned the other cheek.

Ireland's history framed in each carriage of the passing train, passing on and then passing back again.

Men's voices amplified while the silence of "woman" seemed ever-present.

How many young Irish women from the twentieth century wrote poetry that never made it into the history books, a question Darcy asked the glass window that showed her deep reflection, - let alone the wall of a modern form of transportation? Women who could hardly write because it was prohibited or frowned upon. How many women bounced words off the inside chambers of their minds with nowhere to land because they were never taught how to read or write or how to be creative, or taught the beauty of creativity and of how to place it down on paper.

Poems wasted, unwritten.

Caged in a way, like a bird without a voiced birdsong.

At least Emily Dickenson within a pioneering moment, had the skill even if she feared the publication of her life's work to immerse herself in the work and the recreation of the traditional verse, suited to her idea of inspiration. Her poems were chronologically bound, as if self-published, in a drawer for years without seeing the light of day.

Poems, wasted, but written in a way a person sees the world from inside a bedroom, four walls that encased boundless talent. Wasted, but only until the dawn of the poems' power, even though the author of the works had long since passed.

Darcy thought about the art of woman, about the beauty of woman, she thought about the curves and traces of a woman's body. She thought about that quite a lot, in fact.

'Hey, are you listening?' Mina sat again after an unnoticed absence.

'I can't imagine Dom would have the voice for poetry.'

'Oh, I don't know, nothing would surprise me about anyone on this trip.'

Darcy's phone beeped.

How are you holding up?

Darcy frowned towards Jay, checking first that Mina was distracted. Then she replied, *Stop texting me, just enjoy yourself. I'm fine, we'll catch up later.* Jay sipped his beer without looking her way. Jessica sat in the same section as Jay but not directly facing him, she faced Lottie, who sat beside Jay. Both girls seemed engrossed in conversation, sharing phone pictures, Spotify tunes, podcasts, and whatever else.

Darcy had not really spoken to Jessica since her brother's party and the kiss. It bothered her in a superficial way, as superficial things did, heaving with lightness, non-committal and unperturbed. Did it render a conversation? An argument? A shot in the dark? An actual shot of sambuca by the campfire? Who knew?

Darcy would take things one step at a time, without shoes on, or even socks, nothing cumbersome, nothing restrictive.

The conductor walked through and asked for tickets to be presented, scanning them on his machine, one by one. 'Where are you lot off to, the arts, or whatever you call it, the book festival thing is it, the one in Cork?'

'It is indeed, the very one. We have a keen interest in literature, and anything artsy-fartsy, don't we, Darcy?'

Darcy, unamused, just shook her head gently, sipped her wine, and glanced around. She wondered if her grandmother was more coherent today, or if she had eaten without assistance.

'The hotels are packed this time of year, hostels too,

so I hope you've somewhere booked,' The conductor stated, acting concerned.

'Oh, we've tents, pitch forks and alcohol, so we're sorted, ta, sure we're a bunch of organisers, pedantic and anal, in everything we do, except for Jay here, he's a lazy git.'

Jay shrugged. 'Meh.'

Jessica got up from her seat and, while all the attention was on the conductor, indicated with her eyes towards Darcy, a simple head nod beckoning her to follow.

The last time Darcy followed Jessica anywhere, it messed with her equilibrium, so she decided to stay put and send a text instead. Would it be rude, Darcy thought, if she put her earphones on and continued listening to *Ulysses* on audiobook? An endeavour she had begun months previously but put on pause over and over, knowing that Joyce demands acute concentration.

The figures seated around her were all familiar with one another's ways and drunken habits. They shared lectures, assignments and debates on the different lecturers' delivery and content. They sat, in the midday sun, or between light showers, circled on campus grounds, giving opinions on trends, what was trending and current affairs, what books they had read and which ones left an impact, or were worth a conversation following a blow-up on Book Tok and going viral. They all knew each other to a certain degree, but, by the same token, hid parts of themselves. Like the Johari window theory, which teaches interpersonal awareness, recognising that people treat others how they see themselves while hiding parts that constitute the real self. Darcy, in her comfortable hiding space, had managed well enough. It was sustaining the shield, the wall, the veil that had lately become a problem, chipping at her resolve and whatever cheap material her window was made from.

Three hours later, and they all stumbled into the camping site, mostly two by two as if entering Noah's ark, late, but before the deluge. One hour and ten minutes after that, all the tents were pitched, the campfire simmered and the group began to assimilate into their outdoor surroundings. Darcy, from inside her open tent, enjoyed immensely the smells related to sleeping outside. Old pine needles and musky, slow-burning smoke, damp, flattened grass and evening dew. The clamminess created by moving bodies, too tired to wash or just unbothered. The camaraderie of close spaces and the constant exchanges of friends enquiring about friends, a torch, bog-roll, a lighter or a beer. All under the star-studded canopy of night, and sharp contrasting mornings.

Through the flapping door of the tent, Darcy watched Jay in deep conversation with Cora, a medical student, specialising in paediatrics, who was Lottie's best friend and new to the group. His hands moved to express his opinion. Cora moved her head in response, agreeing with whatever drunken gibberish Jay could muster.

The silky zip door blocked, then showed clips of their playful interactions, until Darcy got up and tied the door back, to keep it open and her view unobstructed.

Jay unfazed, did not even look up, which, in some strange way, annoyed her.

She rubbed her eyes and when they opened she was faced with her friend's grin.

'You're unpacked, move your arse.' Mina, eager as ever, clapped her hands together, 'Chop, chop.'

'I'm knackered already, I just want to lay here and watch the world go by, it's so entertaining. And I have a niggling headache.'

Mina kicked mud from her boots, already covered from the outing.

'Well, you can't, we need you, so out you go, my lovely. I've saved a log, a big one, for you to sit on, it's next to me.' She pointed. 'I've been creeping on a group of girls pitched not too far from here. They're understated and look like your type, we should go mingle.'

'Creeping makes you sound, ugh… '

'Admiring then, for fuck sake, Darcy, just get up and take a look, swallow some paracetamol and stop whining.'

Darcy practically dragged herself out of the tent, wrapped in a padded sleeping bag, she reluctantly joined the others by the campfire. Along the outside of the camping grounds, large poles with Chinese lanterns illuminated the evening sky and swayed in a motionless dance full of light, motion and grace. Darcy scanned the area to gauge who was palatic, who was merry and who was just about keeping it together. She had been getting there herself, on the train earlier but, after two bottles of cooled water, was now sober and lethargic. Dom was singing and, in between lyrics, explained the itinerary for the following day. Taking control as if chief organiser. Darcy knew, come morning, Mina would delegate the proper instructions. Darcy had decided against the trip to the previous residence of Sophie du Plantier. For reasons, she was not going to explain.

Jessica sat with Dom, singing, falling over and answering Darcy's text with a *whatever, Darcy,* earlier on in the day.

'I need to use the loo.' A slurred outburst.

Cora broke away from Jay long enough to almost trip over one of the tent pegs.

'Cora, you're not going on your own. Will one of you eejits go with her?'

'Stop, I'm fine,' Cora replied.

'You may be fine now and that's the point. Keeping you fine, keeping you safe. The world is gone crazy. There's no way you're walking anywhere on your own, do you know how many women get assaulted every year in this country, just from being on their own?' Mina said.

'Ah, here we go, the men are all dickheads speech.'

'No, no, not all men, I'm not saying that, I'm trying to highlight a point.'

'Not here, Mina, we're trying to forget about the shit that goes on outside this campsite, even if it's only for a couple of nights.'

'Why, because, if we don't talk about it, then it might go away, is that it… if we don't talk about how women can't go anywhere alone without feeling leered at or stared at or, worse, stalked, attacked, left for dead, then it won't affect us, is that it?'

'No one is saying that; there's no one here going to argue with you over how disrespected women are sometimes in society, we're just saying tonight is not the night for deep chat, it's bound to cause an argument.'

'Well, you would say that, because you don't have to walk anywhere looking over your shoulder, feeling shadowed by a psychopath.'

'Jesus, Mina, that's a bit offensive, sit down and take a chill pill, people might have had experiences you don't know about.'

'Actually,' Jessica casually interjected, 'It's not just men who disrespect women, women, by their own accord, disrespect them too, maybe not to such a nefarious degree but in a sneaky, unscrupulous way.'

'Really, Jessica, you're one to talk.' Mina said.

'We're not opening the door on that one, are we?' Jay drunkenly added.

Darcy had stayed quiet up until this point because her headache, which instead of niggling, now pounded like the beat of a bass drum.

'Guys, please, people are staring over at us, can we please, please talk about something else for now, it's too fucking sensitive a subject, and you're all plastered.'

Darcy hardly ever swore, so the mere fact of it moved the conversation towards a similar topic without the angered tone. Moving away from arguing, between sobering up and getting drunk again.

And, in the stillness of that moment, Jay got up to accompany Cora to the portaloo. The light off his torch flickered by Darcy's face as he passed by.

'It is insane to think that, whoever murdered Sophie, got away with it though, isn't it?'

'I rest my case.'

'Well, a man,' said with air quotes. 'A man got dragged through the mud for that. It was never proven but we all have our doubts and there wasn't enough evidence, so no one knows for sure, it's not a fact.'

'Which could lead into a debate on how men are wrongfully accused sometimes, right?'

'What's the plan for tomorrow, or is there a plan?'

The mood had darkened to emulate the sky, a silent hum of light conversation spread over tent tops all through the camp, but on a lowered vibration, most people turning in for the night.

'Speaking of tomorrow, I'm going to sleep or I won't be able to function.'

'How old are you, fifty? Don't be such a bore.' Mina cited.

'Hardly, I'm not at one of your poetry readings.'

'Oh, that was mean, you're mean.'

'I love you really.'

Darcy's main objective in calming the tension had been to preserve any probity left in the group and to not propagate speechifying alcohol-induced issues any further than necessary. But opinionated college students enjoyed debating on current topics, especially if opinions differed, about sexism and equity and power. So, the chat back and forth was still heightened regardless. And, of course, Darcy understood it was not all men that were anything in particular and, of course, it was not all women, but the air held the sentiments of the previous conversation for ammunition.

Just in case.

And the drunken banter continued, as sleep came and rescued some while the lack thereof tortured or engaged others.

*

Dom was not supposed to be bivvying, as if on a cliffs edge, but ended up sleeping outside, in a drunken stupor. As Darcy zipped across the tent door, he moved and groaned, rubbing his crunched-up face.

'Dom,' Darcy whispered, 'Move into your tent, get some proper rest.'

Dom responded by turning face down beside a cluster of used beer cans, so Darcy parked her good intention, grabbed her wash bag and headed for the camp's restrooms.

The hanging lanterns now extinguished, resembled floating dead balloons without a destination. Suspended, deflated and void of colour. A bit like Darcy's morning head and her thoughts on the pending day. The memory of last night still fresh of how, when Mina climbed into their tent wanting to have a full-blown whispered conversation about Jessica's comments by the campfire, Darcy shushed her and explained tent walls carried voices. The advice went unheeded and Mina continued in a lowered tone than a whisper, a whispered whisper, *that Jessica was bang out of order!* And should be pulled up on her attitude and comments in front of the group.

Mina's instigating and profoundly argumentized comments, were, of course, all but forgotten. An eristic trait in Mina's genetic make-up, Darcy thought, that Mina would deny in a heartbeat.

As if serendipitous Jay exited the male loos, just as Darcy reached the entrance. His head dishevelled and like a curled mop.

'Good morning, I see you're an early bird too. How's the head?'

Other people roamed about half-dressed, some in patterned PJs, some fully clothed. All with a bed head, portraying a lack of essential sleep hours.

'Not so much an early bird as Dom's snoring.'

'Didn't you bring earplugs, I remembered him from last year.'

'I did, but I can hardly remember going to sleep, to be honest.' Jay added.

Darcy shifted in her footing.

'Oh, right, did you stay up much later?' (Did you sleep with Cora?)

'I've no idea, I noticed you left early enough though.'

'Early,' Darcy said surprised, 'It was after two, Jay.'

'Oh, was it, there you go, Jesus, I was pissed. Was there a row of some kind?'

'Only the usual, the annual falling out the first night of camping, to spend the next day loving on one another, it's almost scripted.'

'Well, I'll look forward to that after a nap; what time are we doing stuff?'

'I'm not sure about the others but I'm going to actually attend an event this year.'

'Right,' Jay added, 'most years it's the pub next door.' He smiled.

'There's a bookstore I want to find. Apparently, it resembles Shakespeare's Company in France, shelf for shelf, the shop that published Joyce's Ulysses when no one else would.'

'Oh shit, yeah, I remember you talked about that before. That's really cool, I think I'd rather do that. I'll come.'

'You will not, sure isn't that house you're all interested in, in some remote place, I won't be in any rush to get back for that.'

'You're going nowhere on your own, Darcy, didn't you listen to your own best friend last night? I'm going, just not right now, after a few winks and some liquid to settle the stomach, along with a chicken fillet roll.'

Jay left her standing and walked back towards the tents, lined as if one big attached patched blanket, with big gaping holes pinned to the earth.

By the time Darcy returned, her friends were up and about and chatting as normal, last night's antics forgotten in the fresh morning air of a new day.

Strangers walked through and past their camping spot, think heeled boots unlaced and rara skirts, combat shorts and Veja trainers, flip-flops and bare stained feet. No one cared, no one had to and that was the best part of festival life. Youth allowed freedom and festivals allowed that freedom to have a communal playground. Each pitched tent of self-assured festival goers celebrating life in their own adolescent and ignorant way. The lively, calming atmosphere of selected music picked by faceless figures, tuned to different dials. Some played real instruments and, others, air guitar strums strikes with silent tones. Tie-dye tee shirts and luminous headbands, striking pink and lime green. As if following a strict dress code to tolerate a florescent afterglow, be a thing.

Along the outside of the camping grounds stalls lined the walkway separating two camping fields. Wooden framed mini-shops selling everything from healing stones to carved wooden ornaments and everything in between. Decorated with rows of half-looped bunting, tasselled at the bottom, in every colour. Wind chimes chimed because wind whistled every now and then, as a kaleidoscope light-catcher, folded in on itself, then folded out again.

Darcy searched around for a sock that had been paired in her bag, but was now somewhere else entirely.

'I can't believe you agreed to let Jay go into town with you,' Mina said under her breath, while they rolled up their sleeping bags in unison; a loan sock found underneath. 'That, my friend, is a disaster waiting to happen.'

'I didn't exactly encourage him, he kind of invited himself. I wanted a bit of me time to... '

'Hey,' Jay appeared, being all smiley and energetic, while holding the tent flap open.

'Cora wants to tag along with us, I hope you don't mind.'

Mina, without being obvious, pinched Darcy, not enough to hurt but enough to make her wince.

'Of course, she doesn't mind, do you, Darc? She was just talking about you, actually, and of how spending time with people is the main objective of her day?'

'Uh huh, Darcy does love a chat.' Jay grinned.

'Are you sure you two don't wanna go instead?' Darcy smirked.

'How can I go when I've so much research to do? Oh, that reminds me. There's a book I want. Can you pick it up for me while you're in the village, what's it called again? Gimme a sec, I have it written down somewhere.'

Darcy stepped out and stretched to where Jay held an air of quiet contemplation, as if lost in thought about something needing a great deal of reflective processing before saying yes or no.

'Where is Cora, is she ready? I want to leave soon.'

'You don't mind her coming do you, she asked me off guard and I... '

'Mind? Why would I?'

'There could be a number of reasons, Darcy, but we'll park them for now, I want to talk to you about something anyway.'

'Is this about last night?'

'What... no, it's something else. Something completely different.'

'Guys, just gimme one sec.' Cora appeared, then disappeared into her tent, hair wet from a cool shower, smelling of coconut oil and pomegranate.

'Okay, gang,' Mina said raising from her tent and raising her voice, to a soft screech, 'We leave in ten, anyone coming with me that is, and I'm not calling door to door, you're all adults.'

'Have you seen Jessica and Lottie yet?'

'I think Jessica was sick last light, too much tequila, she's still asleep, and Lottie has gone ahead with Dom.'

Jessica, hearing her name, joined the conversation from her sleeping bag.

'I'm awake, don't dare leave without me, I'll be ten minutes, I just need to find my missing shoe.'

One quaint town later and Darcy followed Jay and Cora into a coffee house, citing caffeine addiction the reason for a rest, as opposed to the truth—an afternoon hangover.

'Can't you put the address into your phone, save us walking up every alleyway in the town.' Jay said.

'Do you think I haven't tried that? The name must be changed, maybe we should just ask people.'

'What and do the thing I suggested about forty-five minutes ago, right.'

'Children, children,' Cora sneered, as if getting practice in for her post-graduate profession. 'We'll ask someone, simple as, we'll get there. Sip up.'

'Have the others put pics up on social media yet, you know what Mina is like?'

'No, actually, not yet.' Darcy replied.

Moments later and Cora and Darcy were alone.

'So, what's the story with you and Jay?' Cora grinned.

Darcy almost choked on her delicious latte. 'Me and Jay?' She raised an eyebrow while catching drips on the end of her tongue. 'That story ended on a cliff-hanger, that no one is paying money to see.'

'Oh, I don't know, I think some people might disagree.'

Jay had gone out to take a call, excusing himself with a slight wave.

'Do you like him?' Cora continued.

'Of course, I do, he's my friend, you know I'm a lesbian, right, you know lesbians can have straight friends?'

'Sure, but not ones they play around with, I mean, that would be confusing for everyone, would it not?'

'What exactly are you asking me, Cora, do you want to know if I fancy him, if I lie about being a lesbian to sound cool, hip, current, because everyone seems to be something queer these days?'

'What? No, I don't care about that.' She added, obfuscating the conversation further.

'You don't know shit.' Darcy added, with an edge.

'I didn't mean that, to question *your* intentions. I like him, I guess, I'm asking if he's off limits. I don't want to over step the mark.'

'I'm not his mother, Cora.'

Cora gave a disappointing shrug, because she did not illicit a confession of undying love from Darcy, and felt placed back into square one when what she really intended was a square much farther along.

Jay walked back into an intense situation but either his phone conversation would take precedence over the obvious, or he was just too tired to pick up on the hovering aftertaste of a seemingly light-hearted bitter exchange.

Why am I feeling bitter, Darcy thought, but she was, and she wanted to leave the shitty café with its delicious coffee and roam the shitty alleyways alone, to look for a bookstore that *she* had researched months prior. As if calling everything shitty would make it so, when, in fact, it was how she felt on the inside. She did not want Jay to be with Cora. There, it was out of the suppressed mind and into a space to where no one else had access. But at least it was out from the pool of denial that swam around aimlessly without any ladder. At least she had named it, not the why of it, or the where to go with it, or the impossibility of it or the significance of it, or who it could hurt or change or maim. Oh no, not the important parts but, still, she looked at him now, differently. A little bit different. And that really pissed her off!

'I just got a text from Dom; everyone is in the pub in some country village havin' the craic, they're asking us to go find them. They couldn't find the house, isn't that gas? So they went to the nearest bar and now Mina is on the table singing political anthems and patriotic songs about independence.' Jay was smiling, 'What do you think?'

'I'm in,' Cora replied.

'Do I have a choice?' Darcy asked.

'It doesn't look that way. Come on, get your jacket, it'll be fun.'

The bookstore would have to remain for another day undiscovered, its floors not stepped upon by Darcy's shoe soles, its book pages unturned and unleafed through by Darcy's touch. She felt panicked after leaving the safety of the café but there was nothing she could do, only follow the crowd, and the man named Jay. Resistance was futile. Anyway, they say resisting something only brings it closer.

Suddenly, in Darcy's world, things, all things, were more than close enough.

*

They jumped in a taxi; Jay sandwiched between two women who barely knew one another, but shared a common interest, a common goal.

Darcy faced the country road instead of the other passengers, she wanted to feel nature through the glass. The green fields were in need of rain because of climate change and the hot weeks of early summer that deprived the roving fields of crucial nourishment. Dull yellow patches and withered stems where ripened fruit and healthy grass should be, changed the landscape of the expansive scenery, asking questions without a voice. And just beyond the lazing grass laid calm lakes, where any given day the ripples rose and fell, rushed fiercely, then rested again. The Irish countryside was never in question when it came to giving the eye a treat.

Cora's phone rang, she answered it on the second ring.

'Hey, yes, yeah, we're in a taxi, we're on the way.'

While Cora entertained someone on the other end of the line, Jay put his hand over Darcy's hand, on her lap.

'I'm sorry about this, I'm sorry you didn't get to see your bookshop, or do the things you wanted to do.' He squeezed her hand reassuringly before releasing it and taking his hand back. His hand, she had hardly noticed before but now looked at it as if it had performed lifesaving surgery. The long fingers and olive skin, his nails perfectly manicured, cleaner than Darcy's after a night in a tent. He had good hands and she knew, knew with everything, that she was being "lost", that she was losing the plot. Maybe it was the small space of the taxi cab, the sitting too close together, the phone conversation bouncing off the walls. Maybe it wasn't but Darcy felt too confined, trapped even.

Pressing the automatic button on the door panel, the window came down and air blew away the mini meltdown beginning to build.

'Ye's must be here for the festival, are ye's?' the Taxi man announced.

'We are,' Darcy spoke, relieved to be given a chance to stop overthinking.

'Our friends are in the pub.'

'Ah, sure, isn't that what it's all about, youth and the like, having fun, no pressure, not a care in the world? Your whole life ahead of ye. Sure, enjoy it while you can.'

With a meek smile, Darcy gathered his wise words. Words that did not apply to her world or her youth but maybe she could turn that around somehow. If youth was meant to be that way, having no pressure, being the best time of one's life, then maybe it was Darcy doing it wrong. There was no doubt the trip away had its downsides but, all in all, she felt relaxed away from the everyday. Maybe she should do more things away from the everyday. But, of course, Pat was her every day and her priority. Time away had only cemented that fact for her. Being away, she thought of home, while at home, her thoughts focused on being away, or, if not away, then away from it all. A thought that had been churning around inside her like butter with no other binding ingredient, with the end goal of becoming something new and cohesive. If she changed, then her environment would too, or at least the created perspective of it. It would be a start.

Life's quandaries still simmered as Darcy and the others disembarked the taxi but, once outside the pub, the gaps were filled with something other than questions about getting away.

Jay smiled towards her as the music, and the sweaty bodies, carried them inside towards their friends.

Jessica beckoned, 'There you are, take a mouthful of this.' Darcy did as she was told, a mix of vodka, orange juice and some other foreign beverage, stained her tastebuds, which made her gag and have to steady herself against a near beam pole.

Jessica laughed, whatever sickness had kept her lounging around this morning, long gone, or replaced with the hair of the dog.

Jay, from the bar, pointed at a beer he held up, Darcy nodded and pushed through the dancing crowd towards him. On her way, she saw Mina in deep conversation with a stranger. The seating booth embraced them and Darcy noticed Mina's t-shirt on the floor beside her, disregarded along with her inhibitions. Engrossed in meaningful banter in only a sports bra and multi-coloured cycling shorts. Mina did not break eye contact with her, from what Darcy could see, androgynous new friend, so Darcy kept moving towards the beer.

The crowd represented happiness, the heaving merriment rubbed off on Darcy and, by the time she reached Jay, she was ready to joy in. She downed the beer in one.

'Here, let me get us another.'

The sun stood still between the point of sunsetting, afraid to leave the party, so it lingered on the horizon. Jay had asked Darcy to walk outside with him and they now sat under a massive weeping willow tree, away from the noise inside the pub and protected from gossip and pointing fingers; to some degree.

Other bodies, as if cast out with the tide, strewed the hill embankment, opposite the pub, flaked out like dots on a cheetah.

'Here, sit on my jacket.'

Both sets of hands held a beer each, until Jay grounded his in order to use his jacket as a blanket.

'I've been worried about you, how you're coping being away from your gran?'

Darcy had all but forgotten about her situation. The sunshine, the beer, the anticipation had somehow pushed down, in earnest, her worries and concerns.

'You sound like an elder uncle.'

Jay half-laughed. 'Do I?'

Was she being friend-zoned? In the moments of letting her guard down, was she about to be relegated, into a lower position than nothing?

'I don't mean to. I'm kinda still on Dublin time when it comes to you.'

Did that mean the feeling happening in Cork did not count?

'What do you mean?'

'Well, seeing you vulnerable like that, it has an adverse effect, it makes me feel uneasy, and I know it's

141

not about me, but you don't show that side of you to anyone and I'm affected by it.'

'In a bad way though?'

'Not bad, unusual.'

'That is bad.' Darcy deduced.

'It isn't, it's ambiguous and means I need to figure it out.'

'You need to figure out what I do that makes you feel unusual?'

Jay chuckled, in between sipping his beer. 'Yeah, I guess... Are you drunk yet?'

'Not yet,' Darcy admitted, 'But I'm getting there, I feel like letting loose a little.'

Jay extended his beer, clinking Darcy's at its rounded curve.

'I'm down for that.'

A moment's silence.

'Oh, what did you want to tell me?' Darcy asked.

'Ah, that can wait, I wanted to run something by you, for advice more than anything else.'

'Well, you can't leave me hanging on that, give me a clue.'

Jay sat with Darcy's demand as if pondering an answer, as he lowered his gaze towards the padded material on his jacket. 'Can we leave it for now? I'll tell you tomorrow when I have a better handle on it myself.'

'Have you told Cora?'

'Cora? Why on earth would I tell her, I hardly know the girl.'

'I beg to differ,' Darcy almost simpered.

Jay tittered, amusingly.

'Are you jealous?'

The question held so much honesty that Darcy had to consciously make an effort to stay poised.

'You wish.' She exhaled a breath, a breath containing fear, doubt and excitement on the out.

'I hate the way you've done that, given me a little and teasing something; it's as if you don't trust me.'

'Okay, Darcy, but I mean it, don't tell anyone else. I've been given a job opportunity, a dream job opportunity actually.'

'What, like after college?

'No, they want me sooner.'

'Well, you can't do that, you've only one semester left, Jay.'

'I can still finish it over there, in the evenings, they'll sponsor that.'

'Over there, what do you mean over there?'

'The job, it's in Scotland.'

'What? Scotland, Scotland?'

'There you are,' Mina shouted from the back door of the pub. 'I need water, do you guys have any out here?' Mina began to take slow steps towards the grassy hill and the resting bodies upon its slope.

'Don't say anything, especially not to Mina.'

'I won't, of course, I won't.' Darcy frowned.

'What are you two up to anyway, out here on your own?' Mina enquired without any tact, through slurred and stuttered speech.

'Drinking, Mina, a bit like you inside.'

'And, talking about inside, I've met someone, uh huh. They go by the name Teddy, they/ them. And they are gorgeous. So I invited them back to our campsite. Them and another girl called Pixie, you'll love her, Darcy, she plays piano.' Mina sneezed then, twice, one after the other.

'Oh, excuse me, yikes. I'm so glad we didn't find that house and came here instead, are you?… I'm going back to get them, cos we're all leaving soon, okay?'

Darcy had learned a trick lately to hide how she was really feeling from the rest of the world. Now that she thought about it, lately, had turned into ages ago without her knowledge. How odd that Jay was planning a future for himself, a grown-up, paying real bills, doing his own washing type of moving on and starting over. A moment earlier, Darcy, in her own future planning had positioned Jay somewhere near the centre. A central figure in her exam preparations, in her visits to the campus library. In the proofreading of her work to advise if her essay needed more in-depth critical thinking, or pulling apart or piecing back together. All hypothetical scenarios that she had planned without ever considering him, or his life or his dream job. Was that what he called it, she thought, a dream job? A job he's been dreaming about.

Something resembling an awkward silence moved by Darcy and in through Jay. They both knew it but continued as if it did not. A secret between them and another thing for Darcy to potentially deny. Getting up from where they were sitting, they followed Mina in.

Darcy, her mind racing, encouraged by alcohol, and a chomp at the bit, closed her month and the phrases of intended thoughts into words merely got choked down instead.

*

Later, as alcohol flowed and spilled, in and out, around the many tented areas, in plastic cups, expensive flasks and recyclable cardboard mugs, Darcy stood in the shower cubical. Rinsing off her annoyance. Cora, as soon as everyone landed back, plonked her inebriated bum down on Jay's lap, pinning him to the ground as if she owned him, one arm rested around his shoulders, anchoring him down. Not long after Darcy legged it and forced herself into believing hot water was the remedy.

'My God, who showers in the middle of a party?' Mina mused as Darcy joined the circle.

'Someone who was sick of smelling like cack.'

Dom belched to show he was still standing, while Jessica and Lottie ate curry chips to sober up a tad, before drinking again.

'Pixie, hi,' Darcy said after Mina nudged her, 'You must be nuts to have come here voluntarily.'

'She didn't, we tied her to us with a belt,' Dom said, gassing at his own silly comment.

'Either way, welcome to the chaos.'

'Actually, I wanted to pick your brains about something, if you don't mind?'

Pixie's voice was soothing. 'Mina said you researched Kafka for an assignment, *Metamorphosis,* to be precise; I'd love to know your thoughts on popular culture and where you think the novella fits in.'

That's very heavy for a campfire, Darcy thought, but Pixie was so damn cute. And Jay had, as if the therapy clinic shut its doors, returned to being Jay.

Somewhere between the words, leaving and Scotland, Darcy cursed herself for being so stupid. For running with a flimsy idea about some gravitational pull controlling her primal desires as opposed to her own judgement. And yet, there had been tense glances. Jay would turn his head to watch her, or catch her gaze, or wink his stupid fucking wink. Or tease her by creaking his neck behind Lottie's back just to zone in and make her smile.

The mixed signals were not only mixed, they were mystifying. And the fact Darcy cared confused her to the point of wanting to pack up and leave. But the biggest surprise of the night was Dom and Jessica, who had disappeared into a tent alone together. Darcy thought she might be bothered by such an unusual pairing but she did not lay claim to Jessica in any way and free love seemed to be the theme of the evening.

The chatter around the campsite lowered to a hum. An odd outburst and intermittent peals of laughter, accompanied low lyrics and arrhythmical tambourines; sounds that echoed as the late night crept in.

'I think Mina tried to set us up,' Pixie blurted out as Darcy, stunned at the revelation, quizzed her further. 'Did she tell you to mention Franz Kafka?' Darcy quizzed. 'She did, didn't she? God, how does she know me so well, she knew I'd bite, I can't believe how manipulative she is.' Pixie, feeling humoured, grinned because she was a co-conspirator in the plan.

'I've really enjoyed talking to you, Pixie, but I'm going to bed before I do something silly.'

'Maybe you need to prioritise yourself sometimes, Darcy, hopefully in the not-so-distant future. You're astonishingly kind and so much fun to be around. Life is too short to take your time, I hope you realise that.'

'I'm working on it, where are you sleeping?'

'Oh, I'm not sleeping, there's a rave one field over, I'm going to follow the others.'

'Not on your own.'

'No, no, Teddy is waiting for me at the herbal stall, you can see it from here, it has bright fairy lights, glowing like nightlight glistening stars. Are you sure you won't come with us?'

'More than sure but I hope I see you again.'

'Oh, I'm sure you will, I've an invite to Dublin, so, it's more than likely.' Pixie skipped away, and Darcy scanned the area before disappearing and zipping out the outside world as much as she possibly could.

*

The train ride home contained murmurs and nods, uh huhs and yeps. Nodding sleepy faces and leaning on shoulders. By the time Darcy put her key in the door, she was glad of the down time. Happy to be alone. The smell of a house left empty made her curl her nose at the edges. The emersion went on and she sat for a while, in the dark, the curtains pulled over the remaining evening light. Trying to put things into perspective, her thoughts immediately brought her to Jay, asleep on the train. It must have been a deepish sleep because Dom, beside him, snored, his mouth open, catching flies. Jay, his arms folded into one another for support, looked comfortable. An odd fitful eyelash flicker but for that his chest lifted effortlessly and rested again, as if a prima ballerina at the end of her performance, on repeat.

Darcy, who had tried to forget about his upcoming travel plans, could not, sitting on her gran's old couch, think of anything else.

Her phone beeped.

I hope you got home okay, I'm sorry we didn't get to talk as much as I wanted, can we meet for coffee? I really need to talk. Jessica must be feeling "the fear", Darcy thought. She did not know for sure but most of the group stayed up all night partying. Darcy presumed Jessica was reaching out through neediness, instead of any genuine longing. Darcy plugged her phone into its charger without responding to Jessica's cry for help.

Chapter Eleven

An hour later and Darcy relaxed in strawberry-fragranced bubbles up to her neck. The almost boiling water claimed her body as if it would dissolve and become floating particles before spiral sinking, then landing on a seabed. Stepping into the bath, she had once again sought out Jay's face. But this time, she reminisced about their first kiss and how she had been "in love" with Jessica at the time and how she had wanted to know what it felt like kissing a boy, because she had consumed copious amounts of alcohol while helping Jay with an assignment that she finished already. And she'd been feeling low, so low, and she imagined a man's embrace, the idea of a man's strong embrace might take away the absence of her father's loving morning hugs.

The holding by Jay, which was welcomed, turned to soft lips upon eager lips and, suddenly, they were passionate and more urgent but the kisses were never demanding. And, for the most part, Darcy lay in Jay's arms, and Jay allowed such tenderness, without enquiry, or looking for more.

But, the next day, the guilt tortured Darcy to a point where she had stopped attending class for a while.

Months later, when she found out that Jessica had slept with Jay, she wasn't surprised but it was now, in the bath, surrounded by strawberry bubbles that she understood feelings had grown in a different direction. The conundrum was figuring out where she fit in relation to those opaque feelings, and where Jay fit into her fitting in. Or the simple question—did they fit? A question just as complex as the one day story in Joyce's *Ulysses*.

As she wrapped her fluffy dressing gown around her damp body, the doorbell rang. A pizza man, his cap tilted upwards, held a pizza box with a note attached.

'Sorry, I didn't order pizza.'

'Well, someone did, it's already paid for, the note is for Darcy, I presume that's you.'

'Oh, right, oh, okay. Thank you.'

The pizza, her favourite, sat on the kitchen table, half-eaten, its cardboard box ripped at the edges because they were too hard to undo without tearing. Darcy opened the envelope of the attached card with care.

It read: *I know you won't eat. You need to stop thinking about everyone else and just put yourself first. I miss you. Jay x*

Even though it was probably the single most adorable gesture anyone had ever done for Darcy, she decided to go to bed instead of calling Jay to thank him. Tomorrow, after a good night's sleep, her thoughts would not be laden down with him and who he was in relation to her. Who he was in relation to Cora, to Jessica, to himself even. She hoped sleep would bring that, a solution, anything that was not as debilitating as now. Tiredness swept in. She walked up the stairs as if holding a hot water bottle packed full of bricks. An imagined weight that made every step, a step she would rather not take. Perhaps, in dreams she might hear whispers, she thought, with words of guidance from those she missed so much.

*

The hospital was not a hospital per se. It was a care unit. The term Old People's Home was never used but the patients who were housed within its walls all suffered from some form of cognitive impairment or another. The professionals deemed Pat's condition as worsening but still manageable. They had instructed Darcy to look into full-time care for a later date when things became not so manageable and provided a list of reputable establishments.

Grey, monotonal grey walls were what Darcy expected to see, noting to herself that every building she'd been to lately was painted grey; light grey, dark grey, another shade of grey, but, instead of such banal colouring, baby pink and mint green paint two-toned the corridors' walls, that made walking along the herringbone floors less daunting.

Darcy walked through the corridors checking for signs of neglect. It was a natural thing to do; observe the place and make sure it was not sub-standard.

'If your grandmother did join us, she would be taken care of in a room similar to this one.'

A nurse with a high bun and red glasses, that rested on her nose, opened her arm into a bedroom.

Darcy stepped inside a space, not too small but not big either. There was enough room for a single bed, bedside locker, wardrobe and T.V. stand. A green vase with fake plastic flowers and a plastic watering can sat centrally on the sill of a small bay window. An alcove of printed wallpaper, made the window look as though it was lost, as if swallowed by a forest, because the print of large green pointed leaves and overgrown shrubs, overpowered the small living area and caused a weird optical illusion. There was no zen to the place. It needs a touch of Feng Shui, Darcy thought, but remained tight-lipped, letting her eyesight take the fall.

'Do you have rooms that are less... well, less loud?'

'Yes, of course, it depends on what the patient likes.'

Do you have cigarette fragrance and butt-end, ashtray carpet, Darcy questioned on the inside, grinning to herself and the immature narrative that was steadying an uncomfortable but necessary interrogative communication, albeit, between her and herself.

Back and forth, Darcy questioned why she was standing in the nursing home. Her grandmother would be home in two days. Back in the house they shared, back to the place where Darcy had lit several scented candles, used shake and vac, to put the freshness back, and bleached every surface.

Who would have thought frantic silences could be subdued? Darcy questioned her reasons for being in the nursing home. Her selfish reasons. How could a stale smell be a reason to put someone in a home?

It is not the reason, not the sole reason, what the hell is wrong with you, she has dementia, she broke her bloody arm, she almost spent the night in a graveyard, you can't take care of her, she lives on breadsticks—and the chat went on, investigating every angle. Even as Darcy was led into another room, a room with light yellow walls and a buttercup bedspread, the internal questioning continued.

Curled up on the sofa later that day, Darcy sent a *thank you for the pizza* text to Jay, and *thank you for caring*, it said, *and being sweet*.

Not long after, texts flowed between them, as if long lost soul mates, trying to reengage. Suddenly, Darcy, if a text didn't come through right away, wondered why Jay was taking so long to reply. Maybe he's feeding his dog, she would scold herself, or picking his toenails!

And, in those empty moments, Darcy let her mind go on a journey, a car ride with many city stops. In a sunny place, with strangers and adventure. It was either that, or think about the pile of washing on the floor.

Why don't you come over to my place? Jay texted after Darcy already refused he visit hers.

That's exactly the same thing, Jay, it means the same thing, Darcy answered.

He laughed and she pictured him laughing.

We're sitting here, each other's company, using a phone, it's a bit impersonal.

It's a bit safe, ye mean.

Okay, well, if not now, when then? Jay asked.

Darcy wanted the confidence to enquire. She wanted to have balls enough to ask him why he was putting so much energy into her. What did he want in exchange, reciprocated truths? A depth-ness that a deep sea diver, with a full tank and one in reserve couldn't reach? Why was he asking that of her when she was known for being super conscious and overly mindful in most areas of her life?

In her diary, a five-year diary, she had written a five-year plan; at least three years ago. Filling in the lines with aspirations, goals, and expectations. She had often wondered if her parents had similar thoughts about their future plans. Plans that never materialised. So, some pages of her diary had been scribbled out, in frustration. Sometimes with a harsh pen, leaving deep indents on the page. As if to hurt it, as if to cause pain to the plans or ideas, or aspirations on the paper. The guidelines in the diary wavered from the truth of it. Life is not something that can be planned to a tee. Like designing a spring garden, some flowers form, bloom and omit the perfect scent, while others wither before being given a chance to brighten someone's day.

Darcy thought back to the fake plastic flowers in the nursing home and shivered.

You can surprise me with something original, Darcy texted, before finally texting goodnight.

*

After work, Darcy would get on a bus and collect her grandmother from hospital with a taxi and an open mind. She was packing boxes when a distinguished man came through the shop door. He walked with a walking stick, the stick's unusual handle some kind of animal's head, a hawk maybe or an eagle. Birds of prey, willing to pluck your eyes out given half the chance.

'Good morning, miss.'

Darcy always felt like a school teacher when customers called her miss. 'How are you today?'

'Hello.'

'I was wondering if you gave out free chocolates, like tasters and such. Samples, that's the word. Free samples.'

'No, I'm afraid you're in the wrong shop, that's another place, where they serve coffee too, cept you have to pay for the coffee, obviously.'

'So, you don't hand out free samples then?'

'No, not here, you have to purchase our products if you want to taste them.'

'Um,' the man grunted. 'That's a pity, a real shame.'

The gentleman hunched defiantly and curled up his nose in a contemptuous sneer of disappointment, it almost made Darcy laugh. Why did he feel so entitled? Why the intractable attitude, hard to sway or even allow? His ideas contrived from a notion that the world should bend to his ideals and self-serving nature, irrespective of rules and protocols.

There are regulations everywhere, even in a bloody chocolate shop! She thought.

Darcy grabbed the sweeping brush as a form of protection, from what she might say, presume or regret.

Not long after her favourite customer Fifi came in, asking to use the toilet instead of buying anything from the display counter. 'I was just passing, you know how it is.' She winked, as Darcy led her out the back, with a full roll of fresh loo-roll.

The clock ticked on and before Darcy knew what was happening Fifi was replaced by Jessica, standing in the doorway, pale and ragged. Her insipid stare, an immediate cause for concern. Her skin colour the tone of ashen Darcy now expected to see in every corridor of every building.

'Jesus, Jessica, come in,' Darcy gently grabbed Jessica's arm. 'Come out the back.'

A cup of coffee later and Darcy sat on the edge of a stool out the back of the shop, with Jessica half slumped over a chair that Darcy's boss liked to sit on when, on the odd occasion, he came to spy and look over the books.

'You can't be sure though, is that what you're saying?' Darcy asked in a soft tone.

'I am sure, but I have no idea who did it, they fucken drugged me, how would I remember.'

'Okay, relax, I'm not saying that, I'm trying to help.'

Darcy, in all her life, had never been speechless, reflective, yes, tactful, yes, but never lost for words. But the conversation with Jessica was so delicate, Darcy held her breath in case her breathing was too invasive. The air felt like it was pushing her and she fought hard to stand her ground.

'All I can remember is leaving the tent,' Jessica whispered, 'I saw Dom there beside me, he was asleep, I wanted to use the bathroom, badly. That must have been what woke me up. So, I walked passed other tents, I remember standing on a bottle, I remember the painful sensation against the inside of my toe. I remember all of that and then, it gets blurred.'

'Did you drink something, did someone offer you something, someone outside of the group?'

'I was still drunk, I mean, pissed, we'd been drinking all day in that pub. Someone, a girl, gave me water when I came out of the cubicle, she said I looked like death warmed up, or words like that, I dunno.'

'Have you been to the doctor, the police?'

'Yes, I'm waiting for results back from the doctor.'

A second later and said with a measure of reticence, 'He made me take the morning-after pill as a precautionary measure. It made me ill.' Jessica gagged, and wiped the end of her nose roughly.

'Jesus, Jessica, I don't know what to say.'

'I just need a friend, that's all, can you be that Darcy? Can you be a friend?'

'Of course, of course. I'm here, whatever you need, I'm here.'

Light-heartedness evaporated and, in that moment, Darcy realised how light-hearted life had actually been.

*

An intrinsic part of healing is in the method of recovery, and aftercare provided. Parting words from Pat's doctors as they left the ward, now homebound, as Pat looked out the window of the taxi, from what looked like to Darcy, seeing the scenery for the first time.

Darcy kept yawning and half yawning. The yawn was simply simulated to prevent an inadvertent phrase or idiom said to pass the time or fill the gaps. She really wanted to ask her gran's advice, she really wanted to say, Hey, Gran, I've been having a rather shitty time of late, my ex thinks she was assaulted, and a guy I think I might like is moving away, and the girl who thinks she was assaulted wants more than friendship. I'm not stupid but I'm truly fucked up and can't seem to get clarity on the important things, on the things that make a difference, and my gran is sick, like really sick, and you remember her, I'm sure, she's the only one left who really gives a shit about me and, well, y'know. Oh, and how have you been?

Darcy wanted a meaningful conversation with the only person left who shared her early memories, and the profound realisation that that was gone, that memory sharer, hit her in the chest like a steam train with no brakes.

Walking through the hallway, Darcy had purposely pointed out the pictures hanging on the wall. 'Remember this one, Gran, you always said this one was your favourite because Peaches was in it. Your dog, come have a look.'

The doctor told Darcy what to expect. A decline, that was the term he used—you'll notice a decline. He never mentioned the vacant stare, the looking around as if searching for something but finding nothing, so continuing the search. 'Come on, Gran, let me get you to bed.'

With a lot to consider Darcy wanted to deep dive into the resources, medicines and support available to her grandmother, to find out what was best for everyone, including herself.

Her gran needed to be supervised at all times and Darcy could not, had decided she would not, be her grandmother's full-time carer. She was not qualified and, without sounding insensitive, she did not want to. Her ambitions stretched further than changing nappies and wiping up dribble, after spoon-feeding someone who had spoon-fed her as a child.

And the guilt of that admission was her own personal juggernaut of despair. By saying "yes" to herself, to her own needs, the "no" to her grandmother's needs, left her wanting to run away and never return. The thing was, Darcy could not put a date on it. As much as she tried, a specific date to admit her grandmother to a nursing home seemed as far away as all the other choices, needing attention in her life.

For now, Philomena would stay when Darcy went to work and Maryann had agreed to help as well. Pat had a hospital appointment to attend the following week, other than that, they would play it by ear.

Opening the fridge, Darcy grabbed a tub of rhubarb yogurt and sat still long enough to let the smooth substance line her tongue. Lifting it up, her palate ignited with pleasure, as she rested her head on the back of the kitchen chair. The simple taste of an own-brand cheap yogurt, tipped the scales in her emotional stability, tipping it towards a meltdown. She could feel it coming, swelling up from a place she had tried so hard to deny. The feminine attributes that society associates with being weak. Don't cry, it will make you seem too emotional, too needy, too teary, too weepy, too hormonal, too passive, fearful, anxious, submissive. The definition of womanhood is to be feminine but that definition can be frowned upon and plotted against. The stereotypical feminine traits that are part of human biology have become weaponised, to use as weapons women use against themselves. Because, somehow, the beauty of women and all that that encompasses has been adapted into a negative rhetoric, a false narrative spewed by people who do not understand and, in doing so, undervalue the true worth of womanhood. And Darcy knew she had played her part, remembering vividly an incident as a child in a swing park with other children. One boy falling over on his knee, a graze that cut and bled and bruised, and another boy teasing him, taunting him—*you're not going to cry like a girl, are you?*—as if being a girl was a bad thing, and crying was even worse. A thing to undermine, an emotion to disregard, to put on the naughty step, to equate with less than, with inadequacy, with othering, with femininity. The resistance of her born gender assignment had begun in an internal revolt against oppression and capitalism and patriarchy. All terms she did not understand back then but knew still controlled the world—even as her father clasped her small female hand in his, and they left the park.

Darcy vowed to be strong like a boy and not neurotic like a girl, crying over spilt milk, or a cut on the knee, or an assaulted ex-girlfriend, or a grandmother with dementia or a boy named Jay with curly hair.

Now, sitting alone, her grandmother sedated upstairs, Darcy expressed her inner demons by crying her heart out without, to a certain degree, being policed by her peers. But the tears turned to frustration because she realised being emotionally policed had become the norm. Being unfeminine had become expected if you were figuring out your sexuality in the arena she had chosen, or had chosen her. Somehow, in fighting every label associated with being a 'cis' female, she had stopped being inclusive and she was repulsed by that revelation. The fluidity of her discovery covered her like a heavy blanket, dampened by a burst riverbank, sodden with decarded water lilypad leaves and soggy debris. Identity, not just gender identity but the identity of "her", had become clouded. She had become lost in her own life. And not by the people who cared about her, they had accepted her for her portrayal of "self", but the pressure from her misgivings, to fit neatly into a category, without rough edges, forgetting that even a diamond, in all its splendour, starts off rough. At least, conversations were changing. People were becoming more tolerant or other's choices even if they deviated slightly from their own. Darcy's problem was letting go of the idea that people cared, because evidently people cared about themselves, and their everyday much more.

The turmoil of the day had taken its toll and Darcy just wanted to crawl under her bedcovers and let darkness in, so she quietly cried her way up the stairs and complied.

Chapter Twelve

Jessica lifted the lid off a smoothie jar she had taken out of her bag, sipped the berry mixture and passed it to Darcy, with a nudge. 'Here, it's full of five a day, your daily sustenance, and a little honey for a kick.'

'No, I'm good thanks, I've already eaten.'

It was a week after Darcy's meltdown in the kitchen and, because the sun was splitting the stones, Jessica set up a picnic in Phoenix Park and insisted Darcy join her. Darcy, whose delight at being there had the depth of a puddle, played along because she had promised to be a friend. And a friend she would be, no matter what.

'Put the book down and lay beside me, Darcy, you might as well not be here, if you're going to read a book in company, what does... ' Jessica seized the book from Darcy's grasp. 'What does... ' she repeated, 'Eleanor Hooker have that I don't have?'

Grace and elegance, Darcy thought, and gently retrieved the book instead.

'How have you been feeling?'

'Oh, you know, still traumatised in a way but, honestly, because I can't recall anything, I feel like nothing happened. It's really fucked up.'

'And what about post-traumatic stress,' Darcy half stammered, 'Have you any symptoms?'

'I feel fairly normal, like myself again. And I don't want to dwell on it and make it a thing, y'know. I'm so happy you're here, Darcy.'

Jessica believed that Darcy worked, studied, slept and lived somewhere in the area. Beyond those simple facts (that weren't true), Jessica never enquired as to how Darcy was feeling, or living or surviving. Jessica was self-absorbed and, while caught up in loving her, Darcy had made excuses for her selfishness. But the outing of such distasteful qualities, now allowed Darcy to see with clearer vision. Friends had permission to be self-absorbed; ex-lovers, not so much.

'Can we cuddle, just for closeness?'

Darcy lay down and Jessica nuzzled under her arm, resting her head on Darcy's shoulder. They were already in a moribund state with only one fully aware of it.

But still, the warmth from their bodies gave the other comfort, and a dangerous safety net.

Darcy began to feel uncomfortable because the tender moment with its outline of pathetic, disingenuous wistfulness disturbed her. She wanted, instead of being where she was, to spend time with Jay. Jay, who had called days previous to invite her to dinner, a "date" she had accepted but later declined because Jessica "needed" her, and she'd promised to be a friend. And telling Jay without seeing his face, knew an injured look was there, a disappointment in her breaking a promise to keep a promise.

'Do you think we could ever make another go of it, Darc?' Darcy knew the words were coming because Jessica was not the type of person to hold back. But, even sitting so close to Jessica, Darcy already knew that the trace, the trace of what was left of them, could not be stored in a place safe from harm, or simply diffused by denial.

Darcy still felt something, but an unnamed "something" was not enough.

'I just, I guess, I need space right now, can you understand that, Jessica?'

'Are you seeing anyone, are you in contact with Pixie, that girl?'

'Who? Pixie, no, no.'

If there was a time to be honest it was now, Darcy thought. Otherwise, she was just a carbon cut-out of the type of person she despised.

'I want to explore... other options.'

'Jay, or someone with a similar anatomy, am I right?'

'I don't know, I... '

'And us, do we have a chance?'

'Jesus, I just said I don't know.' Darcy frowned.

'Is it Jay? Tell me the truth about that at least, because he is a using little shit, he lied about what happened between us and... '

'No, he didn't, Jessica, you lied about that. It doesn't matter anyway. I want to say to you, yeah, sure, let's pick up the mess we call us and continue with torturing ourselves, sure, why not be masochists, but I don't want to.'

'Fine, just say you don't want to then.'

Darcy exhaled heavily without even realising she had inhaled.

'I don't want to go back, just to take the chance you think we deserve. I don't want to, Jessica. But I still want you around.'

'Please don't be so condescending.' Jessica looked away.

'I will be the friend you need.'

*

The picnic, after that, turned sour and, before long, Darcy was on the bus home, deflated but in a saner head space. Even with an indomitable passage of time, Darcy wondered if she would ever shake Jessica, the presence of her.

There had been striking moments of seamless idealism, in a place where Darcy had constructed a future, but that was gone. And she knew it was unfair to Jessica, not to simply just say, *it's over because we've been too deceitful,* and trust is the foundation of any relationship and that's not just some relationship guru telling you what you want to hear but the truth. When trust is gone, it's replaced with all sorts.

Darcy knew about acclimation, about leaving one life to step into another, and the harshness that brings. This was not her first rodeo. The sunny sky of the hours previous now held an odd dark cloud. A travelling cloud, or was it Darcy who travelled, further away from the filled water it retained for another location. Maybe tomorrow, she thought, dry spells meant gratefulness, and having just a tad of that, a sense of satisfaction might ensue and change the landscape of things, just for a little while. Outside, inside a window, as the bus halted, an overcrowded clothes horse untidied the look of the room, the items crooked, displaced. An abstract way to view her afternoon, but a telling comparison.

As the bus neared another stop, on impulse, Darcy made for the exit. The bus stop was the closest one to Jay's flat and, in a spontaneous, effortless move, Darcy decided to pay him a visit.

Jay had a two-bedroom flat. One room he rented out to a musician who spent the summers abroad with the other members of his band. As Darcy climbed the stairs, she confronted her own fears, her shyness, her desires and her intentions. She had no idea what she would say to Jay, only that the urge to see him was real, she felt compelled. And that she moved on that instinct, and hoped he would not leave her standing in the doorway, her mouth agape, like a total idiot.

She stood, fixing her bag strap that had slipped off her shoulder, and she knocked on the door.

Twenty seconds later, Cora opened it and Darcy felt her demeanour shift, physically and visibly shift. Her shock was obvious and presented itself in a physiological manner she could not hide. So, she put her hand out and leaned against the door frame.

'Darcy, how cute, I didn't know you were coming over.'

Jay appeared from the hallway near his bedroom and saw, by Darcy's face, the picture she had painted without any evidence, paint, paint brush, guidelines or advice, and he watched her pull away from the door frame and take steps to leave, to leave what they were becoming before they even had a chance to become. And he couldn't bear it so he moved after her, after her scent and anger and loveliness. Calling her name.

'Darcy, wait, Jesus, Darcy, wait up.'

'No, it's fine. I'm sorry I interrupted you, I can see-'

'Stop, stop it, I'm not having this, Darcy, she just showed up, she was not invited, not by me. I just went to take a piss and I was on my way into the living room to ask her to leave, and then you, and you're fucking standing there in the place I wanted you to be all day, in my flat and you're looking like it's over, for good, that that's it! And you're not even speaking.' He took a breath then. 'And it's not over, no fucken way, no way. I didn't ask her here. I didn't.'

Darcy wanted to kiss him lightly but, instead, she whispered, 'Okay, Jay, okay, I get it,' she smiled, 'call around to me later and I'll buy you a beer.' And they both relaxed into the something obvious, they could no longer hide, or care to resist.

'That smile,' Jay said while shaking his head of curls, himself smiling too, as he walked away. A swell around his heart, alien to him before that exact moment, and not minding it. Not minding it one single bit.

Chapter Thirteen

In the hospital hours later, Darcy tried wiping her eye and its agitation away. The more she rubbed, the worse it got, stinging, becoming smaller the harder she pressed. As if the rotation on her eyelids from her folded fingers would help the memory of the last few hours disappear. Her stomach feel sick, and her brain punched in and tightened from stress.

'Stop rubbing, you'll make it worse, you probably need eye drops from the smoke or something,' Maryann said, sitting a close chair beside Darcy, whose neck and shoulders ached tremendously.

Darcy, while rounding the corner earlier to her grandmother's house, was met with fire sirens and a stationary ambulance van, its doors wide open waiting for someone sick, dying or worse. And, for a moment, Darcy thought she'd rounded the wrong street, a different street in a different estate. But then Maryann was there, paused but standing feverishly, her eyes wide open, her frail hand covering her mouth. And it was then Darcy knew it was Pat. That her dear grandmother was in trouble.

'Why do you think they're taking so long in there, in surgery? Surely they'd have news by now.'

'Oh, pet, she inhaled a lot of smoke, I should never have left her. I just went across the road for some cat food for that friggin stray that does be in the garden, and it must have been her cigarette, it must have just caught fire on something, oh, Jesus, I feel terrible.'

'It's not your fault, Maryann, it's mine, It's my fault.'

Darcy began to pace the tiled floors, unable to sit still.

'And I couldn't ring you because my mobile died and, sure your number was in it and, oh, what a disaster. Thank God, a neighbour called 999 right away, thank the holy lord for that at least, the house was hardly damaged. Thank God for small mercies.'

Darcy wanted to shout, SHUT UP, SHUT UP, SHUT UP, but a doctor walked through swinging doors, that swung behind her, towards Darcy and Darcy's misery and, by her expression alone, Darcy knew that her grandmother was gone.

Grief.
Intense sorrow, especially caused by someone's death.

Some words follow people around, not like a label, but still plastered to the skin in perpetuity. Words forever associated with that person's life. Like, say, a daring mountaineer who has lost a limb through their robust misadventures, being called disabled, his or her word would be disabled and it would follow them around. Or like an elegant prima ballerina, who has fractured her ankle, being called a failure, her word would be failure and

171

it would follow her around. The words might stick to them like glue, like the sticky plant in her grandmother's garden, and become their identity. And, even if they rejected the word, if they determinedly resisted the word, the word would still follow them around, even with their protest, and pleading and protesting. The word, their very own stamp, would be theirs forever.

Darcy, out of the taxi, left Maryann to her gate and walked over toward Pat's partially blackened house, dusted in damp heavy ash. The smell of burning still hanging in the air, along with small specs of dancing flakes. Jay sat on the ground against the wall and, when he realised she was there, he moved to greet her but she slowed him with a hand gesture, mustering energy alone for that and nothing more dramatic.

'Stay, I'll sit with you.' She insisted.

She sat close to him on the concrete ground and he put his arm around her, drawing her in. Then he kissed the top of her hair, and stayed close enough to feel her slow, steadiness against his frame.

'I'm so sorry, Darcy.'

'How did you know?'

'I came around, like you asked, and one of your neighbours told me about the accident. I've been waiting here ever since; I couldn't get hold of you.'

'It's four a.m., Jay.'

'I wanted to be here, if you came back.'

'It's cold and I stink.'

'Let's go back to my place, you can use the spare room, I can contact people for you tomorrow.'

'Contact... people?' Darcy turned her head towards him and half-smiled. 'There's no need, there is no one.'

*

The next morning, Darcy woke up with the feeling of being in a strange room but that was superseded by the sinking ache in her gut and the voice of self-loathing that perched safely on a branch in her head.

She sat but found it hard to breathe, to inhale, to catch, to catch and grab hold of a breath. Then the room, shrinking, the walls moving in, in towards her, and the lack of air, and the difficulty swallowing. And the air, burnt air, dry, choking her grandmother, in her nostrils and down her mouth.

Darcy began to sob, sob from grief. "Grief", her word, that followed her around, and would follow her around in the days to come and forever. Grief, her word.

You'll have to stay here, Jay had said, after the funeral, at least until Pat's house was repaired and habitable again. Darcy agreed.

Mina had attended the funeral alongside Teddy, whom Darcy remembered from the camping trip, oddly enough. There, too, was Lottie, Jessica and Dom, Kate, who stood beside a complete stranger, and other less significant people as well. There to support Darcy who had lost a grandmother they knew nothing about. An elderly lady with dementia whose granddaughter had left her alone, to pop to a park and a flat.

Mina held her up when the casket was lowered, whispering over and over, it's okay, it's okay, it's okay, as much to herself as to Darcy.

No one quizzed her afterwards or acted awkward or even blasé, they simply acted, or pretended or both, because of the day that was in it. Or maybe being deceitful and having lied to them did not matter now, about this anyway.

There had also been a small gathering in the local pub for neighbours and a few others, a solemn affair, as these things often are, and Darcy could not wait until it was finished. To get to a place alone, to deal with things on her own, the only way she felt comfortable.

All her family were gone now. Her bloodline, the blood in their veins, the last of their lineage. She was alone, cut off at the stem. She silently wondered if this summer was the worst summer yet, but then she remembered the other one, the worse than this one, and poured another glass of wine.

Listening to Pat's neighbours exchange fables to one another, Darcy, sat in between two and with her head lowered, was regaled with a tale of Pat's obvious signs of dementia while attending a wake up the road months previous. A lovely women, who lived on the same row of houses, died after a short bout of cancer, a disease that was first diagnosed as being curable, not terminal, but something to recover from.

Sarah, one neighbour said, Lena was the salt of the earth, she was a lovely person, well-loved by us all, kept herself to herself, never hurt a fly, she loved that dog of hers, and she was so young too, taken far too soon, far too soon, it's shocken, shocken.

Darcy listened as Sarah, feeling confident after a whiskey or two, set a scene by description of Lena's wake, in her own sitting room, her body lying in a wicker casket, one she had asked for personally before her passing, and Pat, with her dementia, reaching in to stroke Lena's cold hand, while saying, *God bless you, Sharon, God bless you, Sharon, you're in a better place now*, while Sharon, Lena's sister (who was well and truly alive), stood at the side of the wicker casket mouthing silently, *don't worry, it's okay, I understand.* Another neighbour Marion, said she'd met Pat on a recent walk, Pat who never really left her front door but on this occasion insisted to Marion that she'd been walking every day for the last two weeks. *Better to be out walking than stuck indoors,* she'd inform her faithfully. Even though Marion knew the truth.

And so on and so forth, all through the evening the stories flowed and carried on.

*

The aroma of frying sausages in olive oil on a pan, drifted in through the gaps in the closed door of Jay's spare bedroom. Darcy knew Jay had a kind heart and that cooking breakfast was his way of reaching out to her. But she could not eat, she could hardly get out of bed.

A light knock and he appeared, smiling, holding up a plastic egg turner as if the mere holding of it would initiate hunger in her.

'Just try and eat,' Jay insisted, 'Something small even.'

'Coffee, please, just caffeine.'

Should it be her cooking, Darcy thought, the way to a man's heart is through his stomach and all that? God, what a stupid saying. Darcy couldn't help but wonder if a disillusioned mother made it up to convince her daughter how to keep her husband happy or if it was actually just a man being clever, manipulative even.

Most old adages or saying were outdated and ridiculous. Too radical to contemplate, as if progress had gone around and met itself and thought, this is a total shit-show. Imagine wanting to feed a man, to keep his love. And, in truth, probably giving him heart disease in the process.

Darcy found that, whatever she did not what to think about, but what needed thought, made her ramble, nonsensically, about pure twaddle instead.

'Do you want sugar with this, me lady?' Jay teased.

'Yes, lots, and milk too. Cheers.'

Darcy wanted to and did not want to at the same time, ask Jay about leaving for Scotland. They had not mentioned the "leaving" again, after the first shell-shock moment and, since then, there had not been the right time to bring it up. This was not the right time either, so the questions hovered, like a feather does sometimes before landing.

As Darcy stared from the ceiling to the wall, she had to admit that with everything on the outside going about its business, she felt safe inside with Jay.

About a week after the funeral, Jay produced two tickets to IMMA, near the city centre. Paula Rego, the Portuguese-British painter and visual artist was showing her work titled, *Obedience and Defiance*, and Jay remembered that Rego was Darcy's favourite painter and that she'd talked about going months previously.

'You're so sweet,' Darcy said, 'But I don't think I have the head for it.' Darcy moved towards the kitchen with a half empty mug of tea.

'It's exactly what you need,' Jay insisted. 'An evening of appreciation, it's what's missing, for both of us and I used rent money on these.' He winked his wink.

'Let me think a little on it.'

Darcy had hardly left the flat all week, its confines becoming unhealthy but necessary, and work and her work position would soon need her back because they had called in seasonal staff to cover her absence, again. It wasn't as though her job was a vocation and she was definitely not an indispensable employee. Thus the thin line being walked regarding her position frayed daily without her being too concerned. Was the job worth it, she thought, but then sensed it would be the familiar things, things she'd been used to, that would help reengage her back into what was before. And then there was the burnt out house.

The home that had been her home for a while, and was now a home to melted picture frames and legless two seaters. Darcy sighed deeply and walked back into the living room with uneasy thoughts of visiting her old charred bedroom.

It was time to take the steps, to taking the steps that would move her forward.

'Okay, okay. I'll go,' Darcy shouted softly, feeling that Jay had left the immediate vicinity but knowing he was not too far away.

Darcy understood the concept of creativity calming the soul. Art, building, poetry, prose and even pottery could lift the spirit and place the human condition in a cohesive embrace, replacing whatever was lost with something pleasurable. So, Darcy got dressed in the hope that art might help to reignite faith once again, in her own mortality.

Art on the wall, painted by a visionary, in a studio with a purpose, yes, this is just what I need, Darcy thought, something inspirational.

The art gallery felt hypnotic and spacious. Darcy walked ahead of Jay passing *The Dance* 1988, expressionism at its finest, and stopped to examine one of Rego's esteemed pieces, a woman, with an unfeminine face, as most, if not all, of her paintings depict, in a yellow skirt, holding a sword in one hand and a sponge in the other. With power, sorrow and dimmed light in the subjects eyes. Suddenly, Darcy remembered a documentary she had watched on Rego years before, a late-night Channel 4 production, where, in it, Rego spoke of jealousy, alcohol, free love, orgies and the art of abstract painting. The programme mainly focused on Rego's political opinions surrounding abortion in her native Portugal. And of the subsequent series of paintings titled *Untitled*, illustrating her controversial views through her art, while changing the conversation about abortion and other taboo issues concerning women. Many of her representational paintings featured anger, poise, pain, rage and torment. In that moment, Darcy questioned why she'd completely forgotten about the T.V. show. The passion, after watching it that she'd felt about her own aspirations.

She stood still for a second, caught in the memory, then walked further along.

Darcy felt comfortable in the presence of such majestic artwork, even while Jay raised an eyebrow of concern.

'They're strangely weird, aren't they?' He'd muse.

'Strangely wonderful. You should research her, her ethos. She's so much more than a painter. Her life, in the documentary anyway, was so damn interesting.'

'Maybe I will,' Jay smirked affectionately.

On the way out, Darcy popped into the toilet unaware that Jay purchased a Rego book in her absence. Outside, near the coffee trailer, he produced it, still in its brown paper bag.

'To remember the day.'

'This is too much, with the tickets as well, you have to stop trying to please me. I'm pleased enough and forever grateful to you.'

'Let me at least buy the coffees?'

They sat for a while in the stone courtyard of IMMA's old stunning, stone building. Contemplating different futures and their next unshared steps.

'Do you have a date for Scotland then, is that still happening?'

Jay cleared his throat, a defence mechanism, to retain words he might regret saying.

'Yeah, yes. It is still happening but not for a few weeks yet.'

'Everything is a mess, isn't it?'

'We just take it day by day.'

'We? You're leaving.' Darcy blurted.

'I'm going somewhere to work, I'm not leaving.'

'For the foreseeable future.'

'Darcy… '

'No, I shouldn't have brought it up, because I sound like I'm objecting to your plans, which is so dumb, it's laughable actually, it's the timing, like everything else, the timing sucks.'

'I'm not living there permanently, I'm not giving up the flat here, I'll be back every other weekend.'

'Of course, you will, Jay,' Darcy smiled. 'Of course, you will.'

She sipped her coffee, dabbing the sweet froth left on her lip.

'Let's go get some tapas, I need to think a few things through, I feel tapas might help.'

Tapas, covered in cheese and taco sauce, did not come close to helping Darcy but did provide a level of motivation required to go to her abandoned grandmother's house and retrieve the mail and a few other essentials. The burnt part of the house was boarded up, safety warnings had been nailed to sheets of layered plastic. So the house was insulated and inside protected from the elements and, hopefully, Blanchardstown's growing criminality. Not that there was anything worth stealing from Pat's meagre belongings, and not that Pat cared anymore.

Pat, who had after getting her hair permed put a home colour dye over it the same day, causing her lovely hair to feel like straw, due to the chemicals from the perm. Not able to let the mistake go, she'd taken a scissors later that night and cut every straw curl off at the root. And Darcy had felt so sorry for her because Pat loved her hair, even while forgetting who she was.

The house they had shared now felt haunting and cold.

Darcy had felt alienated from the property but she was not prepared for the content of an envelope addressed to the occupier of the residence, from The Fingal County Council. A letter in the hallway, on a thick bed of ash.

An eviction notice that stated surplus rooms in the property would now house a family of four, instead of one. The housing crisis had pushed this motion forward and that one person living in a three-bedroom house could no longer be justified.

Darcy sat for a moment, in the partially charred kitchen. Perplexed. So the house was not her gran's, not a family inheritance, not belonging to anyone but men in masks, bureaucrats, sitting pretty behind wooden desks. And Darcy had never thought about asking, about planning, about anything significant. About holding her grandmother and whispering, *I love you* or saying out loud, thank you for taking me in when I had no one and was no one but an orphaned adult. But the phantoms had left the charred kitchen long ago, and the memories within were all but forgotten except for a few saved polaroids and framed smiling faces.

Darcy had some money left from a fund her parents had prepared for college fees. But nothing that would be sufficient enough to survive Ireland's rent hikes and the growing cost of living. The country had become more expensive to live in than Switzerland! The cost of living crisis had its clasp and it was not letting go.

*

'They say in the letter that alternative housing will be provided,' Mina read as if Darcy had not seen the printed word.

'I know but can you imagine?'

'I'm sure Jay will not kick you out on your ear; have you guys discussed it?'

Everything that once reeled, calmed down eventually. As Darcy and Mina sat in a café off Fitzwilliam Street, they shared the details of what was happening in their respective lives. Because it had been a while, Darcy thought, it had been far too long.

'I'm not Jay's problem, you know that, he has me staying there by default.'

Darcy would not bring up Jay's news about immigrating, her word, not his, but fitting all the same. That was his sensational headline to provide, when he saw fit.

'What about college accommodation, surely you can be subsidised, with your circumstances the way they are.' (Orphaned adult.)

'I don't want to talk or even think about that just now. I wake up and go to sleep trying to analyse it all, unproductively. I want to talk about you. You and Teddy, is it serious?'

'Oh, they are the cutest, actually, they are performing at the Workman's Club, tomorrow night. I wasn't sure whether to ask you but I think you need to mingle, and it's Slam Poetry, you love that, laced with a little Spoken Word.'

Mina then smiled, enthused at the prospect, 'Say you'll come, Pixie will be there.'

At first, when Mina used the pronoun they instead of he, Darcy, momentarily, forgot Teddy was non-binary and almost, *almost,* corrected her friend's grammar but caught herself just in time. It was not that she wasn't on board for the whole gender identity, call-yourself-who-the-hell-you-feel-you-are concept, because she was, identity was a personal crusade, end of, but, the saying of it was confusing sometimes, the vocalising part. That, to *her*, was still in its infancy. So, she had to concentrate really hard so as not to offend. She wondered about the writing down of it? Is the is changed to are? Even though it's a singular person. Or is that the point, if being non-binary was neither, then what was the actual form? Of course, she could just ask Mina, but she did not what to sound ancient, so she reserved the right to be made a holy show of, and filtered every word that passed her lips instead. Like everything, she thought, these things take time to Au Fait.

'Well, what do you say?'

'Okay, let's go see *them*.'

*

'I didn't think you'd be here, Darcy, it's good to see you,' Dom smiled affectionally, 'Do you want a drink?'

Dom was such a cheeky monkey, and Darcy was fond of him but she said no to a drink because Jessica's admission about being drugged on the camping trip put Dom in the frame and she could not shake that. How many people in the world are convicted of a crime without a trial? Innocent until proven guilty, flushed down the toilet with someone's waste! And she felt awful for even thinking Dom would be so callous and cowardly.

'I hate this kind of shit but it's an excuse to get plastered, so, fuck it.' He said.

The booths in The Workman's Club were all full and the tables, centrally, full of alcohol.

'Hey,' Jay said, as if seeing Darcy, his flatmate, for the first time that day when, in fact, they'd met twice already between a door frame and a boiling kettle.

'Did you come with Mina?'

'Yeah, but she's backstage with the man of the moment, oh, shit, they are not a man, she's with Teddy, he's non-binary, I mean, they're non-binary.'

'Okay, that's cool but what about you, how are you feeling?' Jay enquired.

'I'm good, I'm all right.'

'I wanted to ask you something, one of the lads mentioned it to me earlier, and I wanted to run it by you because it's a bit sensitive. Actually, it's ludicrous, if I'm honest.'

'Well, give us a hint, the show is about to start.' Darcy hyped.

'It's something to do with Jessica, making up shit about being drugged or something. Have you heard? He asked.

Darcy half-nodded, no. 'Uh, umm.' She muttered, feeling her fingernail tap against her leg.

'I don't know how true it is but, apparently, she's being a total bullshitter, again. I don't know why she insists on being such an attention seeker.'

'Well, maybe she's telling the truth, y'know. Try not To be so dismissive.' Jay looked puzzled but refrained from further comment, and sipped his beer.

Through the smoke a lady appeared on stage.

A husky voice came through the mic and was amplified throughout the seating area that was staggered, so every audience member could see the stage clearly. Not so clearly if they had blurred vision from intoxication.

'Hi, hi, everyone, thanks for coming and supporting young artists here this evening. First up is a crazy young lady named Pixie, who will recite her own work for us tonight; a round of applause, if you please.'

It had never occurred to Darcy that Jessica would dare try to manipulate an assault to gain something. The something having no definition because the thought was so absurd. She turned and observed Dom, oblivious to the idea that his name could be involved in a convoluted rumour. A rumour? A word, assault, another label that would stick.

Was it a rumour?

Suddenly, Darcy could not just sit and watch a poetic performance, when inside was not sitting well, in the swell of what was brewing. The inside of her, of her life. She was so sick of everything, of everything only being half-true or only hearing half-truths. Or of not feeling whole, or part of, and the world had turned a shade darker and she knew she was acting okay but that nothing about her was as it should be.

'I think I'm gonna go,' she mouthed to Jay, to which he replied,

'Huh?'

She got up from where she was sitting and walked to where the boys had gathered.

'I'm gonna leave.'

'What, why?'

A group sitting below them, *shushed.*

'You stay, I'll get the bus.' Darcy moved fast, even before Jay had a chance to answer her but, when she turned she faced Jessica, who had just arrived unbeknown to the impatient crowd.

'You're not leaving.' Jessica quietly demanded.

"I was actually; I don't feel well.'

'But,' Jessica said, 'I only came out to see you, let's walk outside for a minute, I'll walk you out.'

The traffic on the street seemed louder than ever. As if warning Darcy of the impending danger. Swoosh, swoosh, swoosh, the cars, all different colours flew by, their headlights bright, astounding in their approach.

'I never got a chance to give you my condolences, not properly. I mean I only just heard that you lost your grandmother a day before and… '

'Jessica. I can't do this, okay? Us, whatever this is, I can't. Not right now.'

'What, I was asking you why you lied to me about living with your grandmother, not anything about us!'

'Lied, no. I never felt confident enough to tell you about me, there's a huge difference, and don't talk to me about lies either. I can't stand it.'

'Lies about Jay, is that is again? Jay, Jay, Jay, the biggest lie is the one you won't admit about him because you lied about your sexuality in pursuit of him. Do you understand how sick that is? When did it stop being Jessica and Darcy and start being Darcy and Jay, I sure as hell didn't see that one coming?'

'When you slept with him and didn't let it go, that's when.'

'*You* can't let him go, you can't, you think you own him or owe him or some shit like that.'

'Do you know how deranged you sound right now?'

'Well, at least I'm being honest.'

'Really, Jessica, because if this is the day you're being honest, then tell me this…' Darcy sniffed, suddenly uncomfortable in her skin. 'Were you really drugged at the campsite? She scoffed.

Jay appeared then, from behind the front door of the club.

'Can you two keep it down, everyone can hear you inside, you're like two cats fighting in an alleyway.'

'That's rich.' Jessica huffed.

'And you can keep my name out of it too.'

'Jay, go back inside. I'm leaving, once Jessica answers the last question, I'm out of here.'

'I'm staying for the answer to that one,' Jay sneered.

'Fuck off, Jay,' Jessica began to lose her cool. 'If it wasn't for you-'

'No, not this time, Jessica, you're not fucking everyone over this time. Dom told me you never left the tent. That, he knows for a fact, you never walked out and bumped into someone who drugged you, or assaulted you or anything else. You made it up for attention because that's what you do. You're a joke.'

Darcy stood in the middle of the two people who had been polar opposites of one another but infused the same contradictions into her divided ideals.

'Enough, enough of this bullshit, the two of you can stay and argue this one out. I'm done.'

'Wait, I'll go with you,' Jay said firmly. 'Let me get my jacket.'

Jessica turned away to call a taxi, she paced the concrete, turned absentmindedly, then turned back.

'This is bullshit, I never said I was drugged, or assaulted, I said I thought I was.'

'Fuck.' Darcy, shook her head, lowering it into the disbelief that had thickened the air around her.

'You made out like you most definitely were, you messed with my head, and I blamed myself, and now, now that's just fantasy, like most things when it comes to you, Jessica. You can't use people the way you do; you've no idea how the impact of your childish antics affect other people.'

Jay reappeared.

'I'm sorry,' Jessica continued, 'I'm an idiot.' Jessica began to gently kick the uneven pathway and repeated, 'I'm an idiot but please don't leave.'

'I should have left a long time ago, Jess.'

'Come on, Darc, there's a taxi across the street, let's get out of here.' Jay waited until he knew Darcy had begun to follow.

Instead of talking about the words exchanged and what they meant Darcy left Jay in the hallway of his flat and gave a look instead of speaking, that she'd rather not go into detail about Jessica and the to and fro, of their endless quibbling.

Jay hadn't pushed, as much as he had wanted to talk, not necessarily about their love triangle, triangle being their word, that followed them around, but about them as a couple, a unit, or something close to that. So, he had closed the door and thought against his pillow, about how he could introduce his feelings, when everyone else's seemed to matter more.

*

The following morning, Jay followed Darcy to an address, the first on her list of prospective dwelling spaces. Of course, the lift was broken and that first impression was enough to make Darcy frown. She lifted her finger to her nose and almost barfed. A flat, on the second floor, was the residence the council had offered. Sent by mail, information on a one-bedroom for rent that was supposed to replace the comfort of her last living arrangement. Nearing the place, an aroma of stale urine, that might not have been urine, bothered her because she could not distinguish what the smell was.

'Inside might not be as bad,' Jay chuckled, enjoying their morning together, even if it meant Darcy could be moving out.

'I don't think I can chance it, do you?'

'Then don't, you don't need anywhere else to live.'

'But, if I don't take what they're offering, then that's it, I'm off some kind of desperado list and I'm on my own. Literarily.'

Darcy had not confided in Jay about how she was truly feeling the last few days, (weeks, months, years). It was easy to act a certain way to keep people at bay and unaware, so, unconcerned. But Darcy was worried about herself. Her thoughts were very dark and contained a voice, that sounded just like her, on repeat. Telling her of her misfortunes, of how life would just get worse and of how she should hate herself because hate seemed to be woven into the very fabric of who she was. And she tried to silence the voice, to distract it, or turn away from its incessant cruelty but, when she did that, the voice only became more powerful, like the engine propellors on the Titanic, the rotary blades turning as if the whole ocean swerved through them, in one interactive motion.

Darcy lay awake sometimes, just staring at the ceiling, because her life had fallen apart. All the people she knew and cared about functioned as normal. Buying bread or train tickets, spending a birthday voucher, browsing through clothes rails, putting washing powder in the machine or putting on deodorant. Going about their every day as if things were normal. But Darcy no longer had parents, grandparents, an honest girlfriend, a proper career, a sexual preference or a home to live in. All the things that stability framed. And she had a feeling, a terrible feeling, that she might just split in two for real this time. Without anything left of her to put back together.

It was a man begging on the street that finally did it, pushed her over the edge. Because his tattered clothes and unkempt, dishevelled appearance, his hollow eyes and pale skin, his limp demeanour and acceptance of faith, could be her in a heartbeat.

'Hey, are you okay?'

'I don't think so, Jay, I might need help.'

'Help, what is it?'

'I'm not sure, but it isn't good, I think I need to go somewhere.'

Jay looked confused but took her hand in his.

'Anywhere, where, just say.'

'St Pat's, I think that's the nearest.'

When the words came out, Darcy's hands began to shake, and her eyes glazed over. The words. The dirty words. A hospital for people struggling with mental health. The mentally ill. The stigma attached to failing and failure, and not being able to cope. And the knowing that the words were nothing compared to the reality of the moment. That the words were eclipsed by the pain of feeling unstable. And that reaching out was her only option now, reaching out before she didn't have a grip, on even the power to lean on anything that was offered.

'It's okay,' Jay said, 'Sit here on the curb until the taxi gets here.' They both cried then, soundless, dry, swallowed sobs. Darcy in Jay's arms, swaying on the curb. And the beggar watching them as if he'd done something wrong.

Chapter Fourteen

What happened was, the world changed.

The room in the hospital was basic, very basic, because Darcy had been put on suicide watch after showing symptoms of self-harm. Nail marks, along with cut marks on the skin a long sleeve had protected. To her, the conversation was about something else causing harm, but in translation, and now that she was feeling a little better, her words were clearer and easy to decipher. She perceived danger from outside, an outside force wanting to cause her pain, when the enemy was within, it was herself. The meds prescribed had saved her life because she had been suffering from post-traumatic stress, a severe case, that had been overlooked and untreated from her parents' death, and the events of the past few weeks had kindled a trigger that her uninformed mind and unequipped coping skills could not handle.

The doctors had recommended she be admitted for at least a two-week stay. It was now day eight.

Jay came to visit every evening. He had become her best friend, placed in——the friend zone – because all other spaces were taken. But Jay, who enjoyed being with her, had moved out of the friend zone and into loving

Darcy. It was a precarious place to place his heart but there was no alternative, admitting to himself recently that he had loved her for quite some time.

'Cranberry juice, just like you asked for.' He was also carrying a magazine, a lad's mag, and his hair was tousled, his denim shirt opened halfway down.

'I would love a walk, come on, it's a sunny day, let's walk in the grounds, I can manage it, I was out for a while yesterday.'

Darcy stretched, then pulled the covers off her body and stepped into the slippers waiting on the floor. The fur from the inside cocooned her feet in warmth, correlating with a lightness that already lived within her spirit.

For practically the first three days and nights, she slept, sedated, her mind resting and peaceful. Nurses checked her periodically, a fact, not an observation, that Darcy learned later. One nurse, in particular, who had an altruistic nature, and brown eyes, usually sat with Darcy in the afternoons, longer than she should. Her name was Kim, or Kimmy, once familiar. She had three large freckles on her face, together in a cluster, that gave her radiant complexion character. Darcy thought she would make an ideal subject for a portraitist. A blond bob cupped her face, except for the small section pinned back by two brown hairclips. Kim was a student nurse, from County Leitrim, or thereabouts and, from the way she carried herself, Darcy would have awarded her a qualification on actions, or compassion, or the way she simply sat and listened, alone.

'What did the doctors say today, did you see one?'
Jay, his caring voice, a soothing remedy.

'Yes, the same really, that the meds seem to have
kicked in. I no longer feel the weight I had been carrying
around. It's hard to describe what that was, but despair
comes close.' And the hiding of it had been so wearisome,
Darcy thought, so trying.

'God, I still feel like a right gobshite, not asking
questions, I should have picked up on the signs. I hate
myself, but you look a lot better, you do.'

They sat on a bench outside, opposite another patient
who sat on a bench alone.

'It wasn't down to you to ask questions. I should have
asked for help, long before I did, the days leading up to the
breakdown, I was spiralling, and I internalised that
heaviness, sure, I'd no idea what was about to happen, so
how could you? As it takes hold of you, and that can be a
sluggish progression, it doesn't say, today is the day, but,
by God, you know when it's arrived.'

Darcy rubbed the palms of her hands together. The
meds dried her skin, the skin between her fingers was itchy
a lot of the time.

'Who is that, do you know her?'

The bench opposite, its dark green wooden slants, the
flowerbed beside it and cherry blossoms trees that
surrounded it, still in bloom, looked picturesque and out of
place but, for the patient sitting midway, staring at the sky.
Smoking a cigarette.

'Her name is India, she's being supervised, if you look over there, you can see the men in white watching her, I think she did something pretty tragic.'

'How come she's here, is it safe?'

'She needs help, Jay, not judgement, that's why she's here.' Darcy realised too late how abrupt her tone was. 'They watch her so she doesn't harm herself.'

'I didn't mean that the way it sounded.' Jay winced.

'I know, I'm sorry I snapped.'

That's why Darcy was here too, she thought, because she needed help. Because on the first night of her admission to the hospital, she'd been given shock therapy, (ETC) to change her brain chemistry, so that she might connect to the present again, instead of just staring off somewhere towards oblivion. The grey walls of her clinic bedroom providing no comfort, only adding to her misery. After the treatment, she had puked all over the floor and Kim told her that that was normal, in a culchie accent that Darcy had completely warmed to, and that getting sick, as contradictory as it may be, was a good sign. And the mortification of it subsided because anguish lingered and anguish was the stronger emotion. And Kim had helped Darcy take a bath, in tepid water, with added relaxation salts, prescribed by homeopathy specialists. Holding on to Kim's hand, Darcy had submerged her troubles and tried to dissolve her regret.

The shock treatment, Darcy decided, would be her secret, not because of shame but because of worry, the worry it would inevitably cause the person she confided in.

'It's just we're the same, me and her, the same but different, both here because we lost our way for a bit.'

Jay leaned forward on his thighs, his elbows resting, his curls falling, so he pushed one side of his hair back, at the parting, his eyes downcast first but then he faced her.

'Have the others been in touch?'

'If, by the others, you mean, our friends, then, yeah, Mina has phoned and texted, she's busy, she's in love actually and I asked her to stay away from my darkened situation, for now, so she's okay with that.'

Darcy wiped the side of her nose.

'All the others have sent texts, Kate and, well, I was going to say Jessica but I have her blocked, I don't want her here.'

'You couldn't keep me away.'

Darcy knew he was teasing. In fact, Darcy, especially in the last few days, realised the bond she shared with Jay. There was no label for it because he wasn't just a friend, or a friend with benefits, or a potential boyfriend, but he most definitely was someone not unlike a person who would be in that mish-mashed equation. He was something more and something less than the hub, the main focal point of where Darcy stood. Maybe she should invent a term that explained their bond, but not while she was under supervision for being unbalanced, no, not just yet.

The term, as unconventional as it would be, would have to wait.

'Just as long as you know, if you skip an evening's visit, that's okay too.' Darcy leaned in, shoulder to shoulder, affectionately.

But, as the words left her tongue, she knew she was lying and that his absence would be sorely missed, would hurt her heart even.

Darcy could leave the hospital ward whenever she wanted to. Kim, on one of her afternoon check-ins, told Darcy that a two-week stint was the normal process for a patient with her condition and, if after showing clear signs of improvement, she would be released. Kim used specific medical terminology but Darcy understood the seriousness of what she'd been through, and what she would continue to recover from, for the foreseeable. She no longer needed shock therapy but she also knew her mental state walked a fine line between okay and not-so-okay. How are these things determined, Darcy thought, by asking the patient? The person who got themselves into the mess they're in in the first place. The ambiguity, the murky water, the grey area. It was always the grey, in whatever capacity, which led Darcy to question her own sanity.

It was the pressure of her life. The sequence of events that she had not processed, or given attention to. The piling of each incident had crashed down, toppling her resolve, highlighting how ill-equipped she was. Kim told her, she would attend a program, that would teach her coping skills and breathing exercises, tools that would benefit her recovery tremendously. Darcy trusted Kim, so she promised to attend the next afternoon.

Feeling thirsty, Darcy opened her bedroom door, a walk to the kitchen, to where chilled orange juice sat on a fridge door shelf and called her by taste bud language. Although the sugar rush would affect her sleeping, she couldn't get the idea of the cooled liquid out of her head.

'Hey,' a voice from behind. Darcy turned and India was standing still, as if an ethereal figure in the shadowy space held up by the walls.

'India, come on, I'm on my way to the kitchen.'

'Oh,' she whispered, 'I can't go in there, that's beyond my limits.'

'You don't have to go in, I'll go inside, don't worry. We're not breaking any rules.'

India shuffled slowly until catching up with Darcy, they then synchronised their footing the rest of the way. A supervising nurse was reading at his desk, as they got closer, he raised a questioning eyebrow.

'I'm just getting a drink, then we're going back.' Darcy volunteered. Two plastic chairs hugged the corridor wall opposite the kitchen entrance.

'Sit here,' Darcy pointed, 'I won't be a sec.'

The dark rings under India's eyes were evidence of scraps of sleep, of shut-eye, where stress hovers, even if heavily altered by prescription tablets, stress put up camp as if an unwelcomed, unsolicited visitor. India's face contained elements of every pain. They walked back the same way after Darcy's thirst was quenched.

'Can you walk around unsupervised in the ward now?'

'I'm on probation, I can walk up and down the corridors, but the kitchen is out of bounds.' India said.

'I don't know why,' Darcy quizzed casually, 'I mean, they have everything locked away.'

'Will you leave soon? So many people come and go.'

'Yes, 'Darcy nodded, 'By the end of next week, I hope to anyway, what about you?'

'Me, oh, no, I won't be going anywhere else.'

Darcy, just out of curiosity, wanted to push for the reason why, but the unproblematic nature of their odd pairing might change with the answer, so she closed the question away and asked instead, 'You're happy though, here, in the safety of the place, I mean?'

'I wake up and potter around and I sit in the garden, and in my room, so I'm happy enough, it is what it is.'

In India's eyes lay the resignation of something resembling defeat. Yes, that's what it was, a deadness to a living thing, that, just then, scared Darcy. The "what?" of the "is" in India's statement bothered her too, but, just like most things, she chose to put it to one side.

Darcy, was herself, fending and that took every ounce of energy she had.

The next morning Kim stood, the door ajar and asked Darcy to be ready in ten. Dr Reilly would see her first and then a therapist would walk through some techniques to help her cope on the outside.

The outside, Darcy thought, the outside of what? Weren't they all either on the outside or all in the inside, somehow? And most people on the outside, walked around unaware that inside existed, until they needed a comfy bed for the night.

Darcy was still getting used to her mild medication. A dose doubled in grams at the beginning of her stay and for the first few days, but now lessened because of her positive reaction to treatment.

So, her mind was less foggy and her body moved in time with orders from the brain. 'Did you sleep okay?' Kim, whose voice fitted perfectly, her chosen vocation.

'Yep. Like a log.'

The breathing techniques were helpful, the meditative state they induced, brought calm, and a welcomed time to reflect but in future tense.

As Kim walked Darcy back, Darcy asked without thinking, 'Why is India in here?'

'You know I can't talk to you about other patients Darcy.'

'I'm not asking you to talk about her, I have a feeling, if I googled her name, I'll be shocked at what I'd find.'

'Well, she's in here, so you shouldn't be too shocked.'

'I don't like the sound of that.'

'Patients in this section are here because of the harm they could cause themselves, or others.'

'But I wasn't going to harm myself, or anyone else, was I?'

'You should ask Dr Reilly, Darcy, you know I'm not at liberty to divulge medical prognoses, yours or anyone else's.'

'Even if the patient is me?'

'Yes, even if the patient is you. Here's your room, come on, before you get me fired.' 'But, ' Darcy stopped and faced her nurse. 'Ye see, the first hours being here, they're a blur, can you at least fill in the blanks.'

'I'm not exactly sure, but I know you kept repeating one line over and over.'

'One line, Jesus, what was it?'

'Something about joining your parents, that they were calling you, something like that, come on now, into bed.'

'Oh right, I get it now. I must have sounded like a right loon.'

Darcy read aloud, then underlined a passage in a book.

"Most people adjust their way of thinking as their lifestyles alter. Some of these life changes have an invitation and others are uninvited but seem to show up, heading for somewhere else but seeing the well-harvested fields and well-bred stock, decide instead to cast an anchor and come on land to colonise. Some people fight against change, while others accept their fate, thus the world keeps turning, and people adjust."

Lately, Darcy's world moved without her input, orchestrated by something outside of her control. Grief had already shown her its moves, how to avoid and manoeuvre through pain. A dancer, with so few lessons, but who had listened intently, Darcy had learned to put pain aside and invite change in.

Chapter Fifteen

The end of the week appeared and, with it, the final days of summer. Darcy sat in the passenger seat beside Jay who had borrowed his roommate's car without permission, to bring Darcy home. In the boot, with smelly football socks and a germ-germinating gumshield, sat a bag with her tablets and a new prescription, enough for a mini drug fest if you were that way inclined. And beside her, Jay, and a prolonged spell of silence as he awaited an answer to his proposition from a minute or two before.

'Well?'

'Jesus, Jay, I can't give you an answer to that already, at least let me get in the door. It's a bit bloody much.'

Jay had stated and then enquired if Darcy would be up for travelling to Malaga, Mijas, to be precise, for a few days. That his parents owned an apartment over there and it was free, unoccupied, and that the plants needed to be watered.

Darcy knew the last part was added on for effect and a complete exaggeration.

'Look, I'm telling you it's what you need. Nice restaurants and relaxation time by the pool, catch up on reading, whatever, the flights are cheap as chips at the moment too.'

'Can you just keep your eyes on the road please.'

Who had money for such luxuries? Darcy thought, money was a small issue for her, but not for any of her college friends, apparently, who all came from upper-class parts of Dublin, rating high on the socioeconomic ladder. Wealth, affluence had never really been part of the conversation before. Wealth, as in the comparison of wealth, was just one of those things, obvious but undisclosed. The trip to Spain with Jay was practically being handed on a plate.

'What about your job, your new job that's taking you away from Ireland, your home.'

'Let me worry about that, Darcy, just say yes and I'll book it. Do you know we've only five weeks left and then our final semester starts, can you fucking believe that, scary, huh?'

Darcy wanted to say, it's not our final semester because you're leaving but she stopped short of being snidey. Jay did not deserve snideness.

'Okay, let's fucking go to Spain then.'

The words were out and they landed with delight, because Jay smiled, either out of happiness or as if he were the cat that got the cream.

*

Gradually, the day got easier. Darcy, who was on extended sick leave from work knew in all practicality, that her P60 was on the way. Too much frivolous time off, even if it was for the reasons stated—to put one's fading sanity back together—had run its course. So, the holiday, for her, at least, would be a time to re-energise and refocus on the future.

The parting anxiety she had encountered from the hospital had been renegotiated, and, now, because of the impending trip, excitement tinged the tender spots.

'I honestly don't think I would have said yes if I knew you had booked this for tomorrow.'

'It was a spur-of-the-moment thing, anyway, it's done now, so just pack what you have. My sister's stuff is over there anyway, all the cosmetics and shit, so don't panic about toothpaste and creams and towels, well, y'know.'

Darcy grunted to herself, as she busied her hands rifling through what summer clothes she had and what was needed for the trip, surmising a visit to Penny's for underwear wouldn't go amiss. She walked back towards the bathroom intending to use the loo, not paying attention, not paying attention at all, to Jay who was undressing for a shower he had not announced and was about to take. Did he forget she was home, back from her hospital stay, back being his roomy? Because he was completely naked, his back to her, reaching for the dial on the inside of the shower, without a care. The stretch extenuating his lean body, his strong muscles, the round lines on his firm ass. His shoulder blades arched inward, showing the olive conures of his skin.

Then, he turned his face and looked at her, grinning, 'You wanna join me?' His expression, bearing no shame or hint of embarrassment.

'Stop, Jesus, can you not close the door, now I've to hold my wee in.'

He walked out, a towel wrapped around his midriff.

'Use the loo, come on, I can wait.'

They were acting like children, the way children act when nothing else matters but the fun forecasted by a preceding conversation between adults. Built up by planning or organising or planning the organisation of what's to come. A day trip to the circus, a train trip to Bray, a trip into town to ride the Viking boat, or Dublin Zoo to feed the caged animals. With the promise of salad sandwiches later on and a flask of sugared tea, sat on the green or upon the many benches positioned strategically for visitors to the park.

And they were giddy passing one another on the way to their respective bedrooms to throw something in an open case, waiting on the bed.

Then, Darcy had an unsteady moment, just a moment, and Jay was there, a glass of water on hand, with gentle instructions to sit and take a rest.

Dublin airport had been a nightmare. Luckily, they had no large cases to check- in, just carry-on bags, so that halved the waiting time. In the duty-free lounge, the obligatory spraying of sample perfume, one spray on the wrist, then a twist from the other wrist to fragrance both arms. Sometimes a dab on the neck behind the ears, sometimes not. Jay stood in another section trying to get Darcy's attention, holding one of those circled neck cushions, his demeanour all but saying *shall I buy this*? Buy something that you won't even use, Darcy thought, and nodded no, while frowning at the same time. That was the thing about airport shopping, the place was filled with items not needed for short flights, at exorbitant prices, exceeding the item's worth, while cleverly confusing the customer's rationale. Consumer persuasion and manipulation at its finest.

With no flight delays, the plane took off and landed on time, each row emptying while letting the one in front go. Twenty-five minutes later, and after a strained taxi ride by a grumpy driver who obviously didn't like tourists, Jay was showing Darcy where the factor thirty sun cream was in his parent's summer home.

'Not on top, underneath.' He pointed before disappearing.

Every wall in the apartment was painted white, pristine white. The furniture was white wicker, with huge soft cushioned underlay and fluffy white and coral cushions lined along the back. Straightened neatly by the previous holiday maker, or a paid cleaner, who had somehow made everything in the place look as though it had never been lived in before. Then the white tablets in Darcy's hand, her medication for anxiety and the contrasting realities between standing in an apartment in Spain, as opposed to a hospital bedroom in Dublin, just days before. And Darcy knew if she began to overthink,

think too much about how, not that Jay had opened the double doors onto the pool area, but how the meds must be making her imagine things that weren't really there, she might question how she, in this beautiful place, on this day, was standing facing the clear blue sea.

'Grab your towel then; there's still plenty of sunshine left to enjoy.'

So, Darcy followed because Jay knew the area, the redbrick walls with hanging baskets overflowing with fresh, big, red begonias. A stoned pathway that opened onto a tiled corridor leading to a gate, that once opened, giving view to a spectacular communal swimming pool, with an odd body on a sunbed, here and there that expanded beyond to show clear blue skies. Palm trees reached the sky and, on the horizon, the glistening ocean could be seen panoramically, if bored with every other sight.

'Holy Lord, Jay, this place is friggin amazing, you kept this secret hidden well.'

'Funny you should say that because I offered the place two summers ago, to the gang, you included and no one was bothered.'

'Did you really, and why did we decline the offer?'

'To be honest, I could have mumbled something after a few too many, but I definitely put it out there.'

'Here's to a few too many. I'm glad I waited.' Their glasses clinked and then opened to a sunbeam.

Sometime later Darcy walked over to a wall that coved the apartment block. The wall, pebble laden with stones that were light brown and glistened in parts, looked as though a stonemason picked each stone by hand, a perfectionist at work, caring about his creation. The wall allowed a spectator to watch the beach below. A small, what looked to Darcy as a private sandy beach. Along the hill, other apartments were fixed into the rocky formation, camouflaged by the natural habitat of the evergreen wildflowers and wild foliage.

Jay came up behind her, his presence immediately felt, and tenderly put his arm around her waist.

'Just what the doctor ordered, right?'

They swam and ordered light snacks, enjoyed the sun and listened to music. Jay said he wouldn't drink because Darcy, with her meds, was advised not to. She laughed and told him not to be so pathetic and he laughed too, but insisted.

He had become perfect. But not perfect for her, and she couldn't undo that. Untie a knot and make it straight.

'What are you thinking?' he asked as the sun entered the ocean for the evening.

'Of how lucky we are. That we're cool and good for each other and that, if I didn't have you, I'd be in the gutter right now.'

'Come on, let's get showered and dressed, there's a quaint restaurant I want to show you, that I think you'll love.'

A light tingling layer of sunburn caressed Darcy's chest, even though she had applied a generous dollop of sunscreen to the area that tingled.

Darcy linked her arm through Jay's as they walked through the cobbled winding road down to the beach. As if castaways on their own island, tropical, exotic and free, sun-kissed and needing no one else but each other. The private restaurant was integral to the beach, hidden behind tall trees, as if part of the natural landscape. White and pink clematis climbed the tree trunk, decorating outside with almond scented speckles.

'This is insane; I can't believe I'm standing in such a stunning part of the world, it's… it's breathtakingly breathtaking. I'm stunned.' Darcy crooned.

'I told you.' Jay walked ahead slightly.

'A table for two, Julian.' He said with a wide smile, as Darcy neared the spacious, candlelit, dining area.

'Ah, so good to have you back with us, Mr Farrell, it's been a while, no.'

'A year or so, I think, this is Darcy, my… my friend.'

'Ah, ha, very good.' Julian pulled out the seat for Darcy and, as she sat, he handed her the menu.

After dinner, both Darcy and Jay walked along the beach, their feet in the warm water, as rippled waves, rippled in the ebb and flow of the shallow tide.

'It's a far cry from home, shall we sit?'

'I'm so tired, Jay, can we come back tomorrow evening, bring a blanket or something? My eyelids are dropping.'

'Yeah, it's been a long day, come on, let's go back.'

'Are you sure you don't mind?'

Farther down the coast, young people sat together, laughing like summer would never end, the kind of vibe Darcy watched on television and dreamed of enjoying. The moment was surreal and Darcy fought back what was coming, not wanting Jay to see her cry, even if the tears were from joy and gratitude.

'Come on, if I'm being completely honest, I feel beat too.'

Darcy could hear Jay moving around once they got back. The flick of a switch, the bolting of a latch, then the whispering of, *see you tomorrow, Darcy, sweet dreams* and the closing of the bedroom door. She sat a moment on the edge of the bed, in a strange room, in a strange place and wondered, if she climbed into bed with Jay, would he hold her without needing something more? Without needing to touch her in a way she craved right now. That union, where skin on skin, takes away the feeling of emptiness, even temporarily. But then the aftermath of such a union would sit at the breakfast table, it would eat toast and ask for juice to be poured, while Darcy looked one way and Jay another. So, instead of seeking comfort in a place that would welcome her company, she pulled down the cotton sheet on the bed and slid under it, closing her eyes to the sound of the ever flowing waves of the sea.

*

The next morning, as Darcy turned her body towards, then away from the bright beams that shone inward, she rubbed

211

her eyes before loosening the strap of her watch to read the face. It read eleven-forty-seven a.m., but that couldn't be right, she thought and sat up blinking. Could she have slept that late? Standing, her feet uneven, she managed to walk over to the nearest window to release the patterned window blind, but it rose too fast and shot up with force, jolting her back unexpectedly. She staggered until she found the dresser and balanced herself against the nearest wall.

'Shit!' She raised her hand up over her eyebrows, as if saluting no one.

When she finally steadied herself, the window beckoned. It overlooked the pool area and she spotted Jay on the sun lounger that they had used the previous evening. Slumbering as if a sun God, unhurried by life. Sipping what looked like a Pina Colada. She yawned, stretched and grinned all at the same time, happy that Jay was letting his curly hair down. Seeing her then, he waved.

Were they on a movie set? she asked herself, some kind of foreign drug heist movie, where the protagonists live the lives of the super-rich before being discovered and jailed, without bail, a frantic gun showdown before being taken, hand-cuffed, into custody, tanned and with a jaunty step.

At least this morning she felt more grounded in her surroundings. Even after the initial discombobulation.

Her mobile rang, the name Jay bright and illuminated.

'Hey.'

'Hey, sleepy head, I got bored so now I'm a little bit intoxicated.'

'You're on holiday, live a little, I won't tell anyone.'

'Come down, I miss you. I'll order food.'

'Only if you rub sun cream on my back.' Darcy enjoined, 'it looks like a scorcher.' Said lyrically.

After bacon and eggs, cranberry juice and seed grain toast, rustic, squared and laden with Spanish butter, Jay lay on his stomach so his back faced the glaring sun.

'Where's the factor fifty? I'm not even joking, that sun is unreal.' Darcy asked.

'Did you bring a vape down? The green one?'

'I'm not your mother, Jay, pass me up that one, the cream by your hand.'

They acted, it seemed, like a normal couple, vacationing in Spain for a few days to get away from the normal humdrum of everyday life in Ireland. Ireland's half-summers in the whole summertime. Putting washing out on the line in the morning heat, then forced to take it in again from the afternoon downpour.

How many times had Pat shouted down the stairs if Darcy was in the kitchen and a sudden torrent opened the skies?

'Take in the washing, Darcy, will ye, love, hurry, just throw the bits on the rads if you've time before work, or college or wherever you're off to.'

Later in the day, Darcy would return from the "wherever" and the dry clothes from that wash would be neatly folded, in a stack on the end of her bed.

Laying back on the comfy sun lounger, Darcy found her mind would regress and ask questions, step back, with cautious steps, to childhood memories, or just poignant memories, of special times. She tried vehemently to avoid the happiest times because those precious memories brought on the worse feelings, a paradox in emotional research, an ongoing survey, that stopped people on the street, in order to fill out data forms that contribute to the reasons why things had to be the way they were. As if data collection on emotions and memories could ever solve unhappiness, or what kept the person unhappy or stuck in an emotional frame of mind.

'What are we doing tonight?' Darcy turned on her side, her right breast half exposed from the cup of her skimpy bikini top. The sunburn line, a two-tone of white and red skin. Jay lifted his head, half dosing. A sunhat on the floor, beside him, flattened in the middle by a lip balm and a white EarPods case.

'Whatever you want, what about skinny dipping?'

'What about a walk along the beach half-dressed, will that accommodate your fantasy?'

'Fantasies come true, Darcy, ye just gotta let em.'

While relaxing, Jay had traced his fingertips along the skin on Darcy's arm, stopping on each mole to say hello. The motion relaxed her even more, while the not objecting to his touch, was something she chose to ignore. They were like every other couple on holiday, except, they were not.

The friend WhatsApp group that had laid dormant for weeks suddenly beeped with enquiring messages from each member.

Where are you two?

Why are you two together?

Is it Spain?

Where is our invite?

Are you two shagging?

Did you see on the news, Spain is in for a unprecedented heatwave.

Good luck with that.

Any nude beaches?

How are Jay's smelly farts?

When are ye back?

Any action, topless, I mean?

'You can answer that one in particular; how do they know we're here anyway?'

'I had to tell Dom, so he could check on the flat.'

'I'm sure they're thinking all sorts.'

'I don't care, do you?' Jay murmured, a straw filled with Pina Colada in his mouth.

Although Darcy agreed with Jay about not caring what the others thought, she knew she was drawing her conclusion from a "holiday perception" and that didn't count, or didn't carry as much weight. The sun could make things seem as if every day would be sunny and, in the presence of it, in the rapture of its warmth, one could believe just about anything was possible. But the need for an umbrella, outstretched and wide, was not to be dismissed. Simply put, the rain never stayed away for long.

'Just one more and that's it.'

Darcy knew she shouldn't, she'd hardly been on the pills long enough to stop taking them for one day but, she wanted to get a little drunk—as opposed to Jay being a lot drunk and her having to watch him that way.

'One more won't do any harm.' He agreed.

They were in a local bar after, what could only be described as, a glorious day in the sunshine. They laughed, a lot. And earlier, while getting ready to go out, when it came to closing the door while showering, Darcy didn't bother because she was young, tipsy and wanted to feel desired, and released from the constraints she put on herself. She lathered soap and washed her tanning skin in full view of Jay and there was something titillatingly raw about the exchange, something profoundly exotic, because she knew he wanted to touch all the parts of her that she touched. And the teasing of it was erotic and dangerous and kind of uncontrollable.

'That girl keeps staring over here at you,' Jay nodded, to which Darcy moved her head.

'She's cute, I think her friend might be staring at you, how cliché, picking up girls in a bar on holidays.'

'Who said we're picking them up?'

'Oh, you know how these things go?'

'I'll only make a move if you do.' Jay said.

Darcy giggled, a laugh letting out any remaining inhibition. Her choices now, she would regret in the morning, but she, they, her and Jay, were too drunk to know that their logical brain had switched into another gear, with no brakes, stop signs or the yield that might break their fall.

Back at the apartment, the lights on low, Nina Simone played on Jay's mother's old-style record player, the circling turntable, the main pickup cartridge at work, the stylus resting against the record, making it possible for Nina's lyrics to fill the room, *For Wild is the Wind, you kiss me, with your kiss my life begins, you're spring to me, all things to me-*. The depth of the accompanying piano, having a trance-like effect on the four occupants in the living area.

After chatting and drinking in the bar until almost closing, Darcy had insisted Aurelia and Maria, natives of mainland Spain but in Mijas for a long weekend, join them in the apartment.

At first, Darcy welcomed Maria's roving hand that caressed the small of her back, then moved up towards her neck, resting in the arch. There seemed to be a consensus on who would couple with whom but, even though Maria was stunning and sexy and inviting, Darcy found her eyes seeking Jay out, where his hands were, on what part of Aurelia's body.

And, when he kissed Aurelia, with a passionate yearning, the type of kiss that would take the couple to a place of no return, Darcy got up from where she was sitting, moved closer and pulled them apart.

'Sorry,' she announced, impaired and with a slur. 'It's time to go.'

'Jesus, Darcy, what the fuck are you doing?'

The girls began to speak to Darcy in Spanish and English and, before long, a row broke out in the living room, not a physical fight per se but a bilingual exchange of rude expletives, that culminated in Darcy swaying, tripping over, then finally leaving the apartment and running towards the beach.

After, what felt like a passing of time Darcy sulked, and sank into the notion that she'd caused an unnecessary scene. She sat facing the ocean, still drunk but not inebriated enough to know she had overreacted.

Footsteps, that should not make a sound on sand, got closer, as Jay sat beside her, manoeuvring until he scooched up beside her, as close as he could get.

'Come on, come back inside, they're gone.'

'I'm such an idiot, I don't know why I did that.' Darcy rubbed the end of her nose. 'You should follow them, go with them, go party.'

'I don't want to be with them; you invited them over.'

'I keep fucking up, over and over.'

'That's just words, Darcy, you're not doing anything that dramatic.'

'I need to tell you something, something I've never told anyone before. I've been sitting here worrying about the whys of why I act the way I do.'

'You're drunk, and I don't want to have a chat about something you won't discuss when you're sober, I don't want to be that guy, I'm not just here to catch you when you fall, Darcy, I want more than that.'

'No, it's not that, I wanted to tell you before, long before tonight and I think I need to talk about this now.'

'Okay, okay, take the stage.'

'It's about my parents.'

Jay nodded approvingly. 'Okay, Darcy, okay, I'm here.'

'It's about how they died, and of how I've never spoken about it before, the how of it, the fact of it even. The specifics that I've tried to bury, I guess.'

Jay, and the other members of Darcy's friend group, had spoken about Darcy's parents but never in a gossipy way, more in an enquiring conversational way. In a way of noting how Darcy never brought up family or of how she opened a book when others did, flicking through pages to avoid interrogation, or a raised brow. So, Jay, along with the others, suspected Darcy lived a life different than theirs but they never pushed or asked for details, not any detailed details anyway.

'Take a deep breath, it's fine, you can do this.'

Darcy inhaled.

'They were supposed to be working that day, y'know, they took the day off specifically for me, to check out colleges, and universities that, in their words, *catered to Darcy's keen interest in History and The Humanities*. So, instead of being at work, they went from college to college, inspecting the grounds, and so forth, because their only daughter and her education was paramount.'

Darcy sniffled but Jay let her continue without interfering.

'Well, afterwards, they decided to grab a coffee, a flat white and a frappuccino, a picture sent to me, in a joking way, to insinuate that they were enjoying caffeine instead of college hunting. My dad ordering his first frappuccino to act cool, for me and I knew it was for me. I knew that, em, the cool dad, because I knew him so well. This part haunts me because they should have just gone home then, home, but, instead, they walked over to a shop window with different-sized smart T.V.s. The fucking really shit part is that my dad told me the night before that, as a gift for passing the leaving cert, he wanted to upgrade my T.V., so they were standing there, their backs against the traffic, against a drunk driver, who lost control of his car and drove right into them, smashing their bodies through the glass window, killing them instantly. The autopsy stated they had no underlying illnesses, healthy but for the internal organ displacement caused by the impact.'

The sea spoke first, its waves light and lively, they whistled, as one wave folded onto another.

'Fuck, I'd no idea, Darcy, that's so-'

'When I read the article in the paper about the accident, the part that bugged me, the part that really affected me, was how the journalist wrote, "Drunk Driver Loses Control", as if a drunken driver has control in the first place, y'know. The headline should have said, *a selfish fuck murdered two loving parents,* the line should have told the truth, Jay.'

220

It was then the tears came, the tears that Darcy had not allowed herself to cry. And Jay held onto her, as a friend, as someone who needed him, his embrace, and nothing more.

They sat there a while until the sun showed signs of beginning a new day. A rosy hue, that caught the ocean and flickered off the rise. A symbolic circle of possibility, that coloured the early morning with brightness but also made Darcy realise she was spent.

'I'm sorry I ruined your chances with Maria.'

Jay shrugged while standing up, then lowered a hand to help Darcy stand.

'I'm sorry you ruined your chances with whatshername.'

They smiled then, both exhausted and hungover. Quietly, they walked back to the apartment hand in hand.

Chapter Sixteen

The following evening, late enough, Darcy and Jay walked through the front door of their Dublin flat, needing a holiday.

'I think I'll just head to bed, I'm wrecked,' Jay mumbled.

'I could make tea.'

'I can hardly keep my eyes open, Darc, sorry.'

On the way home, Darcy noticed that Jay kept his dialogue between them brief, with succinct answers to some of Darcy's questions, as if extra interaction wasn't necessary, similar to superfluous words in an essay, there to fill the word count but adding nothing to the work.

The choked air in the flat seemed to extend to every room, so Darcy opened the windows, standing by one just to let fresh air caress her face. She felt that old familiar feeling of tethered panic, restrained tightly at the helm by taut ropes she couldn't even see.

She retired to her designated room, restless but hoping for sleep. Even though the bedroom was not her bedroom, not really, she felt safe.

Overthinking kept Darcy awake, thinking nonsense. Wondering about the light fixture on the ceiling and about the fabric of the light shade, as if its stillness needed enquiry, as if it was owed something from her mind.

An arbitrary impulse and she sat upright. Jay was probably sleeping by now but she could not help herself.

Opening and closing her door, she reached Jay's door a second later. Inside her stomach, an unsettling she had felt before and not felt before too. She thought to knock but then resisted that urge and, with a gentle ease, pushed down on the handle. Because Jay had left his curtains open, light came in from a street lamp, enough for Darcy to make out his darkened silhouette under the covers. His body still in sleep, his curls, the back of his head. For a moment she thought to leave him, but, just as quickly, told herself, *if it wasn't tonight, it would never be.*

And she wanted him and wanted him to want her.

If it wasn't tonight, it would never be.

'Jay… ' she whispered, 'Jay… '

'Darcy?' Jay moved, he turned towards her, 'What's happened?'

'Nothing.'

The word was said but the word meant say nothing, do nothing, because nothing is wrong, and words are not needed.

Jay saw her then, naked, vulnerable, so he pulled back his bedsheet and beckoned her towards him.

If it wasn't tonight, it would never be.

She lay her head on the warmth of his pillow, a place his head had rested a second before. His body covered her but his weight did not. And he looked at her then, the lines

223

on her face clearly visible from the street lamp's glow. Her button nose and full lips, her structured cheekbones and brunette fringe, wisps of fringe he gently moved across her forehead, and then he softly licked his own lips, and Darcy felt, from under him, him shudder, and she smiled and he smiled and kissed her then. With no urgency first and then with a growing urgency and then with an urgency called passion, a passionate urgency. A want, a perfect want that desire had clearly put in place to lead the way. Their naked skin, and the heat from their naked skin, combined somehow, joined somehow, joined them somehow. And then his head was lowering and his tongue was everywhere, and everywhere had hot air, and open spaces and legs were parted and skin was dampening and then Jay was everywhere inside her and all over every inch of her, and she felt powerful and powerfully combined and in awe and on the edge, completely on the edge of a place she wanted to stand.

It was Thursday morning, three days after Darcy had stopped being a gold-star lesbian. Or a lesbian at all, in the real sense of the word, Darcy thought, as she relaxed into a chair. For years, for as far back as she could recall, her sexual preference had been connected to women, and women only. Getting up again, she put the kettle on and leaned against the counter waiting for the water to boil.

The morning after the night before, the sexual encounter with her roommate, she had put salt into her mug of coffee, instead of sweetener. Now, after a few days of mulling over the night of illicit passion, she thought of the night as having forbidden undertones, hence her reasoning to call it "illicit" which was an untruth to justify her actions. They were two consenting adults, under no obligation to a significant other, or anyone else for that matter.

Darcy felt like a grown-up, not for sleeping with Jay, but for deciding that she could if that's what she wanted to do.

It was like getting something out of the way, so she could move on. Did she want him in her life that way? No, she wanted him the Jay he was before the joining of bodies in the depths of ecstasy. But it was done and regretted but done and not regretted at the same time. The kettle clicked off and Darcy poured the hot liquid into a pink china mug, one of the few things she'd recovered from her grandmother's house; one without the brown stain of a teabag.

The previous evening, while Jay was out at the gym, Darcy received a call from Maryann. There had been a letter hand-delivered into Maryann's letterbox addressed to Darcy and could she come over and pick it up at her earliest convivence? Darcy had no idea who it was from, so, after her coffee, she planned to get the note and then head into town and beg that her position in the chocolate shop be reinstated. Not that she had been sacked, not officially, but she was ready to take on more hours, if that was possible.

After that, she had a date with Mina first, and then Teddy would join them, to catch up and fill in the gaps from the last few weeks of trials and tribulations. Walking by Jay's bedroom, she stopped and stared at his tossed bedcovers. Messy and unmade, empty but for his lingering scent, of Lynx and mild body odour. Darcy closed the door, then walked into her own room to get ready.

After the sex, Darcy lay in Jay's arms, and he kissed the skin on her shoulder, and her shoulder blade, and drifted in and out of a light sleep, then made love to her again, held her afterwards and fell asleep once more, pulling her body close to his beforehand, to loose spoon her, his arm across her waist. In the shower the next morning, she had felt weird. But not a bad weird.

Something had obviously shifted, but, on the other hand, something had not.

The fact that Darcy fancied women.

That was a fact that no amount of penis would change. She slept with Jay out of a place of physical neediness, and she knew that, she understood it at the time. Afterwards, they did not have time to have "the chat" about what happened, but there didn't seem to be any rush.

*

Maryann's kitchen reminded Darcy of Pat's. And sitting in Maryann's kitchen, Darcy could see Pat's house had been emptied already. The outside wall was freshly rendered, waiting for a fresh coat of paint. Hardly a hint of its past occupants, or the damaged souls that lived within the damaged walls.

'I don't know who that note's from; it was in the hallway when I came home one of the evenings.'

Darcy knew Maryann was telling a fib because the envelope had been clearly interfered with.

'So how has life been treating you, Maryann?

'Oh, you know, so so.' Maryann hovered, eyeing Darcy's movements. As she extracted the folded note and read its content.

She looked at Maryann, as Maryann returned the gaze with a suspicious, almost leery side-eye.

'What is it?'

'It's a note from our neighbour, the millionaire, with a key and a rather absurd suggestion.'

Chapter Seventeen

On the bus into town, Darcy twisted the key over and over between her fingers and, in her hand, as the slight smell of metallic, new metal permeated her skin. While, ironically, a song with the lyrics, *Are You Even Real?*, sounded from her EarPods.

The key would allow access into an apartment in a block of trendy flats in Palmerstown, so the note had said. It also said in handwritten scribe that the apartment was empty and was hers to use because of her recent misfortunes and the fact that, when Darcy's grandmother was alive, she had helped their millionaire neighbour through the grieving process after his late wife passed away. Adding that, without fail, every Friday, Pat made steak and kidney pie, mash and cabbage for him to reheat in the microwave, with gravy in a side gravy pot. In his loneliest hours, Pat had been a godsend, and that now, he hoped, in light of *her* passing, that, in some small way, he could do the same for her granddaughter, who, as far as he could tell, was having a bad run of it.

In addition to the heartfelt sentiments written within the note, it mentioned that she could use the place for as long as she needed to, free of charge, except for payment on the amenities and such. That he purchased the place for his granddaughter, who had since been travelling around Europe with no intentions of returning home any time soon. The note concluded with a short P.S, written in different pen colour than the primary text, as a probable afterthought, that he would be on vacation for three months in the South of France with extended family, so not to worry about saying the "thank you" that he knew she'd have planned. That, a thank you, in any shape or form, was not necessary.

Darcy had been floored and, at first, thought it was some kind of joke. That death had somehow come alive and, in the deep mourning of it, the people who were left behind, and breathing, had altered its usual intention by putting hope in death's familiar place of heartache instead.

She pressed with her thumb, the key into her palm, until an indent remained for a brief spell, a part of her.

The hot air outside the bus from its running engine, made her quicken her step into the shop.

Yes, she still had a job and, yes, she could work more hours but not as many as she wanted because they had to employ a new girl, Edie, while Darcy was out sick. Just before leaving, she pinched her favourite raspberry swirl from the cooled display unit and winked at Edie, to keep her thieving ways between them.

Mina was already waiting for Darcy outside a coffee boutique off Drury Street. They hugged, the type of bear hug that was needed and welcomed and reciprocated. Tight then loose, tight then loose, then tight once more.

'Everything, I want to know every minute detail.'

And there was much to share, so much, that both girls fought hard to get a word in edgeways. Delighting in the kind of company that allowed such free exchanges.

'And how are you, I mean your head space?' Mina asked caringly, 'Are you still on meds?'

'Yeah, but a smaller dose now, so, I'm on the mend, y'know.'

'And, you and Teddy, loved up to the hilt, only delighted for ye.'

'It's been a blast, so much fun.'

'How do you think Jay will take the news that you're moving out?'

'Y'know, Mina, he'll be fine, we're not in a relationship, we're far from it and very soon our lives will take different directions anyway.'

'I think he cares deeply about you though, I wouldn't just be fobbing that off.'

'I care about him too, an awful lot but we're not compatible and you can't fit a circle into a square.'

'Have you seen Jessica at all, she's been off the radar for weeks now?'

'Not a peep. I actually came off social media, so I'm not familiar with what anyone's been up to.' Darcy felt like yawning, but the yawn stopped halfway through.

'Oh, sorry, I'm a little tired.' She dabbed her eyes with the edge of her finger.

'I wish I could do that, detox from social media.'

'You can do it, Mina, no one's forcing you to look at celebs being pretentious all day long.'

'Not all of them.' Mina smiled.

'Okay, not all of them.'

'So, when am I going to see this flat then?'

'Good question, I might make my way over there this evening if you're free?' Darcy suggested.

'This evening, no, I'm busy, that's why Teddy couldn't make it today, something came up, so now I'm meeting them for dinner.'

Mina nodded towards the waitress who was clearing away used cups from the table beside theirs. The kiss curls around her slender neck, dyed a faded blue.

'Shall we get a quick top up and a bun or something, you haven't told me what Jay looks like naked yet?'

Darcy laughed, and gingerly added, 'You've seen him in shorts, short shorts I mean, surely you can use your imagination after that.'

They both giggled then, happy to have checked-in and off loaded and glad of one another's lasting friendship.

*

Jay was already in the living room, his feet resting on the table when Darcy arrived back home late evening.

'Hey, I'm glad you're here, I've news.' The strap of her bag fell from her shoulder, so she put the bag down on the floor.

'Oh, really, me too, you go first.' He moved his feet and let her sit beside him. The elephant was in the room, unacknowledged, maybe waiting to be mentioned, but, so far, neither Darcy nor Jay spoke about their night together, acting as if it never happened instead.

'I'm moving out.'

'What, where to?'

'Not far, up the road really.'

'You know you don't have to do that, Darcy, my roommate won't be back for another fortnight at least and... '

'It's done, I've been to see the place. Everything is in order, I'm going in two days.'

'This isn't because...

'Oh, stop, don't be silly, I'm moving because this arrangement was temporary, you and I, we were always gonna be temporary.'

'Jesus, the finality in that, it's a bit brutal.' Jay said dismayed.

Darcy lifted the sleeve of her tee shirt and scratched her shoulder. 'What was your news?'

'Just that I'm heading to Scotland tomorrow, to look at digs and stuff, y'know, get a feel for the place. I won't be here to help you move, that's a shit buzz.'

'I'm going up the road, Jay.'

'It's not up the road from Scotland though, is it?'

They both stared at each other then, in a silence that was filled with questions neither one would ever ask. And, in that precise moment, they both realised, that that was okay.

*

The apartment, when Darcy first stepped foot in it, had felt natural, like nature feels to a soul seeking peace. The décor was contemporary, minimalistic and sharp. Everything had a clean edge and it was not what Darcy was expecting. She was pleasantly surprised. Mod cons, some Darcy picked up and moved to examine because they intrigued her, and she smiled, acknowledging that maybe a YouTube tutorial would be the answer to solving how they worked. It struck her how modern conveniences are supposed to be built for convivence, and not the opposite but, in some cases, without the help of the internet, they would remain confusing; an inconvenience convenience. But the space, she had to admit, would be a peaceful haven. It did lack a homely atmosphere though. And, of course, the walls were painted grey, but it was not her place, and she was blessed to have it.

The vacant rooms had potential to be a potentially loved space to rest in. And that, Darcy told herself, was a good way to start.

Back in Jay's place, he shouted out from the kitchen, 'Do you want coffee, I'm having one?' Darcy helped him pack. As if an old married couple, who understood the moves of the other, as if partnered waltz dancers for the longest time. He could not find a hoody and made that much noise looking for it, that Darcy began helping him fill his case, just to stop the racket that accompanied the fussing.

'The end of an era, hey, kiddo?'

'Oh, shut up, Jay, sentimentality does not become you.'

'We had fun though, didn't we?'

'I like the word fun, it's uncomplicated and suits us so well,' Darcy teased.

'I kinda hate leaving you.'

'And I kinda don't mind you going, so stop.'

'It could have worked for us if, well, if.'

Darcy bit down on her lip.

'It could've for so many reasons, Jay, but, for the fact that if I didn't, every single time, see a woman I desired, make me feel weak at the knees, then yeah, we would have made it, for sure.'

Jay chuckled, shaking his head, 'Yeah, me too, me too. Women, God bless them.'

'I'll miss ye.'

'You make this sound as if it's the end, will ye stop.'

'I know, it's so bloody weird after the last few weeks we've had, I can't believe it's over.'

'You're a great lad, Jay, and you'll find your someone.'

'Ah, I won't be lookin' for a while anyway, all the best ones are gay, or taken.' He winked.

Darcy smiled then. She did not regret her time with Jay, if anything, it showed her what she really wanted.

234

*

It rained on moving day. It lashed out of the heavens, was that bad luck? Darcy's hair flattened onto her wet face, stuck there as she thought, maybe it's good luck, heaving boxes. She did not have many possessions but she still had to make two bus journeys because no one with a car was available to help her.

Part of the bus ride was filled with thoughts of Jay, his leaving, their time together and a thought that maybe she dismissed him, in some unattractive way, and worse than that, had not acknowledged it until now. She flicked a switch on him, on her feelings regarding him, and never really thought about his wants in all of that, or cared if he had any. He was, essentially, a plaything. Her toy. Maybe their affair didn't affect him at all, she mused. And over-analysing their moment was a complete waste of time, the minute had been and gone.

Between one bus stop and another, she condemned her childish behaviour in Spain, the way she had been overbearing in not allowing Jay to make a move on that Spanish girl. And, now, how stupid she felt about her petulance. To appease her thought process, she reminded herself about the meds, and their effects taken with alcohol, and it was the only real way that she could forgive her actions that night. She gave herself the ick, and with too much time to think on the bus, she tried focusing on the things at hand, instead of past mistakes she had no control over. Noting that self-awareness was not all it was cracked up to be. Jay had left, and with him, their relationship. Was he hurt? She had no idea. Had she missed something, his feelings maybe? Maybe the meds fatigued overthinking the topic because it would never be her intention to denigrate his, if he had any feelings towards her, not intentionally but maybe unconsciously. Jay had said as much about the subject as Darcy, and that seemed to suit them both, in equal shares. And that was that.

Darcy had metaphorically taken down the book of her life and was, once again, ready for a new chapter; the pages were becoming tattered but at least they were being turned.

*

With her personal knickknacks around the new space, Darcy for the second time, cleaned around the countertop. She was in two minds about staying, because Jay's place was empty and familiar and, well, empty, so comfortably familiar.

Standing in this empty room had a different tone to it, a different ambience, she thought. It was a room she would have to make her own and she let her imagination paint that exact picture before she popped her head out the front door onto the main corridor of the block. There were four apartment doors on the bottom floor including hers. The number thirteen was screwed to her front door. Her eyeline drifted over the make of the flooring, solid oak, and the light switches, chrome and doubled. Then there was the fire exit and a huge window at the end of the main corridor. A thick blind, hung loosely, attached at the side a pearl draw string, unbroken and ready for use. Darcy noticed there was no particular smell in the vicinity and, for that, she was grateful. A smell of nothing particular, a million times better than the smell of someone's urine up a wall.

She pinched herself, still in awe of her neighbour's generosity and her grandmother's kind considerations. 'Thanks, Gran,' she whispered softly, her eyes raised, before closing the door again.

The T.V. was set up with a Sky installation box that already worked. Never one to have time to just sit still, Darcy began to flick through the programs on offer, convincing herself that a Netflix binge-watch was long overdue.

She felt tired as if the last few weeks had suddenly pulled her down by the shoulders and the sheer force disabled normal functioning, as if an AI machine, unplugged. With nothing on Netflix to tickle her fancy, she settled on a movie instead. *Columbus* 2017, directed by Kogonada, a South Korean with a rare vision Darcy appreciated. Pressing play, she nestled into the padded cushions and let her mind immerse in the splendour of Kogonada's artistic interpretation of wonderfully fretful and curious relationships.

BANG, BANG, BANG, Darcy opened her eyes, in a flutter. The titles of the movie scrolled up the screen, and dusk had begun to call night in to join it.

The banging sound persisted, coming from outside the flat, or maybe from inside the corridor. Darcy opened her door cautiously, just enough. Within that inch, a man, pounded, with his fist on the door, two doors down on the opposite side.

'Come on, let me in, for fucks sake, I'll kick down this door unless you do.'

Darcy stepped back alarmed but did not close her door all the way.

From behind the door of the persistent arsehole, a soft voice insisted he leave, that the person, a woman, would call the police otherwise.

The man engaged with more force, coupled with louder outbursts, and Darcy knew she should not get involved, she should close her door and ring someone. She should do anything but the thing that she did do, which was step outside and interfere.

'Sorry, is there a problem?'

The man turned, a stunned look on his face and a voice that said, *Who the hell are you*!

Darcy, whose mouth dried immediately, was about to answer when, whoever lived behind the door, opened it, directing the man's fury back in her direction.

The door chain clanked, taut, and Darcy thought she recognised the person hiding between what the gap and the chain allowed.

'Go away, Shane, I mean it, you're drunk and I've rang the guards, they're on their way.'

Darcy wracked her brain because the voice was so familiar. Then the figure moved slightly and the cupped blond bob moved too. Kim, the woman was Kim, the student nurse from St Pat's, the kind nurse with the caring personality, now trapped in her flat by a dickhead with a brutish attitude.

'I can hear sirens, if I were you, I'd leave now, while you still can,' Darcy said, unconvincingly.

Shane, the bully, moved then, to Darcy's surprise. Passing her by, he sniggered, childishly, the smell of alcohol practically oozing from his pores, his face so close to her own personal space, she nearly gagged.

And then he was gone.

The door opposite closed, it closed quickly before Darcy had time to react. She mulled over what to do, but decided to step back inside. There, she found it hard to reconcile with herself for leaving things alone, and not knocking Kim's door but it was not her business. Jesus, you're hardly in the block a wet weekend, she thought, and you've enough to be going on with! And maybe the person scared behind the door was not her nurse, just someone resembling her. To a tee. Furthermore, in the aftermath of a domestic, the couple involved had a way of eventually blaming the third party who tried to help. Better to get an early night and, if she bumped into Kim, or the Kim lookalike organically, then take it from there.

Darcy heard a low *meow, meow,* coming from the window area. A ginger cat at the window, meowing in between other cat noises and chirrups. 'Jesus, you gave me a fright there, pussycat. Who do you belong to?'

Down on her hunkers, she looked at the cat through the window, seeing her own reflection first, and through that, the sparkle of cat's eyes, reflected back. The cat had a blue collar and a bell that dangled, chiming softly when it moved.

'You're a little chancer, aren't ye, well, there's no cat food here, you'll have to come back tomorrow. I'll see what I can do.' The fluffy cat jumped off the windowsill as if obeying her command. I've either made one friend and one enemy this evening, she conceded, or two enemies; what a great way to begin.

Then a sense of foreboding hit her, as if she had not thought of it before. A feeling came at her from farther down a darkened abyss, a place no longer on her wish list but one she seemed unable to cross off.

So many things had changed and all without the presence of family. She was alone, without Jay even, in the world and the grip of that on her made the room seem bigger; as if expanding with a breath of its own. So, she stood still and repeated in a delicate hum, you're okay, you're okay, you're okay, you're okay. Closing her eyes and breathing into the words. You're okay, until she was at least, a little bit better.

*

The chocolate shop was quiet, an odd customer every now and then broke the monotony and the rare serenity in between, helped the time tick over. Darcy faced the mirrored back wall, so through the mirrors' refection saw Jessica, her head lowered, enter the shop with an uneasiness that Darcy had time to study, remembering the sweetness they once shared, in what Darcy now felt, was a past life.

'Hey,' Jessica said.

'Hey, how have you been?'

'Oh, y'know, trying to get organised for college, I don't know how it happens but these months between one term and another go faster than any other time of the year.'

'We still have a few weeks left, thank God.'

'I tried contacting you, but I think you might have me blocked.'

'Oh, not just you, I bowed out of all that for a while, my phone just gathers dust now.'

'Oh right, you're probably better off.'

Jessica pressed the tip of her tongue against her front teeth, which was something she did when she struggled to say something that might cause a negative reply. So, the struggle sat in her mouth, swimming in saliva.

'I know,' she began, 'I'm the last person you probably want asking you this but, can we grab a coffee, or a movie sometime? I need a friend, and I know it always seems that way, that I'm a train wreck, but I'd like to talk about you too and ask how *you've* been with everything.'

Darcy wondered who had been saying what, and to whom, and the adding on, and the nonsense that made sense to the gossiper but was not the truth, of *how Darcy had been with everything.*

'I don't need to talk about anything, Jessica.' Darcy answered flatly.

'Well, just me then, can we do that, please?'

This isn't fair, Darcy thought, because her weakness was that she could not say no to people who reached out in a time of need. Genuine or not.

'I think I'm gonna pass, Jess, I just don't think-'

Edie appeared from out back, stoic, but for her mouth that shaped O, and expelled the word, oh, as if it were just one elongated syllable. She stared from Darcy to Jessica, then sheepishly grinned before she spun on the ball of her foot and walked back to where she came from.

'That was awkward,' Jessica said, 'Do I look that scary?'

'She's shy, it's nothing to do with how you look.'

But Darcy did notice in the look of Jessica, that she had a look of someone needing a good night's sleep, a little worse for wear, as they say.

'Do I look pregnant?'

Darcy, who had begun ribboning boxes to avoid eye contact, stared at her as if for the first time.

'Are you trying to be funny?' Darcy coaxed, a tad annoyed.

The tears came then, not forced or dramatic, but silent, from a person pained.

'Come around the back, Edie can take over here.'

After agreeing that the back of a chocolate shop was not the appropriate surrounds to discuss unplanned pregnancy, Darcy suggested Jessica visit her new flat that evening and she would cook dinner, in the way of support.

Now, standing in the veggie aisle of Marks and Spencer, Darcy plucked a bunch of ripe cherry tomatoes, a head of iceberg lettuce and, on her way to the tills, some extra olive oil, back-tracking once she reached the top to grab hold of cat food, in case her furry friend returned. She questioned why she felt the need to listen to Jessica, maybe it was the desperation, or the non-verbal plea for help in her ex's eyes, either way, Jessica would be at her place within the hour, so she climbed on the bus and headed for home.

'It's lovely here,' Jessica mused.

'I only just moved in.'

'Oh, right, where were you before, with Jay?'

They had eaten dinner and, while Darcy put away the delft they'd used, she ran the tap until the water turned cold and prepared a glass.

'Yeah, after my gran died, I stayed with him, as I'm sure you're aware.'

'I don't know that much to be honest, I was kinda banished from the group, a hiatus from all things we had in common.'

'And because you rubbed a few people up the wrong way.'

Jessica shrugged.

'I'm sure they've all made mistakes too, Darcy.'

'So, who is the father, or is that information off limits?'

'I was thinking recently about the group, y'know, our friend group for the last few years, or of how well everyone is doing, their goals on the way to fruition, the way they have carved out a life and, then me, the eternal fuck-up, who just keeps walking into a wall. The same wall it seems, repeatedly. I used to know what I wanted, now I wish someone would guide me, put things in simple form.'

Jessica sat with Darcy on the couch.

'In answer to your question, the father is a one-night stand, some guy, his name is Pete and, I swear, I don't know his surname. I disgust myself. I've been out of control but I don't want to be a mother, I'm not ready. I was hoping you could help me, I'm nervous, I don't even want to ring a doctor.'

'But there's clinics; everything is confidential.'

'Will you come with me, Darcy? Is that too much to ask?'

Two seconds pause, or maybe three.

'Jessica, can't you ask the father? Jesus, I have my own shit, you know, and I don't want to sound insensitive but I don't know if I could handle a place like that right now.'

'An abortion clinic, why? Has how you feel about a woman having control over her own body changed, along with you being a lesbian?'

Darcy placed the glass of water on the table.

'I knew that was coming, so let's put it out there, what exactly is on your mind, Jess?'

'I take it you screwed Jay.'

'Are you really going to lecture *me* right now, after everything?'

'No,' Jessica whispered, defeated. 'No, not at all, what right do I have?'

'This whole conversation is too casual, on subjects that are serious, what's really going on, Jessica? Why did you-'

'I just want a bit back, a bit of the sanity we had before.'

'Back, who in their right mind goes back?' Darcy preached.

'College will inevitably bring us all back.'

'Except for Jay.'

'Why?'

'Didn't you know, he's left us, moved to Scotland to pursue his dream of becoming a renowned architect, I find it hard to believe he left that out while telling you everything else.'

'I haven't spoken to Jay in weeks, Darc, as I said, I've been out of the picture.'

*

The cat did come back, so Darcy opened the window to let it in. Now, as it purred on her lap, an uneasy feeling remained. The feeling had rested while Jessica was there and stayed long after Jessica left the flat. As Darcy pet her new friend, she thought about going to the clinic with Jessica, but at that same it went against the grain and Darcy realised she didn't want to go. The flip side to that was being Jessica's friend, there to support her. No, first thing the next morning she would unblock Jessica, ring her and explain that, she was putting her own emotional state before anyone else's, that she understood Jessica should have someone to guide her, and support her but that Darcy was not that someone. Not this time anyway. Jessica was a strong woman, stronger than Darcy, whose fragile state resembled a walnut. Darcy wondered how much Jessica knew about St Pats. And of how the taboo subject had remained unearthed between them, while everything else had been dug up, brought up, and sat between them on a chair near the sofa. She wanted to be around new people to create a new version of her future plans, because most of the old characters in her life were tied to heartache, regret, pity or pain.

She wanted to take some steps away, not back into.

While backing out the door the next morning, Darcy came face to face with Kim. She faced a woman a little thinner than before, with dark shadows under her eyes, and a certain hollow appearance that Darcy wanted to focus on with compassion but, out of respect for Kim's privacy, faked surprise. So, she micro-managed her approach, while walking towards her damaged mental health care nurse.

'You live here now.' Kim asked.

It was more of a statement than a question, so Darcy explained how her living there was a temporary arrangement.

'It's good to know we're neighbours; you should call by sometime.'

'You're still a patient at the hospital, so that would be unethical, Darcy.'

'I'm an out-patient, and I'm not asking you to sneak me out Diazepam.'

Kim laughed, as did Darcy.

'Just call in later, I'll be watching T.V., it's my new therapy, it's called *Numb Your Brain*, it's a wonderful distraction from real life like.'

'I could be late, Darcy, y'know.' Kim casually replied.

'If you're not too late then, I'll be up, I have a cat now.'

In the outside corridor of the block, Kim walked ahead of Darcy towards the car park, getting into her car, she checked her face in the rear view mirror before driving off. Darcy wondered if now that Kim recognised who Darcy was, would she put two and two together about the other night, and panic, or be embarrassed. Darcy would not push the situation. Her mobile rang, an incoming FaceTime— Jay. She answered, smiling.

'Hey.'

Jay was up a mountain, with spectacular views behind him, roving fields and peaked hill tops. 'This is my friend.'

Jay turned his phone towards a new unfamiliar face, a handsome boy appeared on the screen, both he and Jay wore hiking gear, and matching headbands, and staggered while walking, even on flat ground.

'You both look ridiculous, when are you coming back?'

'I'm not, I'm staying, to explore the Highlands; I'm breathing too much clear air to come back, you'll have to visit.'

'Are you drunk?' Silly question, Darcy thought.

'Listen, because this phone is gonna die, can you leave your key under the mat or something the bloody neighbour has been on; I think you left milk in the fridge or some shit like that, the place is stinking. Anyway, I gotta go, book a flight, come over, soon, ciao.'

Darcy put her phone away and stepped, but noticed the cat by her feet, so, in manipulating her body to avoid a foot in its back, she swerved and fell hip first onto the ground. Most definitely bruising the delicate skin in that region.

'Cat, God damn you.'

'Did you hurt yourself there?'

Shane stood over her, his looming presence larger, because of her position on the floor.

'No, no, I'm fine.'

He walked past her then.

'She's not in.' Darcy exclaimed.

Shane watched her as she strengthened herself out, folding her lined jacket lapel in and over itself.

'Who said I was here looking for anyone, who are you anyway?'

Darcy's ambivalence to engage in conversation further, only seemed to pique his interest in who she was.

'Did we meet already?'

'No, sorry. I don't think so.'

Darcy felt Shane's eyes on her back and, when she opened the main door of the block out onto the fresh air, she was thankful that, because of his stupefied intoxication two nights before, her face hadn't registered, he had no idea who she was.

She didn't like Shane, she didn't like him one bit. He creeped her out, and avoiding him, along with being wary of him, would be her mission.

Chapter Eighteen

Darcy fed the cat, who had jumped in the window as soon as she'd opened it, on returning home that evening.

Hauling paint with her on the bus had not been an option so she paid the delivery cost and now sat on the windowsill willing it to arrive. She felt the cat's tail between her ankles and its bell sound intermittently cracking the otherwise silent air. The grey walls of the flat bothered her, so, she, thinking she was some kind of interior designer, purchased paint brushes, a paint tray, masking tape and *Farrow and Balls* paint recommendation of warm green and stone blue, to two-tone the walls.

'I'm not feeding you any more food, Cat, I'm sure your owner is wondering why you're getting so tubby, and I want to keep living here, so be nice and stop meowing for grub.'

The cat turned its head at a slant, like a mischievous dog. 'Stop, I will not be bribed by cuteness.'

From watching through the window, Kim got out of a car. Darcy sat back out of sight, feeling as though Kim might think she was spying on her, a preposterous thought but it was an initial reaction, that seemed intelligently brain waved, but, in retrospect, screamed paranoia. Behind the car, the Woodie's delivery man parked and opened his truck to retrieve Darcy's paint order.

'Come on, Cat, let's see what we've got.'

A cup of coffee later and Darcy scanned the living room area; she would begin her unskilled paint job the next day. When she opened the door to the delivery man, she caught sight of Kim, just for a nanosecond, entering her front door. There had been no confirmation that Kim would join her later, so she put on the T.V. and settled on a documentary about loving a jellyfish.

Love, in its many forms, is the strangest thing, Darcy assumed. As she mulled over its many forms. And if a deep sea diver could openly reveal tenderness towards a planktonic marine member, then surely she, as an innovative thinking human, could find her way. Her thoughts soon drifted to Jessica, as if the motion of the ocean in the T.V. show guided her thoughts in Jessica's direction and, more pointedly, her situation. A foetus, a termination, a woman's right, a baby's (no, the rights of a foetus) rights, and of how Darcy wanted to remain on the outskirts of that tumultuous brainstorm, and, yet, if past history was anything to go by, she would be dragged, almost unawares into the very epicentre of Jessica's mess—her little foetus, a beating heartbeat.

Grabbing a glass to pour juice, Darcy further pondered on why she put herself and Jessica into the same projected images in her head, who were they really, she thought, Jessica and I? Now that I come to think of it, Darcy sipped, our love was a puppy kind of love. At one point there had been commitment, they had nurtured tepid feelings and let them flourish to a certain degree, but they were never going to last the course because, in the experimental stages of growing up and growing into one's personality, people came in and left again. Early relationships were a place for making mistakes that were, in some respect, supposed to harness learning for both parties. Ultimately, Darcy thought, it's the letting go when things have died, when they have withered and, in that learning, knowing when it's time to reseed. Like the diver, who had somehow managed to make Darcy cry with his emotional story about a dying jellyfish. A devastating ending but an inevitable one all the same.

Sometimes even the water can't keep you afloat.

A tap on the door, light, unassuming.

'I hope you like red wine.'

A glass and a half later and both Kim and Darcy eased from a complex mindset, into an even more intricate conversation about exes. And there was something in the sharing of private information to an almost stranger, with a glass and a half of red wine that made Darcy's words have more leverage; even as her own ears, her own judgements let the words land.

Outside, someone walked by on the pavement, a noise that usually went unnoticed by Darcy, but made Kim jump. Deep, heavy wine drops, most certainly, stained the fabric of Kim's top.

'Shit.'

Darcy sensed a shift. A jarring.

'Are you scared of him, your ex, I mean?'

'I don't think scared is the right word; he's a pain but he is mainly acting out of desperation and I think, when he stays sober long enough to acknowledge how stupid he's been, he'll stop trying to fix things.' The fix was said in air quotes.

'I don't know, Kim, he looked pretty aggressive to me the other night. How long have you known him?'

'We've been dating a little over a year, I finished with him about two weeks ago; I found something on his phone.'

'Jesus, all the signs, the red flags, huh?'

'Yeah, a dating site, another woman, women, sorry. Blah, blah and all the usual. A site he accused me of being on, sly motherfucker.'

'Doesn't it bother you that he comes over, like, to your space, your home, without invitation? I mean that's weird, borderline stalking, no?' Darcy asked without reservation, and with the wine's permission.

'I can handle Shane. He needs a bit more time to accept things are over, for good this time.'

'Um.'

'I think he was in trouble before, so, although I've threatened the guards, I've never called them. It's never gotten that far.'

'But are you keeping track of when he shows up unannounced, like in a log or diary or something?'

'There's no point, Darcy, honestly, I can handle him, things will die down.'

Kim drank the last of the wine, her glass smudged with fingerprints and salt from the crisp bowl they had shared during the evening.

'Anyway, what about you and that curly-headed fella who always came to visit you in St Pats, with the baggy tracksuit bottoms and Converse runners?'

'Ah, Jay, he's a sweetheart but he's my friend. I'm gay, didn't I mention that before?'

'Gay,' Kim jerked back a little. 'Really? I was convinced you two were an item.'

'We kinda were but it's not worth talking about. It was a holiday fling. He has since moved away, living his best life. I hope.'

'Oh, right, I didn't think *gay* people slept with the opposite sex.'

'It was in a moment's confusion; even gay people get confused, occasionally.'

'Um, right.'

Kim moved, slapped her hands on her thighs and sighed gently before standing. 'Okay, that's me, I need to get back. I'm working tomorrow.'

'Oh, God, the whole gay thing didn't ruin us I hope, our budding friendship.'

Kim laughed softly.

'Hardly, half the people I know and love are gay and you're adorable. I'm so happy you're on the mend.'

'Thanks to you, in part.'

'In part. A very small part, and it was a pleasure.'

Chapter Nineteen

Later that night, Darcy stood by the window. Cat purred until she opened it to let him out. A shadow moved and Darcy stepped back, assuming a shadow was attached to a body. The dimly lit street seemed eerie and Darcy thought of Shane and if he was watching the block of flats. Watching Kim through a window without closed curtains.

'Jesus, shut up, Darcy, you're freaking yourself out.'

She checked her front door was locked and bolted, and that the alarm was on. Climbing into bed, her mind raced between Jessica and Kim and how their lives impacted hers. And sleep used evasion as a tool to torment her, as if that was a real thing. As if peace of mind had the power to clude by its own accord.

And then her dad, the silhouette of him in protection mode, and how she had never sought out his protection because, in her younger years, it was naturally present. She had known his protection as malleable, as if coloured maula in her baby hands, his movements following her movements in any direction she cared to go. A given, a gift bestowed at birth. A father's love. But, by the teenage years, his presence stayed out of sight, guarding her from a distance, until he died.

His last sight, a glass shop window and the reflection of a T.V. that Darcy wished he hadn't liked, hadn't thought of buying, hadn't walked over to see. Hadn't stopped to view.

Then the crash, nowhere to go but through.

The glass, a pane, shattered, the pain.

The glass cut his cheeks. Lodged in his cheekbone and in his ear.

The skin, split by jagged edges, his eyes pressed tightly shut, so glass didn't get in. But, in the split skin, it rested; splinters, slivers, traces of the sharp. The pane, the pain. And the car with nowhere to go but through.

They lay still, her parents, unmoving, their hands almost touching. While the drunk driver, paralysed in his seat, glass all over his dashboard, and an off-licence receipt by his feet, sat still but breathing, barely.

Glass all over the bonnet, and the bonnet crushed inward. Perfectly indented to the body shape of her dead parents.

Darcy, restless, sat up. Water, she thought, water might help. Her feet dragged and, as the water ran from the tap, she asked herself why she was, only now, thinking of her father in a way, as someone watching over her. Maybe it was the fact of living alone, the newness of it, or the simple fact of it, because the imagining of shadows along the walls now had a place, whereas before, it was people, real people who laid in bed next to her, or moved downstairs, making tea. And there had been no reason to imagine that anyone was outside, creeping or lurking or wanting to know her moves.

Instead of flicking the kitchen light off, she left it on. 'How pathetic are you?' She asked to the air.

No one answered, so her anxiety remained.

*

Jessica was sure an abortion was the right decision. She had been to the clinic, read all the leaflets, been to counselling, (not with her mother, who had no idea what was going on) and was now asking Darcy, again, if she would just come to the clinic with her, to figuratively, hold her hand.

It had been a week and the termination was booked for the next morning.

Darcy, sat on the fence, unable to agree or disagree with Jessica's decision, and annoyed with Jessica for putting her in the predicament of having to choose.

She, after all, was a woman herself, her reproductive organs were her own, only hers, to do with what she wanted. But what if the foetus was a girl, and she knew how blatantly sexist she was being, how totally inappropriate too, but her thoughts on the subject plagued her? New thoughts that she couldn't handle, that she felt shouldn't be hers to think of, to mull over, in the first place. And the whole thing bothered her and the thinking of it, and the perpetual worrying of it, that shouldn't be her responsibility at all because Jessica was her ex, so effectively, nothing to do with her!. So, there was the annoyance of that too, to piss her off.

Later that evening, she was over in Kim's flat, helping her cook spaghetti Bolognese. They were having dinner and a chat about the situation. As Kim talked, Darcy looked around the flat, how different they were in their style, their shaped ornaments, their coloured toasters. Hers with two spring pop-up trays, Darcy's with four, Kim had carpet throughout the flat, Darcy, thankfully had antique tiled flooring. Kim had cleaning products, fairy liquid and such on the counter, a damp dish-rag ready to mop up a mess. Darcy preferred everything out of sight, behind a press with a metal handle.

Kim's bedroom door was open so Darcy had access to the partial layout of her room. A free- standing wardrobe, wooden, with mirrored doors, inside and out, as if a box with dressed hangers containing nurse's uniforms that watched, a creased reflection, headless and armless, footless even, just waiting to be worn and filled into. So different from her own fitted wardrobe that contained two pairs of ripped jeans, three hoodies, and a denim jacket. Of course, Darcy was living in someone else's styled abode but she still hesitated and consciously noted Kim's personality, somewhat hidden in her simple style choices.

Especially Kim's choice of banal wall paint, cream sheen, throughout.

'Isn't there anyone else who can go with her? Even there, in the clinic, she'll receive great support.' Kim asked.

'I know. Look, I've decided not to go, it just doesn't

sit well with me. I believe women have the right to do whatever they want, but Jessica, she can be so reckless and the way she pulls me into her mess when she feels like it, I seem to always be there, and it's not what I want.'

'Well, there's your answer then, sweetie.'

'I still have to ring her; she won't be happy.' Darcy soughed.

Kim's mobile rang.

'Private number, that's odd... Hello... hello, is anyone there?'

Kim frowned. 'Weird, they hung up, so where were we, ah, yeah? You need to make that call.'

'Yeah, shit, Okay, I might as well go do it now, or I won't be able to relax.'

Jessica was pissed off.

'Now I've no time to ask someone else, Darcy, thanks for being so fecking thoughtless!'

'Everything, everything has to be about you, I don't think you've asked me once the last few times we've connected, how I'm feeling, it's all been about you and I get it, I get that this must be an emotional roller coaster for you, but, Jess, I didn't buy a ticket for this ride, and I didn't because I don't want to go, and you're making me spell it out and that's pretty shit on your part. I said I didn't want to go.'

'Oh, fuck you, Darcy, just fuck off.'

The line went dead and Darcy felt a ringing in her ear. As if her brain was a train platform and an express hadn't stopped for passengers.

*

The next morning it was Cat meowing at the window that made Darcy leave what she was doing in the kitchen and walk over to pet him. She had not slept well again; the conversation between herself and Jessica was like a hamster on a wheel, a catalogue of problems with no solution, and the fact that Jessica had been a dick, and she herself, not much better. And now Darcy couldn't help but feel ashamed of her behaviour, feeling responsible that Jessica might be alone in such a time of need. A delicate, unstable, emotional time of need. It was nine-forty-five a.m., the procedure would begin at ten a.m.

'Damn,' she whispered, as the realisation of what she had to do appeared. In her keep cup, she poured a coffee to go, she tied her shoe laces, grabbed her door keys, before closing the door. In a brief suspension of time she inhaled, before picking up pace, she rounded the corner and made for the bus stop.

The concrete steps leading up to the entrance of the clinic felt cold under Darcy's backside, even with the layered protection from her woolly cardigan. Coldness would be the order of the morning because Jessica's face, once she saw Darcy sitting there, appeared chilly at best.

A hurt was palpable too. If a hurt could be wrapped up in a box and handed to someone, Darcy would need a hefty carrier bag, to help with the weight.

Jessica sniffled, 'I thought you weren't coming.'

'Come on,' Darcy responded, 'Let me get you home.'

In a taxi, Jessica bawled her eyes out, her head on Darcy's shoulder, and Darcy, wavering her own discomfort, allowed Jessica comfort, insofar as she could manage. She stroked her hair, until the bawl turned into a sob on intake, slow and catching, but calmer at least.

And then just silence but for their heartbeats, no longer three, just two.

Chapter Twenty

Back at the flat later on in the evening, Darcy received a text from Mina and then, in quick succession, another one from Dom asking that she come out that night. Not a late one, they had both insisted, to a club where Teddy and his band would play. Fun, funky music and a reason to get bladdered. Darcy had been in a melancholy mood for most of the day, so, with that in mind, she said yes to going out, in an attempt at shifting her dejected, despondent mood. Jessica's sadness hovered. She had allowed Jessica to become a crux in her life, always having a problem to solve and expecting Darcy to be her partner in solving it. In essence, she enabled Jessica's idea that they were connected in some spiritual, other-ly, past, multi-dimensional world or something, at one point she doted on how endearing it was. But now, Darcy thought - as of today, I need to cut the cord, and connect to reality, for my own sense of individualism -.

Darcy agreed to meet the others at the club; it had been a minute since the last time they were all out together. Cora and Pixie were coming out, along with a few friends of theirs, originally from Galway. New faces meant new conversations and Darcy was so down for that.

As she sat in the living room before getting ready to go out, the newly painted walls radiated a warmth that Darcy could never imagine a wall colour would do. The place felt of home, a strange infinity she had not expected. Maybe the ghosts of her family paid a visit every now and then, but, either way, she had settled in well. She thought a moment about the imminence of returning to college and of how it would be her last semester, then "real life", the grown-up life her friend group always teased one another about, would be by their sides. Was she ready? She had no idea, but they were all in the same boat of universal scepticism, perforated with holes of doubt. A sink or swim idiom, that held a specific truth for graduate students. Darcy had recently applied to stay a student, filling in the application on PAC to participate in an M.Ed. Her interview was coming up, which made her a little nervous but it had been her mother's dream to see Darcy teach, so it felt natural for her to pursue that path—and, in doing so, remain out of the "real life" pool a little longer.

Cat purred at the window, but Darcy had no time for cat, she jumped up and headed for the shower.

The club was a small venue, near Portobello, and, because of its proximity, teemed with bobbing heads and sweaty body odour. Darcy soon made out Dom standing, his rizz on point, leaning against a bar over the seating area the rest of the group sat around. Mina, in her usual form, screamed Darcy's name and immediately got up to greet her. Others followed suit and it felt really good, Darcy thought, to be intimate again, to be part of chats and waffle and gossip and nonsense.

'Teddy's band will be on next, come in, sit by me, I've saved a spot.' Mina guided.

Darcy sat in between Cora and Mina and shared stories about what she had been up to, as young people did, describing events, experiences and daily goings-on that had occurred since their last catch-up. Darcy was surprised and not so surprised to find out Cora was flying over to visit Jay the following weekend. Jay and another notch; Jay was Jay after all. Darcy smiled to herself, as she often did where Jay was concerned.

Jessica appeared then and, even over the sound of shared, eager voices, specific in the exuberance and anticipation of a good night ahead, Jessica's hysteria, her banshee cry felt as though it was being projected from a speaker, as she laughed loudly between staggering towards the table where they sat.

'You,' she pointed directly at Darcy, 'I need to see you alone,' the words were slurred but directive.

'Jessica, what the fuck!' Dom, ever the gentleman, 'You can hardly stand, how did you get in?' Jessica sent daggers his way but her gaze soon returned to Darcy.

'Yes, you.'

'Don't get up,' Mina advised, 'She's clearly upset and ready to make a scene; I'll go, Lottie can help me.'

Of course, no one knew about Jessica's loss, no one else knew of the pain Jessica must be feeling and that, even though it had been her choice, her heart must have been broken, if not shattered into tiny pieces.

'No, let me go, I'll take her outside for air, if I don't, I think she'll lose the plot. Here, let me pass.'

Outside, people lined the street, but it was still much quieter than the enthusiasm of inside.

'Jessica, you can't keep doing this, and why are you out, surely you should be in bed?'

'I don't want bed, I want you.'

It was a stupid way to feel, but Darcy felt so sorry for Jessica in that moment. While Jessica's mascara ran down her cheeks and her footing moved unstably, even though they were sitting on the side of the dirty curb.

'I just want you, Darcy.'

'You only think you do.'

Darcy remembered then, some of the good times they shared. The trip to the Aran island, Inis Mhor, and the natural formation in the shape of a massive swimming pool, called The Worm Hole. Its utter magnificence had been a talking point for hours. Hiring bikes to cycle the length and breadth of the place. Meeting locals and enjoying history, in a laughter bubble that they assumed could and would never burst. The shared pizza, and shared stretched cheese, like the animal characters in Lady and the Tramp. The beach walks, her pleated skirt spinning as she twirled. Flexing over stepping stones that protruded from a stream. Back then, Darcy thought Jessica was like the tide, like the tide that she didn't want to go out;

remembering the tracing hearts in the sand, that the water eventually washed away.

But that was then, and a lifetime had happened in between then and now. Now Jessica was to Darcy an empty seat in the cinema, a place she wanted someone else to occupy. Not a body on a curb, leaning on Darcy, while Darcy asked herself, if Jessica wanted her to have nothing. To have nothing for herself.

'My happiest time was with you.' Jessica languished, as if her voice was fading.

'But,' Darcy said, 'Your life will be filled with new happy times, ye just gotta let it happen.'

'I hate myself.'

'Stop Jess, just stop. Please.' Darcy looked around, having had enough of playing a game with no winners. 'You should go home, after the day you've had. Mixing alcohol with anaesthesia; that's really stupid.'

A text came through then, on Darcy's phone. An urgent text because it read as if Kim was panicked.

Are you home? I think Shane is creeping around outside, I'm a bit uneasy.

'Flip, right, I have to go. Come on, we'll share a taxi, let's get you home.'

'Can I stay with you, just for tonight, I promise, I can't be alone, just this once.'

Darcy was left with no other choice than to say yes to Jessica's inappropriate demand. So, she agreed, this once, to let her stay. A decision she might live to regret.

Late autumn weather seemed to have crept in around the apartment block in Darcy's short absence. Kim was waiting by her open door as Darcy, holding Jessica up, and unsteady, arrived.

'I'm sorry, I didn't realise you were on a night out.'

'Just gimme one sec to put my friend to bed, then I'll be over, did you ring the guards.'

'No, not yet, I feel like I might have overreacted now, I got spooked.'

Darcy, who held back, really wanted to say, I think that weasel is around here all the time because I feel him creeping, spying, watching, the hallmarks of a stalker who, if you don't name him to the proper authorities, is going to keep lurking in the ditches waiting to pounce on you.

A tad melodramatic, but Darcy felt something niggle in the small of her back, disjointed even. Something just wasn't right in a non-hysterical way.

Darcy lay Jessica on the bed, who reluctantly turned on her side and closed her eyes. She put a glass of water by the bedside locker and left the bedroom door ajar. Uneasiness accompanied Darcy's steps back to Kim's place, polarising the margins between silent movements and impractical thinking. Her head felt fuzzy, her overall worry patently obvious.

'I feel like a right gobshite now, knowing you were out. You should've said, Darcy, and you've your friend here, I'm sorry.'

'Can you stop, I'm here, Jessica is asleep, she doesn't need anything but sleep right now.'

'Oh, right, the infamous Jessica.'

'What happened, because you wouldn't text if you didn't feel threatened in some way?'

'Something eerie, I dunno. First, the phone rang, private caller, and when I answered, there was be no reply but someone was on the other end, breathing, not heavily, just enough to hear like. Just enough to let me know, as if playing with me. Then I started to hear scratching outside the door, it freaked me out, even as I say the words now I know how overly dramatic I sound.'

'I don't think you are at all, come on, we'll walk around the apartment block, just to be sure.'

Be sure of what exactly? Darcy thought, as they stepped outside, that Shane doesn't have tendencies towards dictating how Kim should act, because he clearly did have control over that. Why didn't Kim see that her fear warranted a call to the guards?

'How well do you know him, Shane, I mean?'

'To be honest, I think I'm un-nerved because the private ID calls have become more frequent, I can't even say it's him for sure, can I? This might be all in my head.'

'Yeah, I've a feeling that's what a lot of women think just before they're assaulted, that it won't happen to them, that it's all in their head, y'know.'

Both women stood outside the main entrance for a moment.

'If Shane is some type of perfidious degenerate, then you need to contact the police, at least to notify them that you suspect something.'

It was then that Darcy realised Kim did not feel confident enough in her accusation, she didn't believe in her own suspicions about her creepy ex and the way *he* was making her feel. In a way, Darcy could not blame her either, she didn't have enough evidence; nothing would be done.

'Shall we go back inside, have a wine or something?'

'What about your friend?'

'I'll check on her and, while I'm at it, grab a bottle.'

Somehow, one glass led to another and, when Darcy opened her eyes, she was still on Kim's sofa. A stale taste on her tongue and a pounding headache that lifted her brain without putting it down again. Kim snored with a humming hiss beside her, moving slowly, she tried to make a quiet escape.

Cat was curled up on the mat outside her front door, snugly within his own furry tail. Her front door was open an inch, the light from the living room window managed to catch the dust falling in the gap, cascades of flowing particles, that uninterruptedly flowed to the floor. Darcy walked through expecting to see Jessica but she was long gone, a mug half filled with cold tea upon the countertop, the only hint that she had even been there at all but for the unmade bed.

'Come on, Cat, let's get you food and painkillers for me.'

The tiles on her kitchen floor felt sticky underfoot, which was weird because, since moving into the flat, she had a strange obsession with keeping the place spotless, especially the floors. Flash floor cleaner, with a hint of lavender, being her new best friend. Maybe Jess spilt juice or something? She thought, Maybe.

'Shit, Cat, I've no milk, I'll have to go across to the shop, or we won't have coffee.'

Darcy could have asked Kim but she did not want to wake her. The path across the road to the shop was not far, the traffic lessened in the estate but heralding traffic sounds could be heard much clearer near the main road. Darcy rounded the corner and walked face-first into Shane.

'Jesus, love, I didn't see you there.'

Darcy must have clipped her lip on the button of his jacket because her lip started to sting and tingle right away. People passed on her left and quickly on her right. She tried to walk past Shane but, if she stepped left, then so did he, as if pre-programmed to follow her intuition, her instinct, her direction. Or was he just being a moron?

He laughed, as if what was happening was humorous. But he was the only one being entertained. Darcy felt ill.

'You should watch where you're going in future, young one.' He openly sneered.

The words were delivered in a tone aimed at causing concern to the recipient, a threat, with honest undertones, regarding her interference in Kim and his "relationship". To put Darcy on shaky ground, a prerequisite to fear, to feeling fearful. His eyes stuck in a face filled with something Darcy could not put her finger on.

She pushed past him then, and he chuckled, unbothered and almost gamey, urging her resistance, her resilience. And as Darcy tasted the red wine in her belch, she moved at a faster pace, fearing she would actually vomit. So, she ran, to get away from her own smell and Shane's lingering crassness.

Gradually, she calmed down, then practically flew back to her flat, to escape from feeling vulnerable and having no one and being alone, a sitting duck if someone wanted to scare her. Why was Shane hanging around the area, why had he purposely accosted her in the street? What game was he playing, was he playing a game? Was she hungover, too sensitive, delusional?

A light tapping on the door made her jump.

'Excuse me, is anyone home?'

A man stood outside Darcy's door, holding Cat in his arms, a stern look, to match his pinstriped briefs and tailored jacket.

'Hey, yes, I live here.' Darcy piped.

'Hi, yes, hello. Em. Are you feeding my cat?'

Darcy wished she had time to brush her teeth, to put her hair in a pony, or even have two dribbles of coffee before this strained encounter, but, no, it was happening, in real-time, without caffeine, toothpaste or a hairbrush, in the middle of the worst hangover she'd had in ages!

'Emm.'

'I don't know if you're aware, dear,' said with an air of superiority, and added hand gestures with his free hand.

Darcy hated the word dear and squirmed when it hit her eardrum.

'But you can't feed other people's cats, I mean, what if they have allergies, or a delicate tummy, or something worse? I mean you can't just do that, feed other people's animals, their treasured pets, just because you feel like it, it's idiotic, down right insane.'

Darcy had no comeback because the man was right. But the lecture was badly timed and Darcy knew if she didn't move away from him soon, her vomit would decorate his black patent shoes.

'Right, okay, thank you… it won't happen again.'

Once the door was closed, Darcy walked into her bedroom. At first sight, the stained patch on her bed, on the bedsheet, looked as though someone had wet the bed. But, as Darcy got closer, she realised it was the water from the glass, emptied to annoy rather than missing Jessica's mouth. But the patch was not there earlier when Darcy had checked and Jessica was no longer there. Now she was being paranoid, her mind completely overwrought with fallacy, with fantasy, with unsupported suspicions.

But her bed was ruined all the same.

Against the door, another light tap.

God, Darcy thought, it's beginning to feel a lot like Heuston train station around here. And she still hadn't managed a decent cup of coffee and a slice of buttered toast.

There, standing side by side a look of innocence and devilment mixed together, was Lottie and Mina, holding, thank the good lord, a Mac Donald's breakfast, with a cardboard coffee tray and, screwed into its sections, a selection of coffee.

'Oh, okay, well, this doesn't look good.'

A double egg and sausage Mc Muffin later and Mina explained that she and Lottie wanted to talk to Darcy about a possible intervention.

'An intervention, okay, for whom, or need I ask?'

The strangeness of the morning continued. After what Darcy could only concede as being a satisfying breakfast that hit the spot, along with the paracetamol, Mina divulged the ins and outs of a dilemma that faced her two days ago.

Apparently, Jessica had been using behind everyone's back, taking Ketamine as if it were going out of fashion and dabbing a bag of MDMA, just to function throughout the day. And why is this anything to do with me? Darcy thought, but knew the answer, so she kept the question, neatly, with all the other undetermined enquiries taking up residency inside her head. Rent free.

Jessica, who was, in many regards, better off than any of them, was the person whose parents were the people that drug addicts sought out help from, when on drugs.

And, yet, she seemed to be the one, more than the rest of them, lost at sea without an anchor, in a habitual state of staying still.

'I know she's been through the mill a lot lately, but I had no idea about any addiction, what about her parents? Maybe contacting them would be a start.'

273

'What, like ratting on her? Really, Darcy, that's your answer.' Mina irked.

'She needs professional help, Mina.'

'She's right though,' Lottie added, 'We can't help her on our own.'

'Or the simple fact that, if she doesn't want help, if she isn't ready to admit she has a problem, then we're wasting our time talking about it,' Darcy added.

'Hence the intervention, she'll have no choice.'

'I can talk to her,' Darcy said, 'I can talk to her first. I'll be subtle, and see where that takes me.'

'Good girl, because it would be an awful shame if she didn't finish her degree, I mean, we're so close to the end now.'

'Oh God, Mina,' Lottie scoffed, 'Do we need to be reminded of a twenty thousand-word thesis right at this moment.'

'Is that all you've to do, you're lucky, I'd be delighted with that? That would be a doddle.'

In the bedroom, once Darcy changed her bedcovers, flipped the mattress over (just in case), slept for three hours and, at last, poured herself her favourite coffee, she sat on her low living room windowsill and wondered how the women in her life were doing. One being a health nurse and the other needing medical intervention, per se. One thing was certain, they both needed help from different organisations. Darcy's thoughts drifted to Shane and the way he'd acted with her earlier that morning. His macho tactics, his type of indirect taunting that Darcy associated with traits of unfavourable toxic masculinity. As if by sheer body size alone, he could control her, and should control her, because that was his job, his entitlement, his innate, predisposed right as a man, because society, on some level, allows such control, by giving him permission. Sometimes Darcy beheld a bigoted thought process filled with sweeping statements that weren't necessarily true but stemmed from her experiences of living so far. Sometimes ridged, sometimes on the bend of enquiry and sometimes so acutely distanced from compassion that apathy's antecedence simply went without saying. It wasn't as though life had pulled her aside and guided her differently; she did not see life through rose-coloured glasses but glasses bearing a hint of frosting, of etched glazing that made things unclear, or clear only to her perception, and she knew that could be dangerous, it could be ego-based and immature. She lived in a time of, what she always believed to be, pro-equality, pro-fairness and pro-freedom. But, to reference in shorthand, why she felt the way she did, felt it to the core, was too monumental a task to undo or work back from.

Maybe it was because a friend of a friend in college had nude photos uploaded by an ex who, by just pressing a button on his keyboard, under the gauge of warped, justified revenge pornography, caused the girl to self-harm, become anorexic and end up in rehab for most of her second year. Never mind the trust issues that accompany such a vile betrayal. Or the fact that a woman, just a young woman, could not simply put on her running shoes in broad daylight and go for a run, without first scoping the area for shady characters, opportunists or men who just leered too long; as if that was okay.

Darcy needed a conversation with Kim about a professional recommendation for Jessica's situation and about Shane's impertinent attitude and failure to move on with his own life.

Darcy wanted Kim to clarify, what she felt was a threat and, when she thought it was time to report someone who she'd already admitted had parked beside her at the supermarket car park, suddenly, and out of nowhere. Or had pretended to be sick, and inconsolable over a close friend's untimely death, just to gain sympathy, or had… the list went on. Darcy could see the signs as if through cling film wrapped around an open casserole dish, but Kim lazed about the seriousness of Shane's insatiable desire to be in her life. Liking all her posts on Facebook, appearing in the same shopping aisle, the one that shelved the lactose intolerant products, along with the stacked dry bean selection; the aisle that most people avoid. No, Darcy thought, something is so off with this set-up, it's borderline disturbing.

Cat purred at the window as if to say, enough already, come pet my coat, and feed me snacks.

Chapter Twenty-One

'Darcy, darling, we haven't seen you in so long, come in, come in,' Jessica's mother said, with an overly eager rasp to her voice. She was ushered in and asked if she needed anything, refreshments, a sandwich, a hot towel or maybe a lavatory break. Darcy wondered if Muireann was drunk or on some kind of happy pill.

'No, thank you. I'm here to see Jessica; she knows I'm coming over.'

'Oh, don't fret, no hurry there, Jessica is in the bath; why don't you sit in the conservatory and wait for her, I'll tell Ursula to go fetch her. You can touch anything in there except for the Macallan, but take as much of the other stuff as you like, fill your glass to the brim.'

'Honestly, I'm fine.'

'Suit yourself, I'll be back shortly, you can put the T.V. on, I think the golf is on and, if not the golf, then definitely the tennis.'

Muireann left then and Darcy felt as though she'd fallen down some rabbit hole. Why did Jessica's mother sound so stoned, why was she acting like a character from the movie *Trainspotting*?

Jessica appeared, robed up, with her ankle in a brace of some kind.

'Do you know how hard it is to wash with an injury?' She said, with a whimpering snarl.

She then explained she had crashed her parents' car, not badly, not a bad crash, but a drunken drive kind of crash, the one that had her grounded at twenty-one. Because the stupid tyre on the car burst, and the tyre alone cost five hundred quid.

'Are you sure it was just alcohol you were on?'

'Oh, now I get it, now I see, Darcy has come to visit, not to be nice, but to lecture, not to console or be supportive.' Jessica raised her hand to her chin. 'Let me guess, the others had a say in this, am I right?'

'We all care about you,' Darcy said, nonchalantly.

'Not to worry, being immobile is my very own version of cold turkey, anyway, I was a recreational user. I'm clean three days, so you can all take a run a jump. And you can tell the others that too… assholes… it hasn't been that bad, mind you, I was on morphine.'

Is your mother on it too? Darcy wanted to ask but refrained from being trite. Muireann was obviously highly strung from her daughter's persistent revolt against her precious life. She would have already been on the receiving end of a barrage of vitriol, unfair insults and anger, no doubt. It was a bit late in the day for teenage rebellion but Darcy knew Jessica had issues that went beyond the norm. Muireann was probably at her wit's end, Darcy figured.

'I have a friend, she's a health nurse, she gave me this number.'

'A friend with a number, how original.'

'I know you think you don't need rehab, but you have to look in the mirror; you've been through a lot, no one blames you for wanting to escape.'

'I can do this without rehab. My mother has me locked up like a prisoner anyway, Practically. Daily blood tests, the whole shebang, what fun, what fun.'

'It's for the best, Jessica.'

'And you? Is this friend your new...girlfriend, boyfriend? I can't keep up. What are you these days?'

'I'm just trying to be me, and, no, she is a kind, loving friend.'

'As opposed to?'

'Can you just stop, can you just be nice and see that I'm here, that I'm here again to help you, and stop being a bitch or some type of badass, just for once, maybe say thank you.'

Jessica licked her lips as if to moisten gratitude.

'Thank you.'

'I have to get to work, use the number if you need to, get yourself right for college.'

'That kip, I can't wait, even if I'm in a wheelchair.'

'And everything else. Are you okay?'

'I try not to think about it, Darcy, actually, I hope I can forget most things about this summer, don't you?'

*

The sun was splitting the stones, it was so warm that Darcy wished she's worn shorts instead of jeans, but she was almost at the chocolate shop now, and entered, glad of the AC.

'You're ten minutes late, I'm telling the boss,' Edie joked.

'Are you in for the day as well?'

'Nah, half a day, then I'm heading out to Sandymount Beach, with some friends, I think we're in for a bit of an early Indian summer.'

'Bitch.'

Darcy poured lemonade from the cooler under the counter.

'It's still the summer, well, early Autumn. I think an Indian summer begins much later.'

'Who cares about the semantics, Darcy, you're such a nerd, you know what I mean, don't you?'

As Edie, in her cute curl bun, served a customer holding an unnecessary umbrella, Darcy was overwhelmed with a sense of uneasiness as if her world was tilted and needed re-grounding. The summer had been, as Jessica suggested, one to remember, or forget, whichever way fits better. But Darcy was still standing and ready to continue, which surprised her.

'I'm just popping out the back to make a call.'

Tapas and the laughter lounge had been just what Kim didn't know she needed. A lesbian, stand-up comic who tastefully dispelled ideologies and notions on sexuality, politics and egotism. A room full of diversity, laughter and genuine transparency. As young people traversed the table rows in order to engage with like-minded, bohemian, ecowarriors, who thought differently but the same as one another. Darcy sipped an espresso martini, half drunk on Kim's company and the way in which Kim laughed, smiled and then chuckled wholeheartedly. Darcy found her very attractive and had done so since meeting her months before, as a patient in the clinic. A lifetime ago.

After the buzzing city swirls of clammy bodies, Darcy suggested a wine bar in Howth, a trendy spot, for clientele that wanted privacy and to hear each other's exchanges of intellectual conversation, at the same time.

Darcy's chat changed, with the added cockiness of the martini, allowing a flirtatious edge, along with the giggling, playful taxi ride there.

She was aware her tone now had underlying connotations, undertones that suggested, she was open to anything.

'Are you flirting with me, Darcy?'

'I dunno, am I, would it be that uncalled for?'

'It would be different, that's for sure, I've never, well, experimented, sexually.'

Darcy laughed then at the way people separated sex into sections, or intimacy as having boundaries. Always the whys of why something had to be this or that, instead of just trusting in the feeling, as diluted by alcohol as that may seem. Why not just follow the urge freely without the questions, the enquiries, the hesitations?

But, of course, Kim had never insinuated that she had bisexual tendencies. Darcy was just chancing her arm.

'You'll never know unless you try.'

'One drink in here and that's all, I'm knackered, I must have been mad agreeing to this.'

'You're twenty-four, not fifty-two, give over.'

The air still had heat within its passing sway, so much so, it gave Darcy an idea.

'Why not forget about the bar and let's just seek out to The Secret Beach instead, a strand not so secret because I know where it is.'

'Oh, I like the sound of that, Darcy Derry.'

'Darcy Derry, nobody has called me that in a while.' She thought about her mother then and of how she had used the endearing term DD as a diminutive phrase. The thought was disarming. Darcy suddenly felt upset and elated at the memory, all at once, in an interlaced moment that she silently embraced.

The beach appeared, after a steady rock climb, which was a small miracle due to the wrong footwear and constant guffaw. The cause of which was nothing in particular. Erupted giddiness relaxed once they sat on a flattened rock, a formation that was perfectly placed for a view of the incoming tide.

The setting could not be more romantic. The alcove of the littoral craggy caves behind, eroded by years of sea salt attack, formed a shelter, that enclosed the couple in romance. Of course, the idea of it, the notion of romance was something in Darcy's head, swimming around in a sea of ambiguity.

'Would you be up for a swim?'

'A swim? Are you seriously asking me, a nurse, to partake in an unnecessarily dangerous situation, just for fun, do you know me at all?'

'This beach is as safe as houses, honestly.'

'But we've no togs.'

'It's still so warm, who said anything about togs.'

Darcy stood and began to strip, not in any elegant suggestive way either. She stripped off all her clothes, as if a kid on an adventure, laughing throughout, feeling liberated and childish, and adulty and immature, feeling reserved and uninhibited, unsure and cocksure, feeling like she was mad to be doing what she was doing, but, on the other hand, needing to let go, completely let go, to the pull of the magical scene.

She ran then, towards the sea, by now not even considering if she was alone or being followed.

Kim copied, and ran too, towards the blue, towards newness, towards Darcy who, by that time, had dived beneath the rippling water.

Damp, but not cold, Darcy and Kim arrived back at their apartment block past midnight.

'Come in for a nightcap,' Kim suggested.

'No,' Darcy smiled, 'I don't trust myself, besides, I smell like seaweed.'

By home time, they'd sobered up. The taxi ride, the back seat, implied touches artistically curved so the back of the hand grazed a leg. A memory, a thought of an hour before, a kiss while the waves pushed them together, their bodies already entwined, a hotness, in the cool water, breasts, cooled skin, a beating pulse, two pulses, and the sand between toes, an insurgence of laughter, an outline with no point of reference, lips catching hold of one another, as if water was impartial, free of the process of choice, free choice, because love is love and lust is lust, even beneath the boundless surface of the see-through water.

'Tomorrow then?'

'Absolutely.'

*

And rehab was rehab. A negative impression, with a positive outcome. Striking a cord. Beginning and getting to the end of something. A face lowly, then enlivened, somewhat.

Jessica, there, under ordered supervision. A stint. Her pleasures sparingly divided into short intervals. Following protocol. A hybrid, of okay and not-so-okay. An empty room of crowded space. And both unrelated, the way of being perceived and the perception. An addiction, that hides behind a conversation about denial. Sitting in a circle. Sipping orange juice, a sugar rush, from sugar-free OJ. In different imaginative forms, anything is real, even sugar. Prominence is obscured and equality is highlighted on the menu, as if the special of the day.

'Why did you bother coming if you're just going to be nasty?'

Darcy put a bag of ripened grapes by Jessica's bedside locker.

'All I said was, these things take time, how was that being nasty!'

'Everything feels nasty in this place.'

'It's only been a week.'

'A week of utter torture, nightmares, sweats, and the yearning, Jesus, it's been worse than craving you.'

'Great.'

'I've been such a leach, are we friends again?'

'Can you stop being so destructive, that's all I ask?'

'I can't promise you that.'

Jessica half-smiled. A half-smile was enough.

Chapter Twenty-Two

The warm weather spell cooled as the feeling of new terms entered the equation, entering the room of a door that, before then, remained shut.

New college terms.

New friendship terms.

New lover terms, yet to be finalised.

The chocolate shop kept Darcy busy all day. Kind customers outshone the rude undertones of others. Gloved hands reaching for salted caramel glazed almond nut and then white chocolate banana squares, one false smile after another and the day moseyed on. Workers, suited bodies, at the end of their day, moved crisscross by the window. Some sauntered along to catch the train, or bus, or bicycle with flowered basket that had been chained to a telegraph pole in an up-right position. Others ambled, strolling, daydreaming, configuring playlists or adjusting loose earphones, all while the sun was beginning to set behind their passing faces. The sound of the beating heart of Dublin city, engines, laughter and the flow of mixed conversation, into a small phone and to the open air.

In between serving customers, Darcy flash-backed her late evening seaside escapades with Kim, the kiss, the naked water skin, that joined naturally without effort, the waves that trapped and the textures that cooled. They had been texting silliness all day.

Kim mentioning, unshyly, that she had never felt the way she did now, and was unsure of what that meant, or where to go with it.

Darcy replied that the unplanning, instead of trying to plan these things, could be just as exciting and to acquiesce in the glory of it all. Darcy admitted she had never felt like it either.

Darcy believed that people should be allowed to explore one another openly, and without the eyes of society's judgements. Furthermore, she questioned who exactly that cohort was. What group in society decided what was what? Was it a group of church-goers, middle-aged and over, reading from an ancient book of contradictions? Was it family members, who held different moral standards, believing theirs to be superior?

Was it an anti-choice group that lived in a high-rise building, looking down on everyone else with contempt? Thus, having "choice" all to themselves.

Who made up these tacit rules, that permeated society but most people revolt against?

Feeling the way she did about Kim, meant questions that would not normally affect her, suddenly, needed to be examined through a different lens.

'Go on, I'll finish locking up, Edie. I'm in no mad rush today.'

'Really,' Edie answered, excited about an impending date, 'You're such a sweetie.'

The bus was packed, more so than usual. Darcy wondered if there had been an event on in the city, causing the extra influx. Hands reached up towards handrails for added steadiness, bangled wrists, multicoloured string, with gold and leather bracelets, lined on top of one another, as if a mini toy mega rainbow spring, embellished.

Some wearing cardigans, some wearing lighter coats than others, not ready to step into heavier layers just yet.

Darcy wondered what the other passengers on the bus were thinking about. Maybe how they needed tomatoes for dinner, or plasters for their heels for blisters caused by new shoes. Maybe of a lost grandmother, missed every day. Maybe a new movie release, or that the book they were reading would excite them more. Maybe the hours previous, or the hours to come. Or maybe, just like Darcy, thinking of a lover's embrace and how that would feel and how it was making her feel, now, on the bus, with strangers and their thoughts.

Kim was working late but that didn't stop Darcy looking towards her window as she neared their apartment block.

The inside corridor, the way it should look but for a bunch of flowers, red roses, left outside Kim's door, on the welcome mat, that Kim insisted on having.

A card attached.

Darcy hesitated.

Would she like it if Kim poked around her delivered flowers, anticipating a salacious message from a secret pursuer?

Maybe the message wasn't uncalled for but an endearing text from a family member.

Maybe, maybe, maybe, maybe.

Darcy walked towards the flowers, she opened the card, which read in capitals,

YOU'RE DEAD BITCH. The words were handwritten.

At the local guards' station, a couple of hours later, and intuition said, in a low, almost unrecognisable voice, *you're not being heard here, here is no place for you.* It came with a melody, a kind of chant, that sang, *go home, go home, go home.*

'I know they're busy, but your life was threatened, and I can't believe they are not taking it seriously. What are you supposed to do, wait until you've actually been attacked, it's really twisted.' Darcy exclaimed.

'Come on,' Kim said, downcast and bewildered. 'It is only a hand-written note, essentially, a piece of paper.'

'Written by a psychopath; you read about these types of things all the time. A guy, an ex, hanging around, watching his ex-girlfriend's every move. She reports it and, by the time the cops have gotten around to caring about it, it's too late.'

'Thanks, Darcy, that really helps.'

Darcy threw her arms up in the air. 'I give up.'

'Listen, they said they would pay him a visit and ask questions; at least he'll know he's on their check-list, it's something. Anyway, we've no proof it was him.'

'Oh, of course, we have, we've both seen him hanging around, at different times, that's proof enough.'

'Look, I'm pissed off too, but let's not let it ruin our evening.' Kim added.

Darcy had planned an evening, but now that would be altered to suit the mood. As they got closer to the steps of their entranceway, Darcy suggested they stay in her flat. That Darcy would sleep on the sofa, just as long as Kim stayed overnight. After some persuasion, Kim agreed. They made Irish coffees and watched an old movie starring Colin Farrell, about an Irish sea trawler and a strange woman he found in his fishing net.

'I enjoyed that, something light-hearted, what was it called again?'

'Ondine, I think, or Odine, are you tired?'

'I'm tired, but my mind is racing a little too.'

'I don't want you to worry, ye gotta stop, okay?'

Darcy shrugged. 'I want to be okay, I want us to chill, but none of this Shane crap sits very well with me, I think we should get some security cameras installed. Just outside in the corridor even.'

'Okay, I agree, we'll look into it but can we talk about "us" now and forget about him?'

'Us?' Darcy teased. 'I like that, "us" I mean, it has a ring to it.'

'I really like you, I thought about you most of the day.'

'Me too, your face adorned all the chocolate sweets I sold, perfect little eyes staring up from a Petit Coeur Pink!'

In any type of relationship, the honeymoon period was exciting for both parties. In the case of Darcy and Kim's coupling, it had avenues of unchartered territory, for both women. All the women Darcy had slept with before, had had sexual encounters with other women. Kim had only slept with men, had only had sex with men and, up until nights previous, had only shared foreplay with men.

Darcy would not rush. She would bide her time, and make it special for Kim because she liked her. A lot. And she had not felt the type of "like" like it, in the longest time.

'I'm not having you sleep on your sofa, when I have a bed across the corridor, I'll go back home unless we sleep side by side,' Kim insisted, beseechingly.

It wasn't that Darcy didn't want to, so she did not take much persuading.

'Okay, but I can't guarantee you'll get much sleep.'

During the night Darcy felt restless. She had kissed Kim, tenderly, they had chatted, cuddled, turned each other on and kissed more. Now they lay back to back, Darcy could feel Kim breathing, and that alone relaxed her.

The next morning, both Kim and Darcy made coffee together, scrambled eggs, with spinach and toast. They thought the day would be ordinary, they thought they were ordinary. A new couple finding themselves within the concept of being one unit. They pushed the counter stools back under the countertop in unison, and buttoned their tops at the same time. They attached looped earrings to their lobes as if the mirror image of the other, Darcy's loops much smaller than Kim's, and searched for their keys within a second apart.

The morning was ordinary until they stepped outside the apartment block and saw the words BEACH LESBIANS painted in red, across the exposed concrete wall of their block. Drops of paint ran down the wall as if the wording cried. On full display for every occupant to see and, for them, Darcy and Kim to be mortified, for many more reasons than the graffiti. Shane must have watched them at the beach before. Their tenderness, their intimate sharing. Darcy, seeing the words, had felt naked in the open air.

Their day now scheduled in a different direction, steered towards photographic evidence, and police interviews. They were positioned centrally in a homophobic attack, but, once again, they had no proof of the perpetrator, only an idea. And an idea was never enough but the police would take the couple seriously and noted, on a pad, their heightened words of worry and concern.

The discriminatory stained wall was painted over in their absence but Darcy knew painting over something so disgusting did not mean the slur did not still remain underneath. Penetrating the concrete until, eventually, it seeped into their living space. The language used on the wall named them as different, labelling them with malice, with vindictiveness. And that, was blatant bigotry.

The slur told others who they were, invading their privacy and their human right to privacy.

Darcy moved in certain circles to avoid homophobia as much as she possibly could. There had been incidences while dating Jessica, childish chants from a passer-by on the street. As if that particular street contained an under-developed community, an ignorant vibe whose only vocabulary contained the words, dyke, faggot, lesbo and queer. Darcy hated when someone commented, *you're so brave for just being yourself and coming out,* which, in and of itself, was jarring because it highlighted separateness, especially from what's standardised as being "normal" and Darcy loathed that differencing, that subtle assumption on other people's part, that she was an outsider belonging to a group of misfits. But Ireland as a whole, was an open-minded nation whose people were inclusive and generally accepting of queerness and people's choices.

But Darcy also understood that by wanting to dismantle other people's arrangement of her sexuality, it named their preference, giving them power, inadvertently giving their opinions a platform on which to air. So, Darcy usually refused to engage, but this, this blatant attack from a jealous ex, well, it was on another level.

It caused traces of fear for personal safety and *that was* new to Darcy.

Worry crept in, but weakness tried and failed to slip in beside it. She was a lot stronger than before. Worry she could and would handle.

Chapter Twenty-Three

A cottage lining the borders of Sligo, Leitrim, and Roscommon belonged to Kim's parents. A summer home, that had become a vocal point after the attack and was now firmly pencilled in the calendar for a visit from Darcy and Kim the coming weekend. They wanted to move forward in their relationship without the prying eyes of Kim's ex who, astonishingly, had proof he'd been working the night of the senseless paint-work job, with police verifying his whereabouts. So, with a kosher alibi, they let him go, citing, along with his release, that it was probably just kids being kids, defaming property and the like.

Darcy had the weekend off but Kim had to put in for a few days' holidays to get the time free.

'What should I bring, hiking boots, I suppose?'

'For sure,' Kim answered, her hand against her chin as if thinking, *what else*.

'Rain is forecast for the whole weekend, nothing new there but it won't be lashing, so we'll still get to explore, there's so much to see. Sligo is Yeats's stomping ground; you love Irish literature, don't you?'

'All literature really; in any form. Joyce, Beckett, Yeats, Synge and Heaney,' Darcy mused.

'They're all Irish, Darcy, and all men.'

'And I almost forgot Wilde, how could I, the queerest of them all?'

'Queer, is that not a slur?'

'No, that's a reclaimed term, apparently.'

Kim frowned.

'Said in jest, and not discriminatory.'

'Still.'

'I love Rooney, and Galloway, Donoghue and O'Brien, Quigley and Boyce, and Mc Keon. Oh and lately I've been reading Gráinne Murphy, her work is amazing.'

'Again, all Irish.'

'Okay, then, you win, I love Irish Literature.'

Darcy sniffled.

'What's your favourite book of all time?'

'Umm, oh let me think, um.' Kim swayed and stopped.

'*On Earth, We're Briefly Gorgeous*, by Ocean Vuong, have you read it?'

'I have actually,' Darcy replied, 'It's exceptional, not only the way Vuong explains displacement of place and culture so poetically, but how being an immigrant, a gay man too, was so hard... '

'... umm, yeah, I got that too, and something serious about his mother I can't quite remember.'

'Should I pack a light rain jacket then?'

'Yes, you absolutely should.'

*

Darcy spent time thinking about her new venture with Kim, concluding they were a new reframing pulse. A pulse that generated a feeling, a feeling that could grow and branch into something vibrant and worth chasing. A new frame to exist in, where both women designed the picture it contained. They would paint their tastes, and colour their life, not as a prescribed, mass-produced copy of someone else's desires and insight—and outcomes, for that matter—but shaped and scripted, from the combined desires of "them" and what they were stepping into. Which would begin with a trip to the West, to explore the tranquil countryside. A foreign land of intimacy, a stone's throw away from unpleasantness. They needed a new landscape to explore one another. An external space without limits, an open, limitless horizon. Where better than the countryside?

Darcy felt excited; she wanted to forget about the disgusting "wall art" and focus her thoughts on escapism, even if the type of escapism was fixed into reality.

'So, tell me more about the place,' Darcy asked, taking a bite from a digestive biscuit.

'Telling you would spoil it, for so many reasons, least of all, you creating a picture in your head and it not turning out the way you envisioned.'

Darcy shrugged. 'Fair enough.'

'Just trust me,' Kim assured, 'You won't be disappointed, it's a simple place, it is.'

'Is it near the beach?'

'No, but there are plenty of lakes around, if you fancy fishing.'

'Fishing.' Darcy laughed.

'Don't knock it until you try it, and, besides, we get into trouble on a beach.'

The thoughts that a man may have watched as private, intimate interconnected moments of sharing between Kim and her were being explored, really upset Darcy. Instead of having a conversation about how seedy, if it was him, Shane had become, they sort of, stepped over it, or around it, sort of. Evidently, Darcy thought, they were going away so as not to think about him, but the conversation would hang around like a bad smell, waiting on attention.

*

Jay texted the morning Darcy was getting ready to leave for her trip. *When are you coming over to visit me? I can't believe how much I friggin miss you!*

Darcy missed him too, in the strangest way, in their way of missing one another, that was always attached to something else, unassuming or unorthodox.

She texted him back that she was busy being a lesbian again and that, if she could afford it, she would try to get over to Scotland before college started in the next couple of weeks. Darcy regressed, only momentarily, back to Mijas, to spending time, romantically, with Jay. She thought it quite absurd now, the breath of him, his touch, his manliness. But she did not regret him, or the lesson he brought to her. Mina had texted right after, a text to invite Darcy to dinner Sunday evening and to bring her new squeeze.

A knock on the door and Kim shouted lightly that the car was packed up and ready to go, could she get a move on?

In each doorbell, a new camera had been installed. Kim and Darcy could watch live footage from their phones through the modern device, which brought with it a degree of ease.

Kim's copper Mini Cooper sat, its engine running, while Kim beckoned Darcy over.

'God. You've only one bag, after all that, come on.'

'I travel light, are you sure you locked your place up properly?'

'Yes, double-locked. There's nothing in the place anyway, so let's bid farewell to Dublin and hit the road, it's time for the smell of cow dung and sheep's shit.'

Once out of Dublin, and off the M50, the scenery became like poetry for the eyes. Words from the every day romanticised with greater depth. Long gaps between cars on a broken-lined stretch of road, litter free and endless. Roadkill for company and Tori Amos playing through the speakers on low; a song about a doughnut hole, a metaphor about something lost. Accountability, more than likely.

Grass blades danced, some shorter than others, fields nestled between golden blankets of patchwork, in as many shades of green. The fields ran for miles, framed by many types of trees, uneven and even. Corn fields, an odd flattened patch. A resting crow on a tree branch, resting crows on farmland, sprawling as if the horizon was make-believe. The outline of orchards further on. Birds' nests as if small mistakes in the formation of a tree branch. Sometimes the city lacked the colour green, but the country had too much, too many shades to choose from.

Verdant meadows and boundless countryside.

Every once in a while, patches of arid land broke the pattern of greenery, as if under the shade of an umbrella in a rainstorm. Rolling hills, a rural setting, right out of a country magazine.

The sky was multicoloured, mixed from a dull palette. Grey, charcoal, light grey and pools of bright blue, rounded outlines of white blossom. Clouds ran a race with no legs, escaping from an invincible force, pushing one another along, as if some carried the weight of dreariness, and others, an opaque emptiness.

'Look at the clouds, up ahead, I think we'll drive into a storm. We need a good storm to clear the air.'

'That's something a country woman would say.'

'Ah, we might drive past instead of directly into it.' Kim proclaimed.

Was life always a storm awaiting, brewing somewhere before it attacked? Darcy thought, or was life made up to include storms, so, when the weather changed and the calm allowed the sun to shine, people appreciated it more? The constant yin and yang. A lucid, cathartic cleansing, no one knew they needed. The calm, hopefully, wasn't always before a storm.

'So, have you any neighbours close to the cottage? I like the idea of being uninterrupted for a day or two.'

'Hardly any, none directly next door,' Kim answered, 'And the people that live farther up are part of the landscape, fixtures, neither coming nor going, you'd have to really look to see them.'

Small towns and villages drifted past the side view mirror. Darcy watched in a lazy haze and only sat up straight when Kim indicated left to pull in at a garage in Westmeath.

'A loo break,' she winked and Darcy responded with a grin.

'Coffee?'

'Absolutely.'

At the beverage machine, choices multiplied; small, medium large. Cappuccino, latte, americano, flat white, cold water, hot water, hot milk, hot chocolate, tea, green tea, fruit tea and cold milk in an insulated stainless steel jug. Buns, croissants, current buns, iced buns. Everything accessible, catering to the busy traveller, or cross-country worker on the go. Even the garage itself was a mini-mall, providing everything from woolly hats to nail files, toilet detergent to birthday cake candles.

'Are you hungry?'

Darcy thought about it. She wasn't hungry but felt obliged to buy something as if travelling across the country gave a free pass to gorge.

'Maybe a protein bar, the salty caramel one.' A treat but not a treat, esteemed in the notion of fewer calories.

Back on the road and Tori was replaced by James Vincent Mc Morrow, an Irish artist, with a soothing voice. His words fit perfectly with the mood. *If I had a boat, I would sail to you. Hold you in my arms and ask you to be true.*

This trip would inevitably bring Kim and Darcy closer. They would be different driving back, either way.

Splitting at the seams, heaving at the brace.

'We're kind of at the halfway point now, so not too bad.'

'Oh, I don't mind travelling, just watching the world go by, it's therapeutic.'

'Wait until you see the cottage then, that's yoga in brick form, if you like that kind of thing.'

'I've never tried, I must.'

Once off the motorway, the winding country roads were lined by land. Large spaces with old brick cottages full of character and old thatched roofs. Some with extensions, changing the look of the vernacular building, others shadowed by red barns, stacked hay, goats, their kid, bucks and tractors. Farmers sat upon machinery, ploughing, cultivating their legacy for the next generation. Cows, tan and white, dotted the thickest grass spots as if cushioned by their very sustenance. Cattle grazing far off the others, who lounged leisurely, staring at people, as if passers-by were intruders, expecting something they couldn't offer.

'Can you smell that?' Kim laughed at her own findings.

'That there is the smell of the country. Mother nature's natural aroma!'

Darcy felt free, free from the anxiety of the last few months. Cut loose from grieving, even if only for a while. Free from Jessica's demands and her own weakness towards Jessica's demands. Free from thinking about her final semester, or her future career, free from blaming herself for her grandmother's death. And free from Shane, and his manic impression, true or false. And mostly free from how hard she'd been on herself lately. Far too hard, she realised now.

'We'll be there in the next fifteen minutes or so, hopefully, my neighbours, the O'Meegans will let us pick strawberries for free. They've a wonderful fruit farm. You'll love it.'

'Why for free? I don't mind paying.'

'Ah, it's a favour for a favour around here, you'll see.'

Darcy nodded, she would fall in and go with the flow.

'See up ahead, the wind turbines, that's how I know I'm almost home.'

In the distance, a row of massive white, wind turners stood that somehow complimented the hill-filled backdrop. The joining of two powerful forces, with a similar goal in the world. Longevity. The wind cascaded the landscape, an invincible friend providing a natural blanket. The land's expansive beauty the length of Ireland and only truly appreciated when observed through a traveller's lens.

Not long after that, a sideroad appeared on the left, a pot-holed lane, to be more precise. Tall pine trees on either side of the road made the entrance seem mysterious, but, simultaneously, without fear or trepidation. Instead, Darcy felt a sense of childhood awe, while driving through the laneway, the magical experience made the hairs on her arms stand up. The stillness of the passing pines, the car sheltered from the outside world, invoked, what Darcy could only describe as, a strange curiosity.

'Are we actually in a forest? Driving through an actual forest?'

'We actually are,' Kim half giggled at Darcy's amazement.

'You kept that one quiet.'

As the trees opened, the car moved uphill, giving sight to open land again before displaying a backdrop of mountainous delight. Hills perched close together, although different sizes, gave the effect of being related. A big brother, or distant uncle, each peak like part of a rock family; steeped in history, holding tight to secrets from through the ages.

Then the cottage, a one-storey red brick structure. At its front, three small windows containing flower-filled flower boxes, with reds, yellows, pinks and greens, still in bloom. The front door was a green barn door, with black accessories. An old-style knocker and post-box. Around the front door, a wooden porch, a small pergola with climbing roses growing from the root and spreading as if it owned the wooden frame, and the square gaps, and the added planks, nailed, adjusted and pierced. By the foot of it, two sets of Hunter wellie boots, stained with dry muck and moss, three standing upright, with one leaning over, slightly so.

'I'm speechless,' Darcy said, her mouth still partly open in amazement.

'I can tell, isn't it the cutest?'

'The whole place, who knew somewhere like this even existed, Kim, I mean it must be a haven, a real place of peace.'

'It is when no one else is around, for sure. Come on, there's so much to show you.'

*

The inside of the cottage was just as quaint as the outside. Whitewashed walls brightened every room but for the unpainted stone around the open fireplace, that still contained ash and burnt turf residue. A wicker basket, with logs and thin sticks, piled high, decorated one side of the fireplace, while old-style fire tools graced the other side. Black soot flakes rested, as if sleeping on the edge of the small fire shovel.

Darcy knew Kim was watching her reaction, and Darcy too had noticed a change in Kim's face; her skin eased, untightened and unworked. Darcy looked on as Kim switched on switches and ignited lamps, unpacked essentials and filled the kettle with water from the cottage's own fresh water well. Under the window, a small round table with a patched tablecloth and miniature clear glass salt and paper shakers sitting on top, stood surrounded by wooden chairs painted bright red. On top of the chair bases, yellow cushions lazed with loose ribbon ties, dangling, redundant and untied. On the windowsill above, a Virgin Mary, mother of God statue, hands together in prayer, rosary beads, link through and around her pressed palms.

Pillared by each side of the statue, were pictures of various saints. St Anthony for lost things and St Francis of Assisi, who, from what Darcy remembered, had a good reputation, unlike some, and probably deserved a spot by the Virgin Mary.

Other holy pictures lined the wall, a lone crucifix secured centrally, a lowered head, shielding a sorrowful face, pained by disappointment.

As if by the flick of a switch Darcy had suddenly been taken back to her childhood. She stood between her granny Pat and Pat's sister Ann facing a big grave site that was their family plot. To Darcy it felt massive, like a white stone court yard one walks over to get to a double doored ancestral house. She was eight and the day was The Blessings Of The Graves, an Irish tradition, on a cold afternoon. Darcy remembered clearly now, an event she'd completely forgotten, holding both Ann and Pat's hand in hers, separately, while a priest raised his dipped holy watered fingers splashing the drops of redemption onto the dead bones underneath. On one side of the plot a gravestone, erected and blocking other gatherers, a granite stone that stood powerfully compared to the other side of the plot, and its empty space.

The priest blessed the left side then just as he was about to bless the right, Darcy's gran aunt announced, 'They're not in there yet father.' To which he frowned and shuffled away, alarmedly. The wasted Holy water dripping, from what Darcy could tell, onto his silly pleated long black dress.

She hadn't understood back then but the family plot had already been paid for, the grave was only waiting for one or more than one, of the other people standing close to its bordered edge, to rest there permanently.

Darcy looked away from the holy statue to the left where a sofa, covered in pink fabric that looked like corduroy, called for her to sit; its armrests shaped like extra parts of extended padding. The contemporary piece did not look out of place in the old-style space but complimented the quirky design. Under the old wooden T.V. stand, books lined the shelf, a layer of dust to keep them warm. An eclectic mismatch of various authors, subjects and genres, for any tastes or intellectual enquiry.

A wide alcove invited people into the small kitchen room. Cupboards, a pink SMEG fridge, a small, dark green Aga stove and a white and black marble countertop, all awkwardly went together and with the blueprint of the cottage. Black raised stone floor tiles, grouted with grey lines, set off the room and somehow made it homely.

The floor tiles ran through the cottage. In the hallway, mats were placed as if stepping stones leading to the bedrooms.

'This is a summer house, isn't it?'

'Yeah, my parents have a place in Dublin too. They still spend most of their summers here though. They're abroad at the moment, Croatia, I think, yeah, Split, then on to Dubrovnik.'

'Very nice,' Darcy nodded approvingly.

'We'll need to pop into the village to get some milk and stuff and-'

'Isn't there a cow nearby that we can milk? I'm just about ready to turn into a country girl.'

'Ha, ha, that would be a sight to behold.'

'You must be knackered after the drive, can't the shop wait, we can relax a while.'

'It's only up the road. There's a hamlet, it has a pub, a butchers, a church and a newsagents, it may have a hardware store there now too, I'm not sure.'

'The pub sounds like it could use a visit more than the hardware store, if I'm honest.'

'Well, if anyone asks, you're my cousin; they'd have a heart attack around here if they thought you were anything else.'

'And do you have any cousins?' Darcy laughed, out of frustration, more than anything else.

'I do now. Look, the place is old-fashioned. The people are church-goers. A dying breed. And, yes, they're full of hang-ups and believe in the Old Testament, but they're also kind and caring. Just set in their ways.'

'And homophobic, I get it.'

'No, that's unfair, I think they just prefer that people carry on that malarky up in the big smoke.'

Darcy laughed then, a genuine chuckle.

'I think I'll take a saint's picture with me then, just in case.'

'That's blasphemy, you're going straight to hell.'

'I'm halfway there already.' Darcy grinned.

'Let me show you around a bit outside; I'm actually not tired and then we'll go into town.'

Kim explained that the five acres around the back of the property, where the fence indicated, belonged to her parents. Adjacent to that, fields of tall barley, the crop almost ripe and ready to harvest. Beyond that, on higher ground, a forest, half living and half cut down. Logs stacked due to invasive species, the woodland, an empty plain but for the workmen, in their florescent jackets. Eventually, Kim had said, the process of forestation will renew the land and restore all the trees that were damaged.

The barley field owners also owned the fruit farm, along with various animals. Kim explained that, as a child, she'd had a field day growing up in such a holistic way, due to the freedom and organic influences of country life.

The couple walked around the property, Kim pointed out what she thought were the most important features of the area.

The car ride into the small town took all of about fifteen minutes. The town was the type of place where everyone knew the other and waved or said hi accordingly. Kids, teens crossed the road, chatting, trying to forget that school days were shortly impending. The day was overcast but certainly not cold.

'Okay, grab a basket, and check the date on things 'cos they could be on the shelf years.'

Kim winked and, for a second, Darcy thought she was winding her up. That the insult of the establishment had an undercurrent of sarcasm towards Jackeens as opposed to culchies.

'Hello there, Kim Mc Givbeen, I haven't seen yee in these parts for a while now, how's da parents?'

'Ah, Brendan, they're the same as ever. This is my friend, Darcy Derry, up for a visit to smell the clean country air.'

'Oh, I don't know about that now, Joe Brady is clearing out his cow shed, the smell ain't so fresh. I can tell ye that much for nothing.'

Brendan pushed his fringe back from his forehead.

'Are ye stayin beyond in the cottage?'

'I am.'

'Micky Dingle is playing tonight in The Rovers beyond, sure you'll have to come and join in.'

'We're only in the door but, you never know, we might make it over.'

With the essentials in two plastic carrier bags that cost thirty cents each, Kim and Darcy drove back towards the cottage.

'I forgot my mam's shopping bags, God, I'd be shot if she thought I had to ruin the environment further by buying plastic bags.'

'These are all biodegradable now, relax, the world is fucked. I don't think using two new bags will save the planet.' Darcy chimed.

'I love how wholesome the town is, there's something so old and charming about it.'

'Ye can say that again,' Kim teased but felt just like Darcy. Oldness, in this case, meant being caught in a better time.

Back at the cottage, unpacked and sipping over coffee and half parted chocolate digestive biscuits on the table, both ladies argued playfully about what to do first, second, and then subsequent to agreement. Micky Dingle was definitely on the cards for later but they would either take a trip to the farm or the lake in between.

In the shed out back, paddle boards, canoes, a kayak, paddles and life jackets, lined the wooded beams, rafters and built-in shelves. The small outbuilding was a mini market for outdoor activities.

'We can take the kayak and canoes out if you're feeling adventurous,' Kim said. Darcy laughed to herself and at herself. The trip was so far removed from her usual life that she was hit with the realisation that her insular world could actually have break-out rooms; it could coexist outside of being a typical college student trying to make it by simply surviving. She knew too that, even if life turned on its axis, there were ways to escape that, ways to comfort the mind and see life as having possibility again.

'How do we get the boats on the water?'

'Ah, the novice will soon be a veteran.' Kim pointed to a trailer under tarp but for the wheels.

'The lake is only up the road, come on, help me get organised.'

Kim gave instructions that Darcy followed with great attention to detail and with submissive caution. She watched Kim who worked like a pro, adjusting, clicking, tying, helping only to attach the trailer, that she'd helped pack with a kayak and canoe.

It was early evening, clouds dotted the sky, and a cool breeze drifted in from the sea but the air still held the remnants of late, late summer, early, early Autumn.

As they approached the lake, Darcy sense its calm. The water was alluring, embedded within the land as if a glass eye on the face of a disfigured hillside formation.

Beneath some trees around the sides of the lake, wooden picnic benches (human error), a tree's natural habitat, deformed into a seating area. A used coke can, dented, rested in long blades of grass around the bench, and the rubbish bin yards away. A pebble dash pathway that eventually disappeared into the water had a warning sign on each side, rusting, deterring swimmers to enter the lake without a life jacket, or lifeguard present.

'Don't worry, it's not dangerous. The signage is a formality, having said that, I always follow the rules here.'

'Rules?'

'Just growing up, I suppose, I never came up here to drink, get pissed and go for a swim, unlike some of the other locals.'

'Do you ever break the rules, Kim?'

'Are we steering off topic, Darcy?'

'Well, you brought me here, to this romantic setting,' Darcy smiled. She did not want to put Kim under any type of pressure but she also felt drawn to Kim, sexually, intellectually, even spiritually, and she wanted to explore if Kim's feelings were mutual.

'This is a perfect place for rule-breaking, that's all I say.'

Nowadays, the autonomous life Darcy had craved and deliberately etched out had room for manoeuvre.

Upon the lake, in the distance, bar-tailed godwits and marsh birds grouped in niches, some on land, others gracefully floating in a slow undisturbed flow of unperturbed silence near the low, water-saturated land, that seemed embraced by sedges and herbaceous wetland plants.

Kim pivoted her slender frame in reference to the task at hand. Darcy followed, standing out of the way sometimes, while, other times, offering a helping hand.

On the water, as both canoe and kayak touched, side by side, so too did Kim and Darcy, in a leaned-in simple peck kiss, too giddy to linger or mean anything, but in the process of flourishing into meaning something. Two bobbled orange life-preserving half bodies, encased on a lake, open and eager to explore one another.

Then the rain came down. The heavens opened, truly, and the couple paddled back in a fit of laughter, enough to lift the birds into the air.

Soaked through, they packed up in haste but in comfort, in willingness and in freedom. The world of time had paralysed, time refrained from mattering. Rain was not something to run from but into. And they both, at one point, just stood, hands outstretched, enjoying the free wash and a cold drenching.

Back at the cottage, the emersion went on, and the open fire at a slow burn, crackled, as splinted wood turned orange and dark brown.

'The water won't take long to heat, then you can have a bath to warm up.'

'I'm not too bad; I'll probably catch a cold but sure.'

'There's whiskey somewhere, if you want, I can heat some up on the stove.'

An old married couple living the country life, Darcy wondered how it was even possible, but she stepped onto it as if a lighted path.

After warming the body, nibbling on various cheeses, crackers and grapes from a miniature charcuterie board, washed down with Kim's version of a whiskey sour, Darcy felt an urge to ask personal questions.

'Do you find me attractive, Kim, are you attracted to me, because I think you are but I don't want to fuck this up, y'know?'

'Are we having the chat?' Kim tittered, 'But, seriously, I don't want this to have some kind of designated timeframe, do you?'

Kim sipped her whisky.

'Why does everything have to follow a certain chain of events, a pre-ordained sequence? Like, oh, if you kiss then the next step is second base and all that. There's one thing I can tell you and tell you easily. I want you around.'

'As a friend, as a… '

'No, Darcy, not just as a friend, I want more but not some prescribed notion of how two people should be intimate or the sharing of themselves, or how to fall in love even.'

'I get it, and I'm good with that approach. I just need some kind of confirmation, I guess.' Darcy downplayed.

'The only thing we've to think about now is, are we staying in or going out, and it's your call. I don't mind either way.'

'But what about Micky Dingle?'

'Ah, I've seen him plenty of times before.' Kim said.

A text came through and both women examined the screens on their phones, as if a natural reaction. Kim frowned but did not elaborate on why, or what the text contained.

'We could toss a coin to decide.'

And toss a coin they did; it landed on staying in. A secret, unspoken, relief to both.

*

Love is love and lust is lust and, even as the evening dusk entered the cottage windows, in separated indirect shapes of light, dust modes danced in a uniquely oblivious moment, intimacy would have its way, would have its say.

As Darcy gazed at Kim, a gaze spoken clearer than any utterances. Words paled in comparison to what the eyes suggested. Then touching, as if for the first time, bare skin, in intimate places. Lips on lips, on lips, on lips, and so on. A bare arm here, a bare leg there, unapologetically, unreservedly, instinctively, passionately. Tenderness, in a display of shared experience.

Two people wanting nothing more than to satisfy one another.

The night, the darkness, the candlelight, the ever-growing need to be close, to be a symbol of themselves, Kim and Darcy spent the whole night in happy exploration. Spellbound and binding, at home, in a place they created, a place of warmth, beneath and above. In and throughout, there was sweetness, enlivened with it all. Until sleep, eventually, held them both.

The shift was like nothing Darcy had ever known before, or wanted to, or needed to, or tried to.

Lovers, Darcy thought, lovers they come and they go, and the falling that enabled that process was usually unprotected and fierce, because at the beginning of any relationship, while in the honeymoon phase everything was fresh and unharmed. Well, Darcy had gathered, this time, this time, the falling was exceptional. The composition of what was before was no longer there. And, in its place, a refreshed blank page, unwritten.

'Good morning, sleepy head, it's a better day out today.'

Darcy approached Kim and kissed her lightly on the lips.

'Rain jackets are probably still a good idea though.'

Kim pottered around the kitchen then announced she needed to brush her teeth. Darcy, whose breath already smelled of mint, walked over to her phone that was plugged into the charger. Beside her phone, Kim's beeped, an incoming text *Enjoy that bitch while you can because you don't have a future.*

Darcy shivered, a physiological reaction to a threat projected in her direction. *Enjoy that bitch.*

Had Shane been texting threats the whole time they'd been away? Why keep nasty texts secret?

Why protect someone like Shane?

Shane's number had been blocked, his number had been given to the police and, yet, he was brazen, or stupid enough to get another phone and text her from that. Did he know where they were? Darcy would not impost on Kim's privacy or push her for an answer as to why she hadn't mentioned the texts, but she was not happy about the surreptitious overtones of the damaging words in his

317

message. Shane was beginning to feel like an encumbrance around Darcy's neck.

What did he mean by, you don't have a future?

As Kim returned, Darcy walked over to the tap and ran water until it was cold enough to drink. Inside she was seething but she would not let Shane win. He would not spoil their time together, and she promised herself that something serious would have to be done about Shane when they got back.

Still on edge, Darcy decided to lead the way, she was extremely agitated but hid her feelings well.

'Can we just browse around the place today and maybe get pissed? I feel like going a bit mad before college work begins again.'

'That's a turnaround but, I have to say, it's one I like.'

They walked the country road with limited traffic interrupting their stroll. Darcy knew Kim's phone was on silent, so internalising her frustration seemed to make things worse for her, because she questioned the phone's incoming in her thoughts. Shane was ruining the country air and he wasn't even present.

'I forgot to say thank you for last night.'

'Oh, no, I don't think a thank you, is called for.'

Darcy reached for Kim's hand then but, just as fast as the touch landed, Kim pulled, no, not pulled, snatched her hand away.

'Not here, Darcy, Jesus, not outside.'

Darcy bit on her lower lip, she couldn't help it. Kim's words stopped her feet from taking steps.

'I'm sorry, that sounded very abrupt, I didn't mean…'

'Listen, it's cool, I understand how some, not all, but some folks think about,' said in a raised voice, 'Homosexuality.'

'Shush, for fuck sake, Darcy, do you want Mrs O'Meegan to shit herself.'

'Strap on,' said with an even higher tone. Then louder again, 'Scissoring, big fat dildo.'

They both laughed then.

'I'm serious, my parents would die and, if they need to be told anything, anything about my choices, then it has to come from me, okay?'

'Okay, I get it.'

'Guinness or Miller?'

'Emm, a bottle of Miller, I'm going in slow.'

The pub was a typical country public house. Dark brown wooden frames, uncomfortable booths with curtain material cushions. Matching curtains lined the bay windows and ugly tiebacks attached to the wall with either screws or a bent-over nail, let in dusky sunlight through stained nets. The wallpaper print was raised and dated. Over the large stone fireplace hung pictures of fallen heroes, rebellious leaders and revered playwrights. In between the frames smoked stained granite, were nailed faded drawings of Hazelwood Forest, and the mudstones and shale of Benbulbin, Sligo's cold-eyed flat top.

Darcy walked over and looked with a head raised, she raised a finger to touch, to dispel, to connect, to history, to her ancestry. She raised the bottle too until she emptied its content down the back of her throat.

'More.'

Two more bottles and Darcy danced to a cool song playing from speakers she had no idea where to find. She did not know the lyrics by heart but, by heart, she knew the lyrics and sang along, mistakenly. Her lips uncoordinated with the singer's intended chorus, her steps danced to their own tune.

And Kim watched, smiled, laughed, gazed, smiled and laughed some more. And when Darcy almost stumbled, Kim ushered her back to the table.

'Tell me more about Jay.'

'Jay? Why, what do you want to know?' Darcy felt tipsy, and so far removed from thoughts about Jay, she had to ground herself into the conversation.

'He's a friend, a good friend.'

'Okay, now maybe,' Kim quizzed, 'But he was more than that before, wasn't he?'

'You really want to talk about Jay now, really? Jay?'

'Just some back story, not every detail, I'm not that neurotic. I'm curious.'

'So was I, I guess that was the point of Jay.'

'Oh, right, so you slept with him, out of curiosity?'

'I don't know, Kim, I mean I didn't sit down one day and say, let's try a bit of dick. I go with the flow, it's who I am.'

'Crude.'

'You asked, I'm telling you.'

'And is it over, or does he creep on you?'

'It was never an "it" to begin with and, no, our friendship is not over. He's supercool and you'd actually really like him.'

'Ménage à trois, interesting.'

'There's no way I'm sharing you.'

They ordered more beer.

'Have you heard from anybody back home?'

Kim frowned, quizzically. 'Like who?'

'Not anyone in particular.'

'What an odd thing to ask,' Kim's voice changed from fun-loving to annoyed, swiftly. 'We don't have any mutuals, so who exactly are you referring to, Darcy?'

'That dickhead Shane for one.'

'What?'

'I saw the text this morning on your phone, and I wasn't pooching, the text appeared as I was getting my own from the charger.'

The mood changed then, from upbeat to sombre in a nanosecond.

'I don't even know if the texts are from Shane, it's a different number.'

'But the content, Kim, come on. It's him, why are you always so lenient with him, with his misogynistic attitude? It's as if you give him the right to act malignant, without repercussions.'

'That's not true, Darcy.'

As the conversation elevated into the domain of disagreement, Darcy knew alcohol was playing a part in their argument. The way Kim juxtaposed Shane and Jay in relation to Kim and Darcy's life was incorrect; both men should have never been named in the same discussion. The illusive Shane and his stalker tactics were a far cry from Jay's caring nature. And, on top of that, Kim was not seeing Shane's behaviour for what it was, psychotic. Shane had purchased a new sim card to antagonise Kim, but Kim was acting as if that behaviour was typical.

'Can we not discuss him right now.'

'I don't want to either but how many texts have you got off him already today? He's interfering in your everyday life, he's trying to deliberately ruin things for us. I'm worried he'll take things a step further.'

'Okay, I promise when we get back I'll report him, I'll do more.'

Kim drank the remainder of her bottle of, by then, warm beer.

'How about a vodka and Red Bull?'

'Block that number and then I'll relax.'

Not long after, a sing-a-long broke out in the bar. Pop music from the eighties always dragged punters out of the woodwork. The nostalgia in the beat, beating back to a better era. When songs had a melody and all that jazz. A group of men about Kim's age came over and sat with her. Kim, through slurred speech and loud music in the background, introduced the men but Darcy could only latch onto the words - old, school, same, and no one's exact name.

Imitation artists filled the makeshift dance floor of the pub. Each trying their best to resemble either Elvis and Madonna or Lady Ga Ga and Erasure.

The room became dense with warmth, with condensation, with people's conversation, with broken glass on the floor, beer seeping into the boards and up through the humidity of the jammed space.

Darcy watched as one of the men flirted outrageously with Kim. She couldn't be sure but, at one point, she thought he kissed Kim's neck. Their exchange of words looked intense or maybe it only felt that way because Darcy was extremely drunk and leaning into paranoia.

It was now late evening and Darcy had begun to feel her head spin. Her head spun within a room that was also spinning, rotating around her head, as if nothing was pinned down.

'I need to go.'

No one heard her plea, so she made her way through the crowded space and found Kim kissing some man at the bar.

The awkwardness of the moment was lost on Darcy, who repeated, in a raised voice, 'I need to go.'

'Go? Already? But things are only kicking off.' Kim mouthed.

'Who are you?' the tossed-haired man asked.

Darcy turned to Kim, 'Who is he?'

'It doesn't matter, come on. Let's go back to the cottage.'

Darcy stumbled out the front door, but Kim stumbled and fell, laughing as she went down and hit her chin on the deck.

'Jesus, you're bleeding.'

'It's okay, it's okay,' Kim teased, 'I'm a nurse.'

With Kim puking in the toilet, Darcy boiled the kettle for tea. The statue of Mary stared at her, full of judgement and hell's fire.

'You can blame Kim,' Darcy said to the still, blessed statue.

'Darcyyyyyyy, help, please.'

Darcy did not feel good, but she knew Kim felt worse. So she put Kim to bed and tried to drink a hot beverage to replenish the lost minerals from her body. She wanted to look through Kim's phone. She wanted to play detective and take Kim's phone and invade her privacy and act like an ass. But, instead, she drank cooled tea and lay down, in a silent prayer that the room would rest and that sleep would take her before the circling twister in the bedroom did.

A split in the curtains, an animal's cluck, a baa or gobble, a chatter and a relentless bark in the distance amplified the headache inside the room, inside Darcy's head. Kim snored lightly, the covers half on half off her body. A vivid dream, with sequences missing, a toe, a touch, a pull-back, an interlude between changing position, then a fading too loose to keep or remember.

Darcy felt as though a layer, a cloth made of stitched haze was placed across her eyes and head. She walked into the kitchen and looked for painkillers.

She thought about the drive home amid concerns of a myriad of different things. But the couple still had today, and Darcy was not angry about anything, she just wanted to put a pin in things to be resolved. Rain pelted the corrugated roof of the shed outside, which danced along to a tuneless beat somewhere not connected but close to the vicinity. A box of Panadol, out of date by a month, would have to do. Darcy punched out two and let them swim to her stomach accompanied by cooling liquid. She heard the toilet being flushed and turned to face a tossed sleepy head, pale-skinned and gaunt.

'Water… '

'How are you feeling?

'A little unwell, but not as bad as I thought I would.'

'Was I really drunk?' Kim asked, to which Darcy smiled yes.

'Ugggh, sorry.'

'I was drunk too, maybe not as palatic but still. We had a laugh.'

'Are you hungry?'

'I don't know, are you?' Kim asked.

'I think so, lemme fry some eggs, and you can tell me all about Shane and why he's still texting you from another number, what exactly he's saying and what we're gonna do about it.'

Kim scrunched up her face to disapprove, but she did not protest.

Texts were not the only thing that Shane sent via text message, no, there was an image too.

Kim tried to explain that the guards would do nothing without hard evidence. (The image had a body but no head.) Until they got back to Dublin, they could mull over Shane's insaneness or they could move on with the day. They chose the latter, to a degree.

When the weather cleared, they wellied up and walked along an ageing, weather-beaten fence, entangled with wildflowers and dying blackberry stems. The ground sodden in parts, but the wellies doing their job, Darcy said that thinking the guards would not investigate was absurd and that she would, if Kim didn't, file some kind of complaint once they got back.

'Okay, all right, but, for today, can we stop talking about this?'

'Did you enjoy your homecoming night?' Darcy changed the subject.

'Oh, the local shenanigans, always fun. Always making a show.'

'What time will we head back, I've a dinner date with Mina.'

'Yeah, back to reality, you had fun though, right?

Fun, jumbled angst, confusion, pleasure, annoyance, then back to fun, I suppose, Darcy thought. And for a second thought about the concept of feeling boxed in. Of how people had tried to box her in before. A one sized box fits all. A place she had sat uncomfortable in, unmoving, hardly able to stretch, until eventually realising the power to leave was hers, and hers alone. And now, a man called Shane was trying to build a new type of box, with Kim, it seemed, handing him the nails and a hammer.

'Sure, who doesn't love country living,' Darcy chanted.

'I hope we come back sometime.'

Only if your parents are out of town, Darcy speculated, an introduction as "the girlfriend", would never happen. Was she okay with that type of denial, hadn't she already overcome such discrimination and bigotry years before?

Some people just have more to figure out in life than others; a mantra Darcy told herself often, derived from the old adage, everyone has their own cross to bear.

'Shit, look over there.'

The sky, bellowing grey, dark grey and a lighter grey tone, amassed clouds which gained speed as if God inhaled, then exhaled a breath to direct a storm their way.

'That looks nasty, we should head back to the cottage.'

'Did you check the weather app today?'

As Kim retrieved her phone, light drizzle, rain droplets covered the screen. 'Damn, thunderstorms are predicted, and heavy rain, like, really heavy rain.'

As the words escaped, so too did the rain, pelting down, without real warning, clouding judgement in the absence of the natural light that preceded the downpour.

By the time they reached the cottage, huge puddles skirted the base of the forest behind, as if black holes awaiting an invasion. Darcy and Kim, both blindly infected by the impromptu cloudburst, ran for cover. Wildflowers became unearthed from their rooted solidity as rubber wellingtons dislodged the safe region of their derivation. The rain turned to hail stones, weapons of mother nature, aimed at any individual crazy enough to be outdoors without shelter.

Kim fell over, as one of her boots was swallowed by an unrehearsed mud suction. Darcy wanted to laugh but composed herself in time to assist her lover instead, doing so with a slight smirk, under a lowered head.

One sodden sock later and they stood under the flowered trellis by the front door, drenched to the skin and needing Horlicks, or something just as soothing.

Wet hands and slippery fingers fumbled with keys, until, at last, the couple sat indoors, a coordinated team, preparing an open fire.

They stripped, wet clothes dropped on top of one another until a pile of damp material, folded in and up, made a small hilltop.

The fire lighting, the warmth it produced, the darkened sky that created an evening glow at midday, and the fact of nakedness, initiated tenderness between the two young women. Passion ensued, as lovemaking turned skin on skin damp, and textured. Heavy panting, passion, hunger and tension, became as sure as the air exchanged in the small space, thinning and heated, until exhaustion, and a light sleep.

And, still, the statue of Mary glared, her rosary beads, her unsaid prayer, caught by unused vocal cords, as she stood transfixed Was she carved from alabaster? Darcy wondered, as her continence bore a stern and unyielding expression. Darcy, while Kim wasn't looking turned Mary so she faced the other way.

Thunder roared from dense clouds overhead. As gusts of wind howled in unison, Darcy got up to look out of the small window. Watching a storm that included lighting and thunder was up there with her favourite things. A tiny spider was busy extruding itself from a threadlike crack in the wall, protruding then disappearing again. Kim wrapped a blanket around her body and informed Darcy she would make coffee, that maybe the roads were blocked now, as they often were after such a deluge, and that they may have to stay another night.

Darcy looked towards Kim's voice and then back to the window where she saw a shadow move. The rain had not eased, so visibility was poor but she was almost sure that the figure's frame was human. She wiped the glass, but the murky blend of darkness, along with the deposited hail stones, impeded correct perceptibility. The figure could have just as easily been an animal.

'Didn't you check the weather?' Darcy half-murmured.

'Sorry,' a vexed, slightly irate voice answered from the kitchen. Kim arrived back, one shoulder exposed to the elements. 'When was I supposed to check the weather exactly? When I was dancing between Padraic Mc Ginty or Ian Walsh, was it, or maybe while I'd my head down the loo, ah, just wait there now until I ask Siri about the forecast for tomorrow.'

Darcy, amused, just smiled.

'You could have asked Padraic, while he had his tongue down your ear.'

'Oh, he didn't, did he? The night's a blur.'

'What about the T.V., switch it on for the weather report?'

'It's not working, it's really only there for show. We're avid readers up here; we read, or walk, or fish, or work the land, sorry.'

Darcy moved away from the window, and they both checked the weather app for details that were confirmed through the window and the endless battering from rain. The weather app announced flash flooding, along with a warning sign not to travel, etcetera…

'When the rain eases off, we'll take a walk down closer to the roadway but I know there'll be no access. I've seen it before, plenty of times, it's a bit of a bummer, ring work if you have to, that's my advice.'

'Did you plan this, Kim?' Darcy teased.

'I'm taking a bath if you wanna join, and I think board games and chats can be what I unintentionally planned, what do you think?

'Worded to perfection, feck the walk down, we know we can't go anywhere, let's just bath and play games. I'm very competitive, so be warned.'

Scrabble, which was usually consigned to the attic, was the game of choice, as the two bubble-bathed women, hot chocolate mugs on each side of the board game, insisted the Virgin Mary be referee and spectator, positioned exactly, so as to be fair.

The weather continued to correlate with the weather app, which was somewhat of a sore point between Irish residents. The T.V. weather person would connote a certain type of weather was on the way, only to have the actual weather rebut most predictions. An Irish person's best bet was just to look up at the sky, instead of trusting a meteorologist!

'Do you cheat?'

'I've been known to.'

'I'll keep that in mind.'

'I like to play dirty, on occasion.'

They both laughed, giddy in the company of one another, in the delight of being trapped, willingly, with nowhere else to be.

The game commenced without clashing until it clashed and became a competition of wills and nerves and patience and endurance, along with a bit of help from sly loo breaks to look up a correct spelling in the dictionary app.

The contention arose because of the authenticity of urban dictionary words, not yet inverted into the mainstream dictionary. Without official credence, or so Kim argued. After pizza was offered and eaten, clamour died down to flippant tittle-tattle about friends and acquaintances.

'So, Mina is your best friend, right, and Jessica is your ex but also a good friend, but an onerous pain in the ass. And you're all bonkers, and almost finished college, am I right?'

'But for the Jessica friend part, yeah. I don't think she's happy with me.' Darcy looked at her watch and jumped up. 'Shit, I'm supposed to be meeting Mina in a while for dinner, she'll be pissed. Let me text her.'

Folding the game away, then throwing more logs on the fire, Kim watched Darcy move around the room on her phone. Darcy caught her eye and winked.

'Okay, where were we?'

'You were telling me about the dynamic of your friendships and I was reiterating your claims for clarification.'

'It's only my opinion, I'm sure they've plenty to say about me, I mean, I've not been honest, the way a friend should.'

Kim shrugged, 'I wouldn't say that. I think you kept things to yourself, especially about your parents and your grandmother, but you made a choice about how to live. I honestly don't think you were being deceitful, private maybe.'

'So, do you think they have secrets then?'

'Oh, Darcy, so innocent sometimes. Everyone has secrets, everyone.'

'I'll take being private then. What about you, how long have you left in your job, training, I mean?'

'Funny, I've been thinking about that lately and of how I'd love to teach nursing instead of the hands-on job. It would mean doing a higher diploma but I could do that part-time.'

'I agree, you'd make a bloody marvellous teacher.'

'I've only six months left in placement, and I've loved it, sure, didn't I meet you?… But I want something else from my career. Will you teach?'

'Well, that's the plan, maybe English and history, and I love Irish architecture, so I'm pretty boring but it's what I gravitate towards.'

'My little academic.'

'We'll see, I need to stop taking trips away and focus on my dissertation.'

'I've every faith in you.'

*

The morning said hi with the sun eclipsing the earth in an apology of warmth. The rain stayed at bay, along with its cousin clouds, and Darcy awoke to brightness, nudging Kim, she offered tea and toast.

'Hopefully, the roads are clear; we need to get up and get a move on.'

Packing the boot of the car with their bits and bobs, Kim locked up behind them, checking everything was off and remained as she had found it a few days before.

'All in all, I think the trip was a success,' Kim smiled.

'A success, you're so funny, it was lovely, but it's time to earn some money and get prepared.'

'Nothing is running out of time, Darcy, it will all happen regardless.'

'I know,' Darcy said, 'But I've been directionless for far too long. In all honesty I'm ready for the next step life has to offer.'

Chapter Twenty-Four

They sang along with broken lyrics to tunes they half-remembered, half knew or optimistically guessed, between them, there was no attempt at cohesiveness but they were jovial in their endeavours. The car ride home, but for the cows passing slowly over a lane in Co. Roscommon, was smooth sailing.

They pulled into the car park of the apartment block in Dublin, just past midday.

'That's funny, I thought I pulled the curtains back before we left.' Kim stared up at the building, concern on her face. As Darcy looked on, Kim removed their bags, still gazing in the direction of the window.

'Hey, you may have just thought you did, we've cameras in, remember, if anyone tried anything, it would have shown on the feed, stop worrying. Here,' Darcy reached out her hand, 'Let me take that, you go ahead.'

Kim walked in ahead.

As Darcy rounded the corner of the corridor, Kim stood in her apartment doorway, her face ashen, her eyes confused, showing confusion, perplexed and dazed. Darcy dropped the bags and ran to her aid. Inside, the apartment had been ransacked, completely wrecked and ruined. Paint smeared the walls, every drawer had been emptied, the smell was putrid, and the furniture fabric was cut, torn and vandalised. Darcy checked the bedroom, it was the same, and the window had a pane of glass removed. The clear sheet lay carefully placed against the wall. Neat against the opposing chaos. Darcy removed her phone from her pocket and dialled 999.

The front door camera showed no signs of disturbance. If anything, the eerie presence of nothing (but recent visits from the postman) in the corridors made things worse. Darcy explained to the attentive ban gardi about recent messages sent from an unknown number. The guard wrote notes, listened, moved her head in agreement, engaged with all compulsory formalities, left a helpline number and asked if we needed anything else. Yes, Darcy thought, we need help putting Shane into jail, so we can feel safe again because he is clearly a friggin lunatic.

Darcy was surprised her own apartment was untouched. Although, she was paranoid that maybe he had installed hidden cameras to spy on them, or something just as twisted. While Kim was at the police station, Darcy checked her flat, unsure of what she was looking for but searching anyway, under pictures, behind electrical devices, under the bed.

The light switch in the bedroom did not ignite when pressed, the room remained lulled in shadows, illumed from the light outside. Darcy wanted to interpose scepticism with logic but she was on edge and doubting the space around her was safe. Leaning against the door frame, she wondered if Jay's place was still vacant or if his musician roommate had returned from his travels.

She changed the light bulb and the room warmed from the false protection emitting from the radiating current.

A text from Mina changed Darcy's mind from eschewal to divergence, to malleable, to resilient, to reality. She had to get her shit together.

When are we meeting up soon, it's been a minute, far too long.

Darcy asked Mina if she was free later that day, to which she replied, yes, in capital letters.

Grounded. Grounding oneself into familiar pathways, friends and conversation, helped to distract, then divert what stared Darcy blankly in the face. Kim was quiet, introverted, when she returned from the police station. Although Kim had been inexorable when convincing Darcy she wasn't to blame for the apartment's destruction, blame was what pinched Darcy's skin, annoying but manageable, like dust lifting off a construction site, and landing, loose particles on the tongue.

While clearing up the mess left by the faceless intruder, Kim regurgitated words said by the officer about Shane having an alibi that evening, and of how the phone used to send offensive pictures and texts, had been reported stolen days before. Kim, while washing walls, remained silent, reflective, not wanting to comment.

Just in case.

Now, sitting opposite Mina, her life before Kim smiled back at Darcy with a real sense of normality.

'So, Teddy asked me to marry them, and I said I'd think about it,' Mina laughed as though a young teenager.

'What, shut up, you're not serious!'

'Oh, you know, I kinda like the idea, I think it's cute.'

'You don't know each other well enough, surely.'

'I might just say yes for the ring and be totally pretentious, and flamboyant and gay.'

'And silly.'

'That too,' Mina teased. 'Tell me all about your trip to the sticks. I'm surprised you made it back after that weather change, and what about Kim, you're keeping your cards close to your chest concerning that relationship. When will I get to meet her?'

'Oh there's a whole situation going on there. I mean, she's lovely, she really is, but there's an ex in the picture and I don't mean she's chasing him or anything but he kinda doesn't want to let her go; it's messy, like, really messy.'

Mina scrunched up her face, 'Ohh, I don't like the sound of that, it sounds unpredictable.'

'That's the word. Anyway, there's not much we can do because he hasn't been physical, or threatening per se, he hasn't touched her.'

'Whoa, that's heavy shit to be dealing with, Darcy, are you okay? I mean, you're still getting over your own upheavals, it sounds like this Kim brings a lot of baggage. I hope she's worth it.'

*

Kim was working nights the following four and Darcy arrived home to an empty apartment and a card from Jessica. One of those occasional inspirational cards, with words of wisdom and, in this case, a poem of apology.

Jessica, who always seemed to have something to apologise for, had signed the card, love Jess x.

Kim and Darcy had discussed renting somewhere new and moving in together, away from Shane to a newer location, but, in retrospect, Darcy now pondered on that idea and it felt uncomfortable; as if she was being controlled by him and his actions. On top of that, she didn't want to move in with anyone permanently. Darcy felt disjointed, affected, once again, split in two. She wanted the new college term to be filled with positive actions, good grades and immersive study. So, as she poured water over a green tea bag, she decided no one but her would dictate her life, the way she lived it or her next move in creating it.

Darcy's phone was switched to silent during the night, so, when the blinking behind her eyes woke her up, she was surprised to see Jay's name flashing on incoming.

'Jesus, Jay, what time is it?'

'I'm sorry, babe, It's early, five-thirty'ish, I fell. I fecking broke my arm and left toe and sprained my other ankle, I think. I'm in hospital. You'll have to come over. I need minding. Please, please, please, pretty please.'

'Jay, don't be a dick.'

'I'm serious, I need help, just for a day or two. I've paid for your flights already.'

'I'm going back to college next week and… '

'Please, Darcy, I wouldn't ask if I wasn't messed up.'

So much for creating your own life, Darcy thought, easily diverted from her strong position the day before.

'Okay, okay.'

Darcy loosened the bed sheets and turned over on her side, avoiding a stain on the top of the wall she'd been meaning to repaint. She tried to go back to sleep but a voice reminded her about the ins and outs of karma, every good turn deserves another. Jay had been her knight when she needed a shoulder, now it was her turn. Of course, leaving Kim, especially with Shane lurking around, would be a conversation. In the dazing early morning light, Darcy was half glad of the distraction. Truth be told, she was annoyed at how Kim was handling the Shane situation and wondered if there was something about the dynamic of the relationship that Kim could, but didn't want to share with her.

Later that day, Kim came over to Darcy for a catch-up and casual debrief. Initially, Kim was unfazed by Darcy suggesting she travel to Scotland to look after Jay and help him rehabilitate. But her mood said otherwise.

'So, you're really going this evening, it's very hasty?'

'Hasty? Kim, he's practically an invalid, he needs help.'

'But there's others who can help, why does it have to be you?'

'I don't mind going, he's a good friend,'

'He's more than that, Darcy,' Kim scoffed.

Darcy inhaled and exhaled frustration on the outbreath. 'He needs my help, nothing more, we go back a long way and I'm going over to help him whether you like it or not.'

'Right, okay. Fine.' Kim answered. Her tone laced with anger that simmered under the surface.

*

Piloted by movements unknown to Darcy, her body just stepped one foot after the other in the direction of her gut's instinct. Off the plane from Dublin, Inverness did not look so different or indistinguishable. In some countries, the hardest part after landing was the initial acclimation, but the Scots were renowned for having a similar outlook on life to the Irish, so Darcy felt settled and oddly optimistic.

A trip to the restroom was foiled by a man holding a card with her name written in black standing just outside the arrivals gate. She walked towards him with a full bladder. She promised herself she would avoid coffee consumption on a short plane ride in the near-future. Texts arrived as she entered the back seat of the Jeep, she opened one from Jay while slipping her seatbelt into its lock, the latch plate clicked as the car pulled away.

The driver will take you directly to the front door. See you soon, J x.

'Is it far where we're going?'

'Only about twenty minutes.'

The driver had a very strong cockney accent and refrained from talking for the rest of the journey. Darcy had always wanted to visit London and the man's accent only reinforced that wish.

She checked to see if Kim answered her previous text. It was still marked as unseen, as it was before taking off from Dublin airport. Kim was annoyed, but Darcy wasn't exactly sure why. Maybe they needed space, time apart to rethink. Maybe Darcy was guessing, projecting or both. Maybe Darcy had no idea who Kim really was, and re-evaluating their coupling was just a normal part of dissecting the coloured parts people put on view. The real clanger, figuratively speaking, was looking behind the façade, behind the layers and, if someone allowed you to dig that deep, then maybe they were worth, going deeper.

Darcy liked spending time with Kim, she liked it a lot but sat in neutral when it came to understanding Kim's acceptance of *her* and what she, Darcy, represented.

The moving vehicle caused Darcy to think about how, after many years, she was open about her sexuality, about wanting to try new experiences, about feeling adamant about being free to do so. Oppression had been something she carried around in her back pocket. So, when it slipped out and fell, she stomped down its grip, until the clasp was broken. She had moved on from answering questions that other people were still asking. So, if Kim was still back there, still figuring it out, all Darcy could do was offer guidance, while staying at her own post, sure and steady.

The car slowed, stopping for a red light, then picked up speed again as Dary shifted in the seat. Pervasive woodland caught the eye. The scenery spanned, not unlike Ireland, heavy with boundless greenery and fields aplenty.

'Oh, I don't take tips but thank you.'

Darcy put her money away and, when the car sped off, she faced a redbrick Edwardian-style three-storey house, semi-detached, white bay windows and a front door partially opened.

She walked up concrete steps that were lined with ceramic flower pots, pushing the door open further to enter.

'Hello, Jay, hello.' She sang.

'I'm here, on the sofa, follow my voice.'

Jay was buried under duvet covers, crisp wrappers, and an array of comfy pillows. There was no arm in a cast, no broken toe or sprained ankle. At best, there was some semblance of a bandage, loosely circled around his wrist.

'Jay, what the fuck!'

'I know, I lied to get you here, but I did injure myself playing rugby, I swear.'

'You're such a little shit.' Darcy shrieked, exasperated.

'I know, I know, but you're here now and the weeks are flying by so I knew you wouldn't just visit.'

'Oh, right, so you think I've nothing else to do.'

'My bad, my bad. I'll make it up to you.'

'Two days, that's it!'

'I know, I'll show you around, you'll love it. I'm being needy, I know it. Please just play along.'

That wink.

A homemade cappuccino later and both Darcy and Jay gossiped on every topic. Jay said he remembered Kim from the ward but not clearly and that the nightmare scenario concerning Shane sounded far too much hassle than it was worth.

'I'd run from that if I were you, I mean, it's nothing to do with you, not really.'

'No, but I like her, why should I run?'

'You may not be aware of this because, sometimes, and I'm not being funny, Darcy, but you're a bit of an idealist, and, sometimes, people don't share exactly how they feel, they hold things back, for whatever reason, y'know.'

'Like you, ye mean?' Darcy smiled broadly.

'Yeah. Like me and like you too, and that's okay, it's how it works when you're not committed to the other person.'

'Maybe from a male point of view.'

'That's sexist and untrue; you lied to Jessica and she lied to you too, remember?'

Darcy looked at Jay then as if to say, *needless to say, smartass.*

'Anyway, how can you find commitment based on lies?'

'You can't really, and that's it, your answer, if something is built on a foundation of lies, it won't survive, it's doomed.' Jay agreed, philosophically.

'Well, I haven't lied to Kim and that's what's so friggin annoying; the first time I'm honest, Karma is waiting to bite me.'

'Forget about home for now,' Jay sniffled, 'Let's hike in the morning, honestly, the clear highland air will decimate this heavy load you're carrying.'

'I thought you were injured, remember.'

'I'm still mobile, would ye give over.'

'I'm just back from a trip down the country, I don't need to see any more hills, for serenity's sake, but if you insist. What about this evening? Netflix would without the chill?'

'Sure ,we'll see what happens.'

'And no funny business, I mean it.'

Jay casually laughed. 'As if.'

Darcy's phone chimed.

'What the hell is that?'

'A delivery man, I've a camera installed.'

'Well, you can put that on silent, Sherlock.' Jay patted the empty sofa cushion beside him. 'Come on, sit close to me for a cuddle, I've missed you.'

As Darcy sat down, Jay put his arm around her and she let him, feeling his warmth made her feel considered. He always felt and smelled so familiar to her. She checked her phone before putting it on silent, then reached for the goodie bag on the table and relaxed into Jay's Scottish life.

Darcy woke up to the smell of spices, aromas from distant lands and, for a moment, she had to catch herself from panic because, just for a second, she had no idea whose room she was in. A delayed confirmation lasted seconds because Jay's curly hair moved with his youthful face, back and forth, from the kitchen table to the oven and so on.

'Ah, you're awake, I had you snoring in my ear and I swear your exhaled smelly breath spoke to me, saying "feed me, feed me".'

'Oh, shut up, it smells nice though, whatever I subconsciously inspired. What time is it?'

'It's almost eight p.m., sleepy, the evening is almost over. I doubt you slept much in Sligo, ye dirty hussy.'

'Are you jealous... I'm sure there're women in and out of here on the constant.'

'I've been having a good time, I won't lie.' Jay's eyebrow arched.

'Do you have roommates?'

'Yeah, I told you, Beibhinn, the girl from Kerry studying nursing, or midwifery or something, and Charlie, a lad from London, up here in college, both mad yokes but a great craic. They'll be in at some stage. Anyway, it's me you're here to see.'

'You and the Highlands, of course.'

'Of course.'

Jay came closer holding plates filled with scrumptious rice and meats and sauces. He had wrapped, in ripped-off sheets of kitchen roll, cutlery for them both. Darcy was impressed by his hospitality but not so much by his lack of injury!

'You're such a chancer, broken arm, my arse.'

'Do you want me to break my arm, would that be better and then you could stop trying to guilt me and just accept that I wanted to see you?'

The living room was clean but sang with an old décor love song. The wallpaper had a velvet, paisley pattern. The ceilings were high, painted white with decorative cornices along the edges. A fake crystal chandelier hung centrally, and it too was circled by a decorative medallion, embellished with solid leaves and roses. The sofa was large, and Darcy ate her dinner while its cushions held her in a padded embrace.

'There is such a thing as FaceTime, or the truth. If you wanted to see me, why not just say.'

Darcy raised a fork filled with Cajun chicken and sliced chilli, letting the food rest on her tongue, the spices jumped as if just lit, rotating sparklers in her mouth.

'Okay, look, you're going to kill me for this, Darc, but I've tested positive for Chlamydia.'

Darcy stopped chewing and her body staggered, even on the seat. 'You should see your face,' Jay laughed, 'It's priceless.'

'You git, and it wouldn't surprise me either.'

'That's very unfair, we used precautions so at least give me some credit.'

Darcy continued to eat as her stomach eased itself back into pre-shock mode. A key turning in the door vibrated through the tiled hallway, steps, then a happy face appeared by the living room door.

'Hey, you must be Darcy, at last, we meet.'

'This is the lovely Beibhinn.'

A quirky girl with red long wavy hair and freckles extended her hand for Darcy to shake.

'Jay has mentioned you quite a few times in the last couple of weeks.'

'That's only because he's feeling lonely and needed Tayto crisps, don't mind him.'

'Are you coming out tonight, a few of us are heading to The Sheep's Head?'

Jay looked at Darcy. 'What do you think, it's really up to you?'

'I don't want to be a bore but I'd rather just chill here.'

'Oh, no bother,' Beibhinn said, 'Just be aware you'd be chilling there too, it's a laid-back old man's pub, hassle-free, trust me.'

'It's early yet anyway,' Jay said, 'We'll follow you up if she livens.'

'She's cute, is she gay?' Darcy asked once Beibhinn was out of earshot.

'You tell me, do you not have the gay radar on?'

'You are such a loser, Jay, honestly.'

'Not as much as you, if I see you check that phone once more, I'm binning it. What happened to you, you used to be anti too much time spent on the phone, my God. you've changed.'

Kim had now seen Darcy's message but still left it unanswered. Darcy didn't know which was worse.

'What's going on? Now that you've relegated me into the friend's zone, you can tell me all your relationship issues, I bet you're in a nasty mess as we speak.'

'Nothing official, and I guess that's the point.'

'Ah, the grey area, I see.'

'Look, the best advice I ever got is simple; If they wanna be with you, they will, no excuses, they just will, simples.' Jay said.

'I don't think we even got that far, to be honest.'

'What do you mean?'

'Things were going good but she's annoyed I'm here, with you, so there's that. I hate that kind of controlling, manipulating, mind game shit.'

Darcy looked at her phone again.

'Oh, wait, shush, look, there she is.'

On the phone screen, Kim could be seen leaving her apartment, heels, lipstick, stripped dress and hair styled into a neat bob.

'Son of a bitch,' Jay teased, enjoying Darcy's discomfort.

'Where is she going?' Darcy asked.

'As if I know. Put the phone down, Darcy, Jesus, it's so distracting, and you're spying, which is pretty seedy.'

'How am I spying, it's my doorbell camera?'

'You sound neurotic and everything you hate in a person, just so you know.'

349

'Okay, I'll put the phone away, but I need to check that creep isn't snooping around, I told you what he did, I feel unsafe.'

'I think we should head to the pub for one or two, you're wound up and no fun, you're a stress bomb, you need alcohol to chill the fuck out.'

*

As Darcy and Jay walked the main street of red brick buildings, neatly placed, edged and matching somewhat, Jay pointed out different landmarks, as if an avid sightseer. The town was busy as was the pub they walked into to unwind. Two pints of Coors went down a treat and Darcy was able to loosen up. Jay became tactile, touching Darcy's hand as she spoke, moving closer to her on the seat, the more she drank and less she cared.

'Well, wherever Kim went, Darcy noted, 'she hasn't returned, and by the way, nothing is happening with us, okay, nothing, no matter how much beer you buy.'

'I don't want anything to happen, you remind me of home; I miss it a bit.'

'You've still time to come back, a week left until college begins, not too late to change your mind.'

'No, I love the work here. I just miss you guys. I think Dom is coming over in a couple of days.'

'And I heard Cora came over too, right?'

'Yeah, yes, she's a good girl.'

'You're some piece of work.'

350

Jay laughed then, out loud. And Darcy smiled at him and into their acceptance of one another.

Darcy's head was somewhere other than the beautifully decorated old pub, in the historically laned and cobblestoned curling pathways of the Scottish town. Even with the introduction of new friends with tales and fables, Darcy found herself wanting to ignore the words flowing from their lips, unstripped and eager, moving far too fast and, at some point, intangible, especially to the empty layers of her engagement. She wanted to, instead, let her mind fantasise, flashback or dabble in creating a future, all with people who weren't in her company right now.

Kim was still out, but out where, Darcy wondered, and why had there been no contact, no answer, no call, no text?

Maybe Darcy had felt something for Kim that, in hindsight, had not been reciprocated. Darcy had only presumed, and now the detriment of that was how insecure her doubt bounced from one haphazard unfiltered truth to the next. Her own mind had become an enemy.

'You're not having fun; you've hardly spoken to anyone, Darc, you gotta snap out of this.'

'I'm sorry, I'm going to walk back, it's not that far, you stay.'

'No way, I'll come with you.'

The mild air, the dimly lit street, the odd man, the odd woman, did not interrupt the silence that linked arms with Darcy and Jay as they strolled back to the house. A linked chain of confusion, the relief coming from someone unknown owning a lock to the rusty bolt at the end.

Jay stopped walking and turned to face Darcy, he had words of advice. 'You just have to ask yourself, is she worth it, she hasn't made contact with you and you've done absolutely nothing wrong, so, you don't deserve to be treated like this? I know you and you would see through this kind of crap before, you said she's not even a lesbian. She's probably off looking for some male satisfaction, there's nothing wrong with that, you don't own her.'

Darcy wanted to deck Jay, even though what he said was true, he sounded like a misogynist, a caveman, an idiot, a truthful idiot. His words were her words, her ethos in life repeated back to her. The words seemed more effective coming from someone else and directed towards her.

'Okay, I'm done talking about her. I'll have a good sleep and then tomorrow you can take me on a small and, I mean, easy trail. That will clear the cobwebs.'

'Great, let's go back and I'll make you a cocktail, just one. I promise.'

*

The flattened pathway, a desire path left by the many footprints of hikers' boots, became a guiding line followed by many morning walkers. Before going to sleep Darcy checked her phone; on waking, she did the same. Like a stupid robot, with no sense or morals. Through the phone app, the corridor of the apartment block remained empty, void of action or people but for one neighbour walking towards the window, rolling the blind down, and walking back up the corridor again. Kim had not returned to her flat, so she slept somewhere else or didn't sleep at all, depending on how things panned out. Darcy rested on the latter and as that sat, she trudged along, heavy set and heavy-footed, making the walk, around the perfect scenic route, fairly unbearable.

The night before, she had let Jay kiss her, on the mouth, with tongues. Today, she felt pathetic because Jay was not the answer and he never would be. Looking at him now, his back farther along the uneven path, she felt a pang of guilt at, what seemed to her as, a type of reoccurring incestuous snogging, which was not healthy. She told herself Jay would keep trying if she insisted on feeding his ego, and that their "mistakes" were on her as much as him. She also wished he would come back to Ireland, but she wished it for selfish reasons. Jay was her safety net.

Out of breath, Darcy called to Jay to rest and for the water to be passed. A plastic bottle half full and tepid that, quite satisfactorily, quenched her thirst.

'I need something stronger than this.'

The sights of The Scottish Highlands, daunting in their magnificence, became a feat, unattainable. The conquering stature of the mountainous region, encased Loch Ness and Darcy's quickened heartbeat, instantaneously. The view made her feel as if walking barefoot on glass, because of its beauty, and the fact that she was miserable in its vibrant echoes.

'Can we head back and get drunk?' Jay didn't need much encouragement.

'Yes, Darcy, we can.' He answered.

'You're flying back tomorrow, so you might as well just make the most of it today.' Jay's words of wisdom while handing Darcy a bottle of beer. They still wore hiking gear that smelled of sweat and damp moss.

'I'm just going to concentrate on me; it's been a crazy summer, thinking about everyone else. My grandmother, you, Jessica and now Kim. Somewhere in between all of you lot, I lost me. So, I'm flying back tomor-'

The beep on Darcy's phone indicated movement outside her flat door in Dublin. Kim and Shane, two bodies without reserve, without shame, or the embarrassment Darcy thought they should emit, especially knowing they were on camera, walked close together and disappeared behind Kim's front door. The door closed and clicked.

'What, what is it?' Jay asked, after noticing Darcy's face change.

Darcy thought a moment, a blank, not filled with garbage or excuses, or gibberish; all that was left was a blank space, so the answer to Jay's question was obvious.

'Nothing, nothing at all. Let's switch to cocktails.'

People moved and shoulders danced, they ruffled, touched and moved to allow movements of uncoordinated spasms, the type that consuming alcohol encouraged. No one cared if tipped-over cider stained their blouse, shirt, ripped jeans or new trainers. By the time Darcy and Jay returned to Jay's house, Darcy stopped trying to fit a circle into a square and decided she wanted to stop wanting something she couldn't have.

And maybe in the not wanting part of that, she might find herself wanting again, something more attainable and suited to her tastes.

Chapter Twenty-Five

The hangover from hell kicked in as her eyes opened but Darcy still managed to pack her meagre belongings and, with little help from Jay, she prepared for the airport. Saying goodbye was easy because Jay promised he would come home to Ireland and visit by midterm. He told her he fancied her, that he couldn't help himself and maybe it was the fact that he knew he couldn't have her that made her more appealing to him, but, still, he understood, she would always be the *one that got away*. Darcy laughed lightly at his accurate but silly idiom because, in conjecture with her own love interest, it played a part. She was flying home into a situation, one that was over, and would stay over, but for the conversation. Darcy felt the pangs of that, of that ending before a beginning, but, in her heart, she knew Kim was not a lesbian, a lover of women, she was not even bisexual. Kim wanted a shoulder, after a terrible experience, and what Darcy gave was a full body, a full naked body, at that. An experiment, a muse for Kim to experiment with, and, if Darcy thought, which she had momentarily, that experimentation was anything more than that, then it was Darcy who messed up, big time.

On the plane journey back to Ireland, it was easy to reflect, to think about her journey and what was left to do and with whom. If life unfolded by itself anyway, then why try to alter it towards a lane unlit or in darkness, laden with thorns or broken branches, unmoving, but for the pain they could inflict if disturbed? The grass was not always greener, the flow runs anyway, better to let it have a natural path to traverse.

Jay would be just fine, his infatuation with her would fade and he would find his flame, with a woman whose ideals emulated his own. Sometimes, Darcy surmised, as she zipped up her coat, life can be superficial, so trying to force another narrative into a story that already has an ending, simply goes against the grain.

Darcy kissed Jay on the lips and told him she loved him dearly, which was true. He smiled his cheeky smile.

Saying goodbye, she closed the door and with it that chapter in her story and headed for home.

On the plane ride, she pictured different reunions, but Darcy had not expected to see Kim walking out of the apartment block as she was walking in. They both stopped on the stairs. There was a dry awkwardness, as dryness turned to distance and the unremembering of skin on skin, and the remembering of how that felt, was over.

'I'm sorry, I never got a chance to text you back, I-'

'Oh, I know you were busy, I saw.'

'Oh, right... listen, he's apologised and-'

'Oh, no, no, no, you don't have to explain anything to

me, especially about him, I don't care enough. It is what it is, and we were a couple of casual friends, I get it.'

'I'm sorry if I confused you. I confused myself for a while there, anyway, we're moving. I mean, I'm moving in with him, across the county.'

'So he can keep a closer eye on you.' Darcy sneered politely.

'It's not like that. I drove him crazy, and I knew what I was doing.' Kim blinked too fast.

'Kim, you didn't do anything. You followed your heart for a minute. Don't apologise for that. I knew we were just a thing.'

'And you, will you be okay, I know you've started to come off the meds?'

'I'll be more than okay. I'm figuring it out. Every day, just figuring it out, and I feel on the outskirts of better, which is so much safer than in the middle of its vortex.'

'That's good, really good. I think you're gonna be okay.'

'I think so too.' Darcy said, honestly.

Darcy watched Kim drive away. One part of her would worry about Kim's well-being but the other part understood that, as individuals, we all make our own mistakes, to learn from, grow from, grow into and regret. Darcy felt the truthful pang of her thoughts, as she pondered further that Kim's choices might take her down the road of regret but there's no one else that can take that road but her.

For now, Darcy was done with regret.

*

Darcy walked into her final semester ready for an ending and the new beginning it would bring.

'Hey,' Mina called from across campus, as if on loudspeaker. 'We're in the canteen.' She pointed as if Darcy needed directions. Kate, Cruz and another unknown or two moved in the distance, their heads growing smaller, as Darcy covered her brows with her hand to get a better view.

Mina, nearing, enthused, 'It's so good to see you, it's been weeks, literally forever, you've been so damn low-key. I can't believe we never got to reconnect again after that coffee date. I've loads of news, and so have you, I gather.'

'Slow down, I need to go to the bookshop before class, and I'm over idol gossip even about strange marriage proposals. We're grown-ups now, after all, so I need facts.' Darcy smiled, and so too did Mina.

'We're hardly grown-ups just yet,' she stated, 'Only almost grown-ups, don't push it... okay, we're still meeting for lunch though, right?'

'Sure, but not after college, not today anyway. I want to go back to my place, sorry to be a bore but I'm planning. I'm gonna put it out there, on my unambiguous virtual vision board. A plan. I'm in future mode, no more looking back. I'm on.'

'Oh, of course. Same, it's all about the vision board! Just as long as you're still going to the gig this weekend, you can't miss that. Kate making a right fool of herself again.'

Mina began to move away, 'Oh, and Jay text, he's over for the night, that lad, he hates to see us all having fun without him.'

Darcy smiled. 'I'm going. I promise.'

'Good, because no one likes broken promises.'

No, no one liked or deserved broken promises, so Darcy had made a promise to herself. To get to know "her" and all her eccentricities. To explore her individualism and accept she/he/them/they/herself before letting others try to understand her or label her, through their tainted lens or divisive opinions.

She was her own personality; an identity unique to her. And, she, in turn, would do the same for them. It was a work in progress, a step-by-step way of taking each day as a reward, as a way of learning, sharing and being part of.

Life was better.

Life was honest.

Life would get complicated again.

No doubt.

Because life was supposed to.

Life was tender in places, and rough in others but life's participation was worth both and Darcy was willing to forgo the worry of disappointment in place of optimism.

The split girl, split in two, was mending, sewed up halfway, which was better than nothing, right?

She reached the door of the bookshop and turned in time to see Jessica waving from across the recently mowed lawn.

Darcy nodded and smiled as the light made her squint, then she pulled open the door and walked inside.